# Love, Lies and Family Ties

### By

## Florence Keeling

### Cover design by
### Florence Keeling

*To my family and friends*

*For where would I be without them.*

# CHAPTER 1

**M**iserable! That was the only way to describe the day. Cold, wet and miserable and that was exactly how Bea felt. She'd had the worst day at work ever and to top it off it was now pouring down with rain, she'd forgotten her coat and the bus was late. Maureen, the woman she shared an office with, had been extra prickly today.

Bea worked as an accountant and even though she'd been at Rock and White's for over four years since finishing her degree, she was still the most junior one there and Maureen took great pleasure in reminding her of this daily.

Maureen was a little woman with a big complex. The office they shared wasn't particularly large but Maureen's desk took up over half of the space and she sat behind it, pompous in her own self-importance. She was a senior accountant in the firm and had been there for over thirty years, a fact she repeated at any given opportunity.

Bea often had to cover for the receptionist Jen when she needed a break and as she was Mr. Rock's daughter she had no qualms in taking advantage of this and was sometimes gone for half an hour and usually found chatting to Josh, the handsome accountant in office ten on the first floor.

This had been the reason for Bea's roasting today.

Maureen had been off with her from the moment she'd walked in. Her car had been playing up and she been forced to accept a lift from her brother, so instead of arriving in her huge Jaguar she was dropped off in an ancient Mini that misfired continually. Bea had loved watching the scene from her office on the second floor.

The Mini was a myriad of different colours held together by rust, and swerved into the car park with a loud bang. Maureen had flung the door open so hard it had rebounded onto her legs and pushed her back into the car. It took her three attempts to physically get out of the car and with a toot of the horn and another bang, the Mini took off with an over-enthusiastic screeching of tyres.

Bea couldn't wipe the smile from her face as Maureen toddled into the office and dumped her extra-large briefcase on her desk, but she kept her head down so Maureen couldn't see. And this was how Bea spent most of her day until the usual call from Jen summoned her downstairs.

It was an exceptionally long break and after almost an hour, Jen returned, all smiles and apologies. Bea stood up to get straight back to her office and this was how Maureen found them.

"I knew you were just down here chatting." Her face was red. "You are a waste of space, Beatrice Winters, and I shall be having words with Mrs. White." And with that she stormed off upstairs.

"I'm so sorry." Jen was mortified.

"It's okay." Bea picked up her laptop from the desk. "She's had it in for me since the day I moved into her office, no wonder poor John left." John had been Maureen's previous victim.

"Do you want me to have a word with Dad?" Jen was already picking up the phone.

"No, it will only make her worse." Bea smiled wryly. "I tried that, remember, Mrs. White just told me I was being silly and then told Maureen what I'd said. She's been insufferable ever since."

"I'll try not to be so long in future." Jen smiled again. "And why did she call you Beatrice? That's not your name."

"I know it isn't." Bea was at the door now. "But she's never asked me anything about myself so she's just assumed. Anyway, off to face the Bitches of Eastwick."

Maureen had gone straight to Mrs. White and within two minutes of arriving back in the office, Bea had been summoned to receive a rather long-winded telling off with not even a chance to reply or give any evidence in her defence. She sat there looking as contrite as possible wishing she could just hand in her resignation, but as jobs these days were few and far between she wasn't about to cut off her nose to spite her face.

Even after the severe reprimand, Bea forced a smile onto her face and spent the rest of the afternoon being polite and courteous to Maureen which seemed to throw her off guard, and she headed off early with the excuse of picking her car up from the garage. Bea relaxed her face with relief as she left and counted down the last hour till she could leave herself.

The number thirteen finally arrived and a dripping wet Bea stepped on, flashed her bus pass and then sat down towards the back. For the tenth time today she wished she'd brought her car, but it was so easy to get the bus and she hated driving in rush hour traffic. Anyway, she liked to sit and write on her journeys to and from work and she couldn't do that driving a car.

Bea had always written, it was her way of escaping the real world. She had hundreds of stories and ideas but not one was finished, she could never seem to plot a whole novel from beginning to end but she wrote anyway. It was far easier to accept the lure of a new idea than slog away at an old one that was going nowhere, and she hoped one day inspiration would strike and she would at last be able to follow her dream of being a published author.

The traffic was even worse today and Bea knew it was going to be a long journey, so she plugged in her head phones and pulled out her notebook. Her current story was a fantasy series for children about a magic world and as she pictured the scene in her head, the characters came to life and she scribbled frantically.

So engrossed was she that she didn't notice the dark-haired man staring at her. Didn't notice as he walked past her and accidentally dropped his newspaper by her feet. In fact no one seemed to notice him as he melted into the crowd of people getting on and off. It was only as the bus pulled away and she looked up that she realised she was three stops past her house, and as the bus had already driven off she knew she was going to have to go to the fourth.

Standing up, she trod on the newspaper. It was open at the job page and a large red circle had been drawn around one of the adverts. It was for an accounts manager at a small publishing company in a place Bea had never heard of. She felt light hearted all of a sudden, like fate had lent her a hand, and with a spring in her step, she got off the bus oblivious to the rain thumping down on her head, and skipped the half-mile home.


After a hot shower and a bowl of thick tomato soup, Bea sat in front of the TV, her laptop open and the damp newspaper by her side. She re-read the job advert, racking her brain for any recollection of a place called 'Bloomsdale'. It sounded like a made-up name but when she typed it into Google she found it to be a small village nestling in the middle of Yorkshire. As Bea lived in the Midlands she was unsure why there would be an advert in her local paper for a job over a hundred miles away.

She flicked to the front page to check that it was indeed her local paper and upon discovering that it was, shrugged her shoulders and resumed her search for the little village. There was hardly any information on it at all, only that it had a canal running through the middle and held an annual classic car festival every August.

She found the local estate agent and was shocked to discover that a one-bedroom flat was twice the rent she paid for her little house and she wasn't in the most desirable of areas as it was. Her heart sank as she realised the pay advertised would not allow her to live in the centre and after reading the advert properly to the end it stated that experience in the publishing industry was required.

Slamming shut the laptop she put the newspaper onto her recycling pile to take out in the morning, resigned to the fact that she was doomed to stay at Rock and White's forever. She flicked through the channels, settling on EastEnders before scoffing endless amounts of junk food and despairing of her current situation.

She didn't even have the motivation to write. In her current state all she wanted to do was veg out and eat rubbish, which did nothing to lighten her mood, in fact by the time she went to bed she felt utterly miserable and extremely sick after all the chocolate she'd pigged out on and she hadn't even noticed that the newspaper had disappeared.

# CHAPTER 2

Bea literally had to drag herself out of bed the next morning. She felt sluggish and ill and wanted nothing more than to phone in sick but wasn't going to give Maureen the satisfaction of thinking she'd upset her. It was raining again when she stepped out of her front door, in fact it hadn't stopped raining since yesterday, *typical British summer* she thought, but at least she'd remembered her coat and umbrella today.

The bus was already full and she found herself having to stand, crammed up between the stairs and a rather large man who smelt of sweat and cigarette smoke and who took great pleasure in bashing against her boobs every time the bus braked or moved in any way. Thankfully after two stops he got off, a smarmy smile on his face.

Feeling even more miserable than she had done the day before, Bea was grateful to find Maureen was out for the day visiting clients and even more grateful when Jen told her during their lunch break that a new junior was starting on Monday. The day seemed to be getting better and better, even the rain had stopped and the sun was shining brightly through her office window.

Jen buzzed up for her to cover reception and she headed down the stairs, a skip in her step.

"Maureen's just called in, she's out for the rest of the week." Jen knew this would please Bea and from the huge smile that spread across her face she was right.

"Well, seems like things are finally looking up at last." Bea sat down at Jen's desk and for the first time in many months was actually looking forward to the future.

Bea's optimism didn't last long. By Monday afternoon she realised that the new junior in the office was just that, a new junior. His name was Wesley and although he was a very pretty boy, he knew absolutely nothing about accountancy and even less about answering phones. He was fresh out of school and had been taken on as an apprentice, not like Bea who had her degree and was 21 when she had started work.

Maureen and Bea were in the board room having a meeting with one of the company's larger clients. It was nearing the end and Maureen had asked Bea if she would fetch the files from the office for the client to take away with them. Bea knew how many boxes of accounts there were to bring down and groaned silently.

"Shall I ask Wesley to give us a hand?" At least then Maureen could stay down here with the client while they lugged the boxes down the two flights of stairs. Maureen nodded, so Bea headed upstairs, grabbing Wesley as she did.

It took them over fifteen minutes to bring all the boxes down and load them into the waiting Range Rover. Maureen was still talking to the client and Bea enjoyed five minutes of peace before she came thundering into the office slamming the door behind her, the glass shuddering in its frame.

"What makes you think you're above carrying clients' books?" Her face was like thunder as she slammed her fist onto Bea's desk. Her hands were deceptively large compared to the rest of her body, as was her nose which was now only inches away from Bea's face. "I dread to think what Mr. Yakamoto must have thought."

"But…" Bea was lost for anything to say. She hadn't thought for a second that Maureen would react like this. "I was just trying to save you having to carry them down with me." And it was the truth, although why she should have cared about Maureen was beyond her.

"Well that's not how it came across." Maureen stormed across the room, throwing herself down into her chair. "You really have got to sort yourself out, Beatrice." Bea sighed again at the use of what Maureen thought was her name. It was no good correcting her, she never listened to anything she said anyway. "You're not going to amount to much if you continue with this attitude of thinking that you're better than everyone else. I've been here thirty years now, and when I was your age…" Maureen droned on and on. Bea drifted off, she'd heard this story a hundred times at least.

"Maureen?" There was a knock at the door and Bea looked up, grateful for the interruption. "Can you pop down and see Debbie in accounts when you get a minute?" It was Mr. Rock's secretary Linda at the door.

"I'll go right now." Maureen followed Linda down the corridor, Bea despairing once again at the injustice of it all.

Bea couldn't wait to leave the office that evening, her head was thumping and she was determined to apply for all the jobs on the internet that were even vaguely suitable. When Maureen had returned from seeing Debbie she was white as a sheet, had snapped something at Bea, then made some kind of excuse and gone home.

Half past five finally arrived and she gathered her things angrily, grabbing a handful of files off her desk that she needed to work on at home. She kept her head down as she walked along the street towards the bus stop, dodging past the other commuters as they went about their journeys.

"I'm so sorry." Bea found herself on the floor after she'd managed to crash into a couple walking arm in arm. The files were scattered around and she hastily grabbed at them.

"Let me help you." A dark-haired man knelt down and started picking up the files, handing them to her after helping her to her feet.

"Thank you." Bea looked into his handsome face. He gave the impression of being quite a mature man, well into his sixties, but his hair was jet black and his face completely free of wrinkles except for a few tiny ones around his grey eyes. "I really need to look where I'm going in future."

"I'm just glad I was here to help." And with that he walked past her, disappearing into the crowd.

The bus ride home was quick and uneventful, Bea was grateful for this as she microwaved a meal for one and poured herself a rather large glass of wine. She didn't think she could have stomached being on a bus full of people any longer than was necessary.

She sat at the table in her small dining room and opened up the files. The first thing she saw was a crumpled page from a newspaper.

"Well how did that get there?" Bea unfolded it and smoothed out the creases. It looked familiar and upon closer inspection she discovered it was the job advert she had looked at last week. The date at the top of the page was from last week and the advert was still circled in red but this time when she read it, it quite clearly said experience not required.

Bea wasn't sure how she'd managed to misread it and didn't have a clue how it had found its way into her work files. The pay was still poor but she fired off an application straight away and began to plan.

Her house was rented so she would only have to give a month's notice and when she checked her employment contract it was only two weeks' notice she had to give. She was due more than that in holiday so if she got the job she could finish virtually straight away. She prayed she got the job. She needed to get away from Maureen as quickly as she could. It was getting her down now and making her ill. She dreaded work each morning unless Maureen was out on audit, those were days she relished.

Clearing away her plate and glass she headed into the living room. Her phone pinged, telling her she had a new email and she was pleasantly surprised to find the publishing company had already replied to her application and invited her for an interview on Friday afternoon. All she had to do now was hope that she could get Friday off work: she would ask Mr. Rock first thing in the morning, he was far kinder than Mrs. White.

Decision made, she started browsing local hotels in the area. She didn't fancy a two hour drive then heading straight into an interview, so she booked herself into a delightful little B&B that doubled as the local pub called The Angel Arms for the Thursday and Friday night. She could drive straight down after work and have a little scout around the area before and after the interview.

She slept like a log that night, the best she'd slept in a long time. The next day Maureen was off sick, so she headed straight to see Mr. Rock. He was a portly man with the kindest face Bea had ever seen. He welcomed her in and gave her the day off without hesitation, even telling her to get herself off early on Thursday to avoid the traffic. Bea had a feeling Jen had told him what was going on with Maureen.

He wished her good luck with her interview promising not to mention it to anyone else, and Bea went back up the stairs to her office, looking forward to a whole day without Maureen breathing down her neck. She was so happily wrapped up in her daydream that maybe she would soon be getting away from Maureen that she didn't notice the dark-haired man with the grey eyes watching her from the empty office by the stairs.

# CHAPTER 3

Thursday dawned hot and muggy. The air was so heavy it was like walking with lead boots on. Bea was thankful she wasn't taking the bus today and smiled smugly in her air-conditioned car as she drove past the packed number thirteen, its passengers visibly melting in the sultry heat.

She pulled into the office car park, her smile fading as she saw Maureen's Jaguar parked in its usual spot. She'd thought it was too good to be true that she would be off all week but at least Bea only had three quarters of the day to get through.

She walked into the office to find a very white-faced Maureen, she clearly wasn't fully recovered but it didn't stop the usual tutting and snapping that was part of her daily routine where Bea was concerned, and she couldn't wait for lunch time. Maureen headed into the canteen but Bea decided to stay in the office and just a few minutes later Jen came in to join her.

"Something's going on." Jen sat down in front of Bea, her face eager with untold secrets.

"What do you mean, something's going on?" Bea pulled a face. "A what something or a who something?"

"Both." Now Bea was intrigued. "I heard Dad talking on the phone last night, it's something to do with Maureen, a client and the police."

"The police!" Bea squealed then hushed her voice. "The police?" Jen nodded.

"Dad didn't know I was listening so I can't go asking him about it." She leaned closer to Bea so she could whisper. "But I'm sure it's something to do with her being off sick the past few days and why she's so quiet today."

"She's not that quiet." Bea raised her eyebrows mockingly. "Trust me."

Nothing more was said and nothing else discovered so with a cheery 'Have a good weekend' to a bewildered Maureen, Bea headed out of the office early. The heat hit her as she stepped into the car park. It was three o clock and the sun was at its peak. She got into her car, started the engine then sat there for a few minutes waiting for it to cool down because she couldn't even touch the steering wheel to drive away.

Turning on the Sat Nav she punched in the post code of The Angel Arms before ignoring it completely until she was actually on the motorway. Bea was feeling happy and positive. She wasn't expecting to get this job, wasn't even sure she actually wanted to move away if she did, but it was a good excuse for a short break.

The Sat Nav's electronic voice told her to take the next exit and she moved back to the inside lane after overtaking a rather slow lorry with a precarious load of crates wobbling around. Bea concentrated hard, she was always a little nervous when driving in new places.

She was now in Yorkshire, according to the sign she'd passed a few miles away. The landscape was breathtaking, endless green fields, the odd farmhouse and rolling hills made the long drive worthwhile. She had a quick glance at the Sat Nav and saw she was now only a few miles away from her destination.

The road had suddenly become very curvy and as it was a single track Bea had slowed right down. She couldn't see past the corners and hoped she didn't meet any vehicles coming the opposite way. After a precarious ten minutes of almost crawling she came upon the most beautiful village she had ever seen.

Pristine cottages with neat gardens lined the road, neighbours chatting over low fences or mowing lawns completed the scene.

Bea was so used to living in the city that she'd forgotten what a country village looked like.

She carried on along the road pulling into a car park as the Sat Nav announced she had reached her destination. The Angel Arms was a large Georgian building built in golden Yorkshire stone. It was three stories high with an oak wooden door in the middle, narrow rectangular windows and was perfectly symmetrical even down to the chimneys at either end of the slate roof.

Switching off the engine and grabbing her small suitcase from the back seat she walked to the front door admiring the beautifully painted pub sign hanging proudly on its wooden post. A glorious angel dressed in white hovered above a perfect replica of the pub, endless moors dotted with sheep in the background.

A young woman with a pram walked by and nodded hello to Bea as she walked through the front door into a tiny hallway. To the left was a black door with the sign 'Bar' written on, to the right another black door with the word 'Lounge' and in front of her, which was the one Bea followed, was the same black door with 'Reception' neatly written in gold.

The stairs were narrow, painted in neutral cream with a black handrail along the right hand side. As she reached the top, the stairs opened onto a narrow landing with five closed black doors numbered in sequence, another staircase at the far end and an open room which upon inspection housed the reception.

A middle-aged woman, smartly dressed in a black suit and red shirt, smiled as Bea walked in.

"Have you got a reservation?" she asked in a friendly voice. Bea was expecting a Yorkshire accent so was a little surprised to find the woman spoke with an Irish lilt.

"I made a booking online." Bea stepped towards the desk. "Winters."

"Oh yes, here you are." The woman tapped on the computer then passed Bea a heavy old-fashioned key and asked her to sign a form. "You're in room nine which is up the stairs on the top floor. Breakfast is served between seven and nine in the lounge downstairs and we offer discounted rates for dinner to our hotel guests." She rang a bell and almost instantly a young man dressed in the same colours as the woman appeared. "This is Andy, he'll take your luggage and show you to your room."

"Thank you."

Andy picked up Bea's suitcase.

"Any questions, there's always someone here in the day, or ring the bell if it's after ten at night." The woman went back to the computer. "I hope you have a lovely stay."

Bea followed Andy up the stairs and along the landing to room nine which was right at the end. The door was currently open and after depositing her bag on the bed, Andy bowed neatly, his heels pressed together and disappeared, closing the door behind him.

The room was stunning. A white marble fireplace was the central attraction with a four-poster bed coming a close second. The walls were white except for the chimney breast which was covered in luxurious silver paper with large black flowers. This pattern was repeated on the bed coverings and curtains giving a rich feeling to the room.

Heading over to the window she ascertained that she was at the front as her view was remarkable. She could see what appeared to be the whole village. A small courtyard was surrounded by shops and houses with lots of other little streets leading off from it and in the distance the moors stretched as far as the eye could see.

She couldn't wait to explore and after changing into her jeans and trainers she locked her door and almost ran down the two flights of stairs and out the front door.

It was starting to cool down but the air was still muggy. Bea walked straight across into the centre, nodding to people as she passed. Considering it was only a small village there seemed to be lots of people around. Checking her phone for the name and address of the publishing house, she followed the directions on her phone and found Summers Day Press was on the top floor above a coffee shop at the end of a particularly long street called North Avenue.

The coffee shop was still open so she headed inside and ordered a large latte, cheese panini and a delightfully stodgy-looking chocolate chip muffin. She sat by the window and for the first time in days pulled out her pen and notebook and started scribbling. A new idea was forming in her head and she wrote the basic outline and characters before staring out of the window thinking of how to begin.

A bespectacled man with messy brown hair walked in and caught her attention. He looked about twenty and carried himself with an awkwardness that Bea found endearing. He was carrying what looked like a laptop case and after buying the largest cup of tea she had ever seen he sat in the far corner, pulled out his laptop and then sat staring out the window just as Bea had been doing.

This was when she noticed that most of the people in the coffee shop were sitting alone and had either a laptop or notebook open in front of them. Bea supposed this was what you got when you owned a coffee shop underneath a publishing house and wondered which one had come first and whether all of these budding writers actually lived in the village.

The young man caught her eye and she smiled nervously at him before turning away, embarrassed to be caught staring. For the next hour she kept her head down pretending to write even though she still couldn't even think of a killer first line. At ten to nine the place was virtually empty so Bea picked up her stuff and headed back to the hotel. The young man in the corner watched her leave before packing up his own things and heading off in the opposite direction.

# CHAPTER 4

Bea sat at the breakfast table the next morning feeling stuffed after a huge plate of bacon and eggs, followed by toast and washed down with mountains of orange juice. The serving staff were all dressed as the Irish lady and Andy had been the day before. Apart from Bea, there was an older couple and what appeared to be a business man in the dining room. The older couple were taking their time over their food as Bea had done but the man had already finished even though he had sat down almost ten minutes after Bea.

Pouring another cup of tea, she checked her watch, assuring herself that she had plenty of time to get washed and changed before her interview at half past twelve. As she knew exactly where it was now she could afford the luxury of a long soak before a bit of last minute swotting up on the company.

At quarter past twelve she found herself sitting in a small waiting room attached to the reception of Summers Day Press. Everything was open plan and Bea could see everyone at work. She wasn't sure she would like to work this way at Rock and White's but supposed everyone here worked together on the same projects so it was probably easier.

One thing intrigued her and that was the spiral staircase that sat slap bang in the middle of the floor. She hadn't realised the building had another storey, there wasn't any indication of one from the front. She had declined the offer of a drink, not wanting to risk spilling anything down her suit before her interview. Bea checked her watch, still ten minutes to go—and it was then that the raised voices of two men could be heard.

Bea looked around: everyone else had their heads down, couldn't they hear the shouting? She caught the receptionist's eye, who just smiled and went back to her typing. There was more shouting and then heavy footsteps before the man from the coffee shop last night stormed down the spiral staircase, slipped on the last few steps and landed on his backside at the bottom, the files of paper he'd been carrying flying out everywhere.

A few had even managed to find themselves at Bea's feet so she picked them up quickly before heading towards him, collecting more papers as she went. No one else helped. They all sat there at their desks, heads down as if they hadn't even seen the incident.

"Are you okay?" Bea knelt down in front of him as he scrambled around on his hands and knees picking up the remaining few papers.

"Regular occurrence." He paused for a second to push his glasses back up, his brown eyes lowered in embarrassment.

"Happens to the best of us." Bea handed him the messed-up papers as they both stood up. "I'm Bea by the way." She stretched out her hand.

"Eddie." He almost dropped the papers again as he tried to shake her hand. "It's Edmund really, but I've never been a big fan. I'm not sure where my parents picked it from, I think it was my great grandad's name or something like that." He was aware that he was rambling and stopped talking.

"I'm not a fan of my full name either." Bea found herself instantly liking Eddie.

"Well I think Beatrice is a beautiful name." He had started trying to turn the pages all the same way but this was proving impossible so gave up.

"Oh, it's not Beatrice." Bea was so used to this common mistake. "It's…"

"Mr. Summers is ready to see you now." The receptionist called from her desk. "Straight up the stairs."

"I'd best go." Bea straightened her jacket and skirt.

"Perhaps I'll see you later, in the coffee shop," he said hopefully.

"Perhaps you will." Smiling, Bea headed off up the stairs.

"Miss Winters, so lovely to meet you." She was greeted at the top by a smartly dressed, blond haired, blue eyed Adonis. "You've definitely got the perfect name for working here."

"Thank you." She couldn't think of anything else to say as she shook his hand.

"Just take a seat over there, I'll grab your file and then we'll get started." He indicated a group of soft looking arm chairs then headed in the opposite direction towards some filing cabinets. Bea walked towards them and sat down, finally taking in her surroundings.

The office was beautiful. The whole of one side was made of glass giving an unspoilt view of the countryside. A large mahogany desk sat facing the view and Bea found herself day dreaming about such a work space. It was the only desk up here so she assumed he had the whole floor to himself.

"I planned it all myself." The Adonis sat himself down opposite her. "I prefer things informal and open. I don't see the point of hiding away in little offices with tiny windows, not when you've got a view like this anyway." He opened up a brown folder and pulled out her CV, *he must have printed it off,* she thought. "Where are my manners? Scott Summers." He held out his hand again. "Not the one from the X-Men."

"Bea." She said simply, shaking his hand again and finding herself believing that with a body like his he could quite easily be in the X-Men.

"So, what's made you apply for this position then, Bea?" Every time he spoke she found herself watching his mouth move. "You're a little far from home if you don't mind me saying."

"I feel the time is right for a change in my life." She launched herself into her practised interview responses, trying to keep eye contact with him even though each time she did her legs went to jelly. "I've come as far as I can at the accountants and I'd like to broaden my horizons. As you can see I'm a fully qualified accountant but I'm also up to date in payroll and Human Resources."

"And I see here that you are a writer?" He lifted an eyebrow quizzically. "What do you write?"

"Everything and anything really." That was the only way to describe it. "I start a story never really knowing where it will take me."

"I'm the same." He almost jumped up in his enthusiasm. "Have you read any of my books?"

Bea knew she could lie here, she'd done enough research on him to know he wrote crime and thriller novels but did she know enough if he was to question her on a particular book?

"I must confess I haven't read any of the Robin Sparrow Mysteries." She saw a look of disappointment on his face. "But I do know that your last novel 'Cuckoo in the Nest' is currently top of the best sellers chart and your first novel 'A Bird in the Hand' has been released in over ten countries."

"I see you've googled me." He was smiling as he said it. "Well at least you're honest." He put the file down on his lap. "I like you Bea, I like you a lot." He smiled again and Bea found herself smiling back. "Now the job is nine till one, five days a week and the salary is just under twelve and a half thousand. Now I know that seems low but it is only a part time position."

Bea nodded, she hadn't read the part time bit in the advert. At least that meant she could perhaps get something else to prop up her wages and it also explained why it was on the low side.

"I've got a few more interviews this afternoon and I'll make a decision over the weekend and let you know." He stood up and shook her hand once again. "It's been an absolute pleasure." He walked her towards the staircase. "I'll be in touch."

"Thank you, Mr. Summers." Bea almost forgot to say it as she headed back down the stairs. She walked out through reception, passing a rather busty blonde in a tight shirt on her way who stated to the receptionist that she had an interview at one o clock. Bea sighed. Well, there was no way she was getting the job now, not after Mr. Summers caught sight of Marilyn Monroe.

"She's not there about the job you know." Bea turned to find Eddie sitting on the top of the stairs that led outside. "It's written all over your face." He still had his papers with him but now they were back inside the folder. "Thought I'd wait for you."

"That's very kind of you." They started walking down the stairs. "What's she there for if not for the job?"

"She comes every few weeks, trying to get a publishing contract." Eddie opened the door when they reached the bottom and they both headed out onto the street. "I don't know why she bothers, I've read her writing and it's terrible. There's just no soul in it."

"Do you work for Mr. Summers then?" Bea was intrigued.

"You could say that." The Star Wars theme tune started playing and he sheepishly pulled out his mobile phone. "I've got to take this," he said, putting the phone to his ear and handing her his folder of papers.

After a stilted conversation, Eddie put his phone away and took the folders back.

"I've been summoned," he said rather regretfully. "And I haven't a clue how long I'll be."

"It's okay, I was going to check out the village anyway." She was a little disappointed at losing his company so soon, and with a quick goodbye he was gone, back through the door.

Bea decided it was time to visit the estate agents and see what properties were even half way affordable. She walked back into the centre and headed down East Avenue, finding the cutest little office in the tiniest little house she had ever seen.

She was greeted by a small middle-aged man who shook her hand vigorously as she entered.

"Good afternoon dear lady, and how can I be of service on this fine day?" Bea took an instant liking to him.

"I was hoping you'd have something very, very cheap available." Bea flashed her best smile.

"And what exactly do you mean by cheap?" The man's friendliness didn't falter. "I've got a delightful one-bedroom cottage on the outskirts. It's been empty for a while now and the land lord is looking for around £800 per month."

Bea shook her head. That would leave her just over £200 for everything else.

"How about this?" He headed to the window. "It's just become vacant and rather a steal at £750." Bea didn't even look at it and just shook her head. "£675 for this charming..." She shook her head again before he had even finished. "I'm afraid that's the lowest rent around here my dear."

"Well, thank you for your time." Bea headed back outside feeling utterly despondent. Even if she was to get the job, she couldn't afford to live here. A life filled with Maureen stretched out in front of her as she walked back to the hotel. "What are you doing there?" A small black dog had suddenly appeared on the pavement in front of her. "Where's your owner?" The dog seemed to smile at her. She looked around but there was no one about so she went to pick him up.

"Come back." The dog had run off back down East Avenue. "You'll get run over." Bea chased after him, she hated seeing lost dogs. She followed him as he turned a corner and then another, Bea had no idea where she was. She caught sight of his tail heading down a small alley and followed him but just as suddenly as he'd appeared he had gone.

# CHAPTER 5

"What on earth do I do now?" Bea asked herself. She hadn't a clue where she was, the dog had vanished into thin air and she was half way down an alley way. She turned to try and re-trace her steps when she heard the sound of an engine coming from the other end. Curiosity got the better of her and she walked down the alley wondering why on earth it had a name sign proclaiming it to be called Watery Lane.

Out of everything she had expected to come across when she reached the end, canal boats was not one of them. On one side was a long row of terraced houses, their small back yards backing on to a tow path. On the other side was a brick wall stretching as far as the eye could see and down the middle a canal filled with brightly painted narrow boats completed the scene.

Bea felt like she had been transported back in time. There was nothing modern anywhere. The houses were built of stone, weathered and aged. They didn't have gardens, just small paved areas surrounded by stone walls. The boats themselves were all traditional in nature, painted in different shades of red, blue and green. Most were stationary, tied up to large metal rings on the tow path but the engine noise was coming from one boat called 'Mavis' that was just chugging gracefully past, its driver waving cheerily to her as he went by.

Feeling suddenly inspired, she wished she had her notebook with her but as she didn't she decided to walk along the canal and see where it took her: after all she could always double back on herself. It was a beautiful day and she needed to think how on earth she could possibly take the job if it was even offered to her, if she couldn't afford to rent anywhere.

After half an hour of walking she came across a delightful looking pub called 'The Plough' and as she hadn't eaten since breakfast she went in and ordered a cold glass of cider and a ploughman's lunch which she devoured in the garden overlooking the canal.

The sky was beginning to turn an ominous grey so she called for a taxi to take her back to the hotel. Five minutes later she was sitting in the back of the cab when the heavens opened, grateful that she hadn't decided to walk. After pulling up outside the hotel, she ran in, just those few feet got her drenched and she stripped off as soon as she was in her room.

She wrapped a fluffy white dressing gown around her and started to towel dry her hair, staring absent-mindedly out of the window. The rain was torrential, falling in sheets down the glass. A loud rumble of thunder and a flash of lightning made her jump and she decided against any further exploring of the village, settling down with her notebook and pen instead.

When Bea checked out the following morning, it was still raining but the thunder and lightning had disappeared sometime in the night, much to her relief. Her drive home was far more eventful than her drive there and after eight long hours of traffic jams and floods she finally walked back in her front door at half past six. She was absolutely starving and dying for a cup of tea but after checking her fridge there was nothing there and the milk was off.

She found some bread, slightly mouldy but she picked it off before toasting it and suffered black tea which made her pull a face each time she took a sip. Lounging in front of the TV, she sighed heavily when the doorbell rang. She really didn't want visitors.

"Mum!" Bea opened the door in shock.

"Surprise!" The blonde woman opened her arms and with slight jazz hands almost screamed at her. She was well into her seventies but dressed and acted like someone half her age, Bea sometimes thought she looked younger than her. After two air kisses on her cheeks her mum turned around to the waiting taxi. "Come along, Carlos." Bea moved to one side as her mum swept past quickly followed by a very tanned, very dark, very young man. He babbled something in Spanish to Bea as he pulled two heavy suitcases behind him.

"Mum?" Bea shut the door and walked into the living room.

"How many times, Bea? Don't call me Mum." Her mum was already sitting on the sofa, the rather perplexed Carlos by her side. "I don't go around calling you by your real name, do I?"

"Well if you'd called me something normal I wouldn't mind." Bea really wasn't in the mood for her mother. She'd hardly been around when she was young, her older brother and sister had virtually brought her up but now her mum thought she could just impose herself on each of them whenever she felt like it.

"Your brother and sister don't complain." Her mum turned to Carlos. "This is my daughter Bea." Carlos looked at her, bewildered. "Poor boy doesn't understand a word of English but he speaks the language of love so very well." And with that she launched herself at him kissing him passionately. In seconds they were both half undressed and Bea took herself off to her bedroom, plugging in her headphones to block out the noise.

Her phone vibrated and she found a text from her brother.

*'So sorry I didn't warn you earlier, just found out Mum's on her way to you. Thought she was off to Em's as she was flying into Gatwick but got diverted to Birmingham so you have the pleasure I'm afraid. Al x'*

*'She's already here, with a plus one x,'* she replied.

*'What poor sod this time?'* The shocked emoji face followed this text.

*'Some Spanish lad who looks about eighteen and can't speak a word of English.'*

*'Still doesn't beat Gino the Italian stallion she brought to mine the other year. Good Luck x'*

Not for the first time she asked herself why she couldn't have had a normal mother and thanked her lucky stars that her brother and sister were reasonably sane and had managed to instil their values and morals into their little sister.

Al and Em were almost twenty years older than Bea and had unfortunately been passed from relative to relative as they were growing up. All three of them had different fathers and only Al was in contact with his, Em and Bea didn't even know the names of theirs.

From past experiences she knew her mum wouldn't be moving anytime soon so she snuggled under the covers and due to the long drive earlier she thankfully fell asleep quickly, only to be awoken a few hours later by a warm body cuddling up to her.

"What the hell?" Bea switched on her light to find Carlos stark naked trying to kiss her. "Get out!" She pushed him off the bed, pulling the covers right up under her chin.

"What's all the noise about, I'm trying to sleep." Her mum was standing in the doorway, her face plastered in some green slime, her body covered in a see-through black nightie. Averting her eyes from the sight Bea got out of bed.

"Your boyfriend just tried to kiss me." She was so shocked and angry that she was shaking slightly.

"Poor boy just got confused that's all." Her mum beckoned to Carlos and he took her hand before walking out of the door giving Bea a wink over his shoulder as he went. Bea slammed the door shut behind them, pushing a chair under the handle to stop any further unwanted interruptions.


Sunday morning found her up early and out at the local shop for a few basics. When she came back it was to find Carlos, clad only in tiny white boxers standing in the kitchen waiting for the kettle to boil.

"Good morning beautiful." Although his accent was thick, his English was perfect.

"Mum said you couldn't speak English?" Bea put the heavy bags down on the counter.

"Kathleen has never asked nor do I believe she even cares." He poured boiling water into two mugs before reaching for the milk from the bag, brushing his nether regions against her as he did.

"Then why are you with her?" Bea tried to ignore the blush that was slowly spreading across her body.

"If I had known what a beautiful daughter she had I would not be." He was looking at her so intently that Bea had to look away. "Your mother is beautiful in her own way but her body is old, yours is...how do they say? Fit as?" With these last words he made the outline of a women's body with his hands. "We could have fun, *Senorita*." These last words were a whisper in her ear and despite herself she shivered.

"Morning everyone," her mum shouted as she came down the stairs and into the kitchen. Carlos immediately went back to making tea and Bea looked away lest her mum should see the guilty look on her face. "Thank God you've been shopping Bea, your cupboards were empty."

"Morning Mum, I mean Kath." Bea corrected herself at the reproachful look her mum gave her. "How long are you staying for?" She busied herself making bacon and eggs.

"Just a few days, we'll head off to London soon. I've lined Carlos up for a job in Kings Cross." Her mum headed into the living room and Bea gave herself a mental note to forewarn Em of her impending arrival.

"We will carry on later, *Senorita*." Carlos ran his hand over her bum before taking the two mugs of tea into the living room.

"Heaven help me." Bea looked to the sky, unsure if her life could possibly get any worse.

# CHAPTER 6

By half past nine on Monday morning, Bea realised that in fact, life could get worse. Her mum was in a foul mood after she'd received a phone call saying the job in Kings Cross had been filled and Em had texted Bea practically begging her to keep their mum for a bit. Her husband was still recovering from the last visit and had gone ballistic when she'd told him she was coming again. Apart from that, Bea had spent the whole of Sunday avoiding being alone with Carlos who tried to kiss her every time her mum left the room even if it was for just a few seconds.

Whatever had been wrong with Maureen was obviously over and she was back to her normal spiteful self, making snide comments and putting Bea down in the first five minutes of her being in the office. She'd never been so happy to receive a summons from Mr. Rock to visit him immediately even if it was accompanied with "What have you done now?"

Walking into Mr. Rock's office she was surprised to find Mrs. White in there as well and really did begin to wonder what she had done.

"Ah, there you are Bea, please sit down." Mr. Rock indicated to the chair in front of his desk, unfortunately next to Mrs. White. "I've been told that you're not getting on very well."

"What?" Bea was caught off guard. "I'm not really sure I understand what you mean, sir?"

"Mrs. White has been telling me you've been causing trouble with Maureen, undermining her in front of clients, getting things wrong in the accounts, we can't have this I'm afraid." Bea looked over to Mrs. White who was smiling smugly.

"It's not a recent thing either." Mrs. White spoke up. "Maureen tells me it's ever since she moved into her office." This first comment was directed to Mr. Rock but now she turned to Bea. "You had such promise when you first started but you just seem to think you're better than everyone else here."

Bea didn't really know what to say, it looked like her card was marked whether she defended herself or not. What would she actually say anyway? It was clearly her word against Maureen's and who would believe her over one of the most senior accountants there?

"Perhaps I could speak with Bea alone now?" Mr. Rock asked Mrs. White who was not best pleased about being dismissed so quickly. "She doesn't need an audience for what I'm about to tell her." Once the door had been shut his tone and demeanour changed instantly. "I'm so sorry about that Bea, but have to keep up the pretence you know." He winked at her.

"I've told Dad everything." Jen had entered from the adjoining room to Mr. Rock's office.

"There's not a lot I can do I'm afraid, but I had a rather interesting conversation with a Mr. Summers first thing this morning and may I suggest that you take the job if he offers it to you?" Bea still couldn't find her voice. "It seems like an excellent opportunity, get yourself off to see a different part of the country, enjoy your life while you're young."

"But it's only part time sir, I can't afford to live on the wages." This really was the biggest hurdle.

"What do you need money for at your age?" Mr. Rock was getting animated. "As long as you've got a roof over your head and food in your belly what else do you need?"

"I don't suppose I'll get the job anyway sir." Bea was quite sure Mr. Summers would have chosen someone with experience of the publishing industry.

"Well then the man's a fool." They were interrupted by a buzzing and Mr. Rock waved them both out as he picked up the phone to answer the incoming call.

"You'd best get upstairs." Jen waved her off. "And pretend to be all contrite, remember you've had a good telling off." She laughed as she went down the stairs and Bea went up.

The look on Maureen's face was a picture. She was absolutely positive she knew what had gone on so with a solemn face, Bea sat down at her desk and kept her head on her work all morning. Lunch time came and without a word Maureen went off to the canteen and finally Bea lifted her head up, rubbing her neck to rid herself of the ache in it.

She pulled out her phone to find a missed call and voicemail message from Scott Summers. Half of her was dying to listen to it, the other half didn't want to know. But with Mr. Rock's words echoing in her ear she pressed the voicemail button on her phone to hear the silky tones of Scott Summers being delighted to tell her that the job was hers if she wanted it but could she start a week today.

Bea couldn't stop the huge smile that spread across her face and the excitement that started coursing through her veins. He'd even said that after speaking with Mr. Rock he'd like her to cover reception over the lunch time period so that would mean an extra hour a day and an extra three thousand pounds a year. It would still be extremely tight but perhaps she could just stretch to that property that was £675 per month.

She ran down to reception where Jen always stayed for lunch even though the office was closed for an hour. However, Bea was surprised to find Josh also in reception, his trousers round his ankles and Jen's legs around his waist. They both looked at the door guiltily as Bea stumbled in and averted her eyes hurriedly.

Josh hastily pulled his trousers up and Jen rearranged her skirt and top as she slid off the desk.

"I thought you'd locked the door?" Jen hissed at Josh.

"I thought I had," he hissed back.

"Just be glad it was only Bea." She kissed him passionately before sending him out the door.

"I'm so sorry." Bea still didn't know where to look. "I mean I knew you were seeing him but I didn't know things had progressed that far. I thought he had a girlfriend?"

"Oh he does." Jen sat down behind her desk, Bea sitting in the seat opposite, trying not to touch the desk. "But she's an absolute cow, Josh says."

"Well if she's that much of a cow why is he with her?" Bea always wondered why women were sometimes so gullible when it came to attractive men.

"He won't be much longer." Jen was busy reapplying her lipstick and brushing her hair. "Josh says he's just got to wait for the right moment to tell her." Bea just nodded, not believing Josh for a second but not wanting to burst Jen's bubble.

"Do you know what time your dad's back from lunch?" Bea changed the subject.

"Dad didn't go out today, he's probably in his office still. Why?" Jen looked over at her and saw the huge smile on her face. "You got the job, didn't you?"

"I did, and it's a bit of extra money as well but I'll still have a few hours in the afternoon to concentrate on my writing." Bea hadn't consciously made the decision to accept the job but from the way she was talking she knew now that she had. She couldn't turn down the opportunity of a fresh start in such a glorious part of the country, not with so much wrong in her current life.

"Go and see him now," Jen urged her. "He won't mind." Bea stood up and walked out the door. "Congratulations, by the way." Jen called as she disappeared out of the hallway.


Mr. Rock had been overjoyed at her news but sorry to see her go. He apologised over and over again for what had happened and promised her that Maureen would have no further juniors in her office. He assured her that finishing on Friday would not be a problem under the circumstances as long as she got all her work finished.

When she returned to her office Bea had immediately rung Mr. Summers to tell him she would accept the job, then set about making a list of everything that she needed to do over the next week. When Maureen returned after lunch it was to find a very smiley but very quiet Bea.

"Had some good news, have you?" Bea could tell Maureen was curious but she wasn't about to tell her a thing. Mr. Rock said he would keep it quiet and Bea knew she could trust Jen not to say anything.

"Wouldn't you like to know?" Bea muttered under her breath.

"I beg your pardon?" Maureen had been heading for her desk but she did a double take at Bea's words.

"I said, not that I know of." Bea knew she didn't believe her but at this moment in time she really didn't care.

"Humph!" She sat down heavily in her chair. "Well we've got the Osbourne account coming in on Wednesday so I'll need you to start prepping."

"I won't be able to do that I'm afraid." It felt so good to speak to her like that.

"Too big to do the mundane work are we?" Maureen picked up the phone. "We'll see what Mrs. White has to say about that."

In seconds Mrs. White was at the door, her face as purple as a beetroot.

"Get yourself down to Mr. Rock right now." Everyone else on the floor had looked up at the raised voice. "How dare you answer a senior member of staff back like that? After your warning this morning as well."

Bea was almost marched out of the office and down the stairs by Mrs. White with Maureen following closely behind.

"Maurice, you have to do something with this insolent young girl." Bea had never heard Mrs. White use Mr. Rock's first name before.

"My dear Caroline, please calm down and tell me what an earth is the matter." Mr. Rock was the epitome of quiet as Mrs. White, helped along with Maureen began their offence against Bea. "Well she's right, she won't be able to do it."

"I'm glad you agree with me." Mrs. White obviously hadn't been listening. "I'm sorry but what did you say?"

"I said that Bea is correct, she won't be able to start the Osbourne account. In fact she won't be starting anything new for a while." Mr. Rock clasped his hands together as Mrs. White and Maureen's mouths fell open in shock. "She's starting a very important project on Monday and needs to get everything else finished off beforehand."

"May I go please sir?" Bea had been silent all through their tirade. "I've got such a lot to do."

"Of course you can my dear." Mr. Rock smiled at her as she left then turned to the other two women in his office. Bea didn't hear what was said but when Maureen returned to the office, her face red with anger, Bea was sure Mr. Rock had told them a few home truths.

When Bea returned home that night it was to find her mum dressed as a French maid performing a strip tease for Carlos in the living room. She rushed upstairs into the bathroom, running a hot bath and turning her music up loud. She'd had enough of bursting in on other people's sex lives today.

She relaxed into the warm bubbles and began to plan her next move. She would have to stay in the hotel unless she was able to move into a property straight away. *But what about furniture,* she suddenly thought. This house was rented fully furnished and Bea was pretty sure the other property wasn't. In fact she didn't even know what the other property was, she hadn't let the agent finish telling her about it.

For the first time that day, Bea wondered if she was doing the right thing. How could she give up a secure well-paid job and move miles away on what felt like a bit of a whim? And in less than a week as well. She had no idea where she was going to live, she couldn't afford to buy furniture. No, she would have to tell Mr. Summers she couldn't take the job.

Decision made, she stood up to get out of the bath just as Carlos burst in, completely naked. Her towel was on the other side of the room so she covered herself with her hands as best as she could.

"Get out!" she screamed.

"But sweet *Senorita*, there is no need to cover yourself from me." He tried to prise her arm away from her breasts. "We will be seeing so much more of each other from now on." His face was level with hers. "Your mother says we are to stay with you for a few months."

"Isn't that wonderful news." Her mum came swanning in behind him, also completely naked except for black stockings and suspenders. "Do cover yourself child, you'll catch a chill." She handed Bea a towel which she accepted, wrapping it around herself quickly. "It's all been arranged." Her mum was smiling, as was Carlos and Bea averted her eyes as they started kissing again.

"Will you please get out of the bathroom?" she begged and without an answer they backed out, lips locked all the way. "Well that settles that then," Bea said to herself as she wiped the condensation from the steamed-up mirror. "I'll sleep on the floor and eat beans on toast every day if it means getting away from this madhouse."

# CHAPTER 7

The next few days flew by and for once Bea was enjoying work. It had never been so much fun. She was thoroughly enjoying winding Maureen up on any and every opportunity. No one in the office had a clue what was going on but most of them seemed quite pleased to see that the normally opinionated Maureen had been silenced for a while.

Home life on the other hand was slightly worse. Her mum wasn't best pleased that she would have to pay the rent, she'd been hoping for free board and food as she normally did but Bea knew she had more than enough tucked away in some bank or another. There was no way she could afford all these foreign trips without money.

But finding a suitable home in Bloomsdale was another matter. The property that the agent was advertising at £675 a month had already been taken but he was looking to take on a one-bedroom maisonette later in the week that he would let Bea have for £625. She arranged to meet him for a viewing on Saturday morning, pinning all her hopes that it would be suitable. She still wouldn't have any furniture but maybe she could pick some things up from charity shops.

It was Friday afternoon before she knew it and all her work had been completed and signed off by Mr. Rock. She'd packed all her clothes in a suitcase that was now sitting in the boot of her car, along with a few bits of cutlery, towels and anything else she was able to sneak out from under her mum's watchful gaze.

Her mum had hardly spoken to her last night as she'd packed up her things, she didn't like not getting her own way and tried everything she could think of to dissuade Bea from leaving.

"Where are you going to live?" Her mum had stood in the doorway to the bedroom, arms folded. "And how are you going to live? You said yourself the money isn't very good." The conversation had been pretty much one sided. "Why would you want to move to a tiny village where everyone knows everyone else's business?"

"I think it will be lovely to have a bit of community." Bea was looking forward to a different pace of life after living in a city. "No one talks to their neighbours around here and I only know the surname of next door because I took a parcel in for them just before Christmas."

"Well I think you're making a big mistake." Bea knew her mum only wanted her to stay because she didn't want to have to look after herself, and after a stilted goodbye she had locked herself away in the spare bedroom leaving Bea to fend off Carlos for the rest of the night.

"I could come with you, *Senorita*." Bea had laughed out loud at this, not in a nasty way but almost a hysterical way.

"I don't think that's a good idea, do you?" She was folding her clothes as neatly as possible into the suitcase.

"Why not?" Carlos had sat opposite her on the bed. "I am hard worker, I will get job and provide for us."

"Oh Carlos." Bea couldn't help laughing.

"What is so funny? You laugh at me all the time." He appeared to be hurt.

"You're so young." He was only a few years younger than Bea, but it was all she could think of to say. "It would never work." She didn't even want to try, he was handsome and charming but Bea could never be with anyone like him.

The conversation had ended there as her mother had called him and she didn't see either of them again, neither got up to say goodbye to her or wish her well so she had headed off to work early.

It was now three o clock and Mr. Rock had told her she could leave early. As everyone was still in their offices, she made the rounds to say goodbye to them all before heading back to her own office to collect her things.

"What on earth have you been doing all this time?" Maureen hated not knowing what was going on. "You may have pulled the wool over Mr. Rock's eyes but you don't fool me."

"I don't need to fool you, Maureen, as you put it." Bea was finally going to have her say. "I have never met such a spiteful or opinionated woman as you in my whole life. You seem to delight in hurting people, even take pleasure in putting others down." Maureen seemed to be shrinking in size under Bea's words. "I tried to work with you, I really did but you had something against me from day one." Bea took a slight pause. "I think you're jealous."

"Jealous?" Maureen spat. "Why would I be jealous of you?"

"Not just of me." Bea knew she'd hit a nerve. "Of anyone that's younger than you, cleverer than you or just taller than you." She carried on with the size issue. "You sit there, behind your huge desk lording it over anyone that will let you, thinking you're better than everyone but really Maureen, you're just a little woman with a big problem and I feel sorry for you." Bea turned around, grabbed her bag and walked out without a backward glance at Maureen who for probably the first time in her life was completely and utterly silent.

It felt so good to be back in Bloomsdale. This time when she pulled up outside the hotel the sun was still shining and the village looked beautiful. She hadn't noticed all the hanging baskets and planted tubs around before and they just added to the charm of the place.

She was given the same room that she'd had the previous week and after quickly unpacking a few bits and pieces from her overnight bag she took a walk to have a look at the maisonette that was up for rent.

It was about a mile out of the village but she enjoyed the walk after being cooped up in the car. She turned down the road that Google Maps told her to go down and her heart sank. Instead of a pretty little street like all the others were, Bea found herself on a dirt track that led to an old cottage.

"Well, this can't be right." She spoke to her phone, checking the map again and again but it was insistent so she walked closer. A tiny sign in one of the downstairs windows proclaimed it 'For Rent' and Bea was no longer in any doubt.

The numbers on the battered front door were 10 and 10a and she wondered where on earth all the other houses were if this was the tenth one. The upstairs of the property looked marginally tidier just because there were curtains at the windows, but the whole of the outside was in need of a good lick of paint. The garden looked like it hadn't seen a lawn mower in years and the pathway was cracked with weeds.

The door opened suddenly and a man dressed in a dirty vest that just covered his stomach stepped out and began to light a cigarette. He noticed Bea after his first drag and walked over to stand behind the rusty metal gate.

"You looking to rent this place?" he asked with more of a Lancashire accent than a Yorkshire one. "I'm the landlord Mick, I live upstairs." He looked Bea up and down and she felt naked under his scrutiny. "It went up with agent t'other day but I'd be willing to make ya a deal."

Before she knew what was happening Bea had accepted an offer to have a look around and her worst fears were confirmed. The walls were so damp that the wallpaper didn't even stick to them anymore. Mould was growing on the window sills and the kitchen was thick with grease. The whole place smelt musty and old. The lounge, kitchen and bedroom were all just one big open plan room and she couldn't even look in the bathroom, just one whiff when he opened the door was enough to send her scuttling into the relative fresh air of the hall way.

"Here's my lovely wife." A female version of Mick had now joined them. "Ruby this is…er…sorry love I didn't get your name?"

"Bea." She held out her hand then immediately wished she hadn't. Ruby's hand was thick with dirt, the nails cracked and yellow.

"Ruby love this is…" But he didn't have chance to answer.

"Moonbeam Winters." Ruby's soft voice was in complete contrast to her appearance. "Returned at last."

# CHAPTER 8

"What did you say?" Bea surely hadn't heard her correctly.

"I said, pleasure to meet ya." She spoke with a broad Yorkshire accent, where had the soft voice gone? Had she imagined it?

"But, you just said my name." Bea wasn't letting it go.

"I don't know your name." Ruby looked to her husband. "She alright in the head?"

"Don't worry yourself Ruby love. Get back upstairs and make us a nice pot o' tea." Mick guided his wife towards the stairs then turned to Bea. "Ruby likes to play little games with people."

"How did she know my name?" Bea wasn't at all convinced. "No one knows my name."

"I told you, she likes to play games." Mick was ushering her out now. "Like I said, it's up with agent so you'll have to see him if you wants the place." And without even a goodbye the door was firmly shut in her face.

Bea just stood there for a few seconds, had she really just heard that? Had that woman really just said her name? And what on earth had she meant by 'returned at last'? Bea had only been here for the first time a few days ago and she was sure she'd never seen Mick or Ruby before.

She headed back to the hotel, informing the receptionist of her intention to stay for the foreseeable future, luckily they'd offered her a discounted rate. She had to find somewhere soon though, there was no way she could have lived in that place. Apart from the crazy woman living upstairs the maisonette was a health hazard.

After leaving a message for the agent on his phone, cancelling the appointment for the following morning, Bea headed off to the coffee shop, she needed some caffeine to calm her nerves.

Her face lit up when she saw Eddie sitting at the same table he'd been sitting at before and after ordering a large cappuccino and a slice of chocolate cake she headed in his direction.

"Hello stranger." Eddie looked up from his laptop with a huge grin on his face.

"Back again I see." He pressed a few keys, Bea assumed he was saving his work before shutting down the lid and moving it to one side. "I heard you got the job."

"That seems to have been the easy part." She ripped open a sachet of sugar and poured it into her cup, quickly followed by four more.

"You need a sugar rush?" Eddie handed her a plastic spoon. "Even I don't take five sugars."

"What?" Bea looked at the evidence on the table, she hadn't even realised what she'd been doing. "I normally only take one." She laughed.

"Want to tell me about it?" His face was full of concern.

"Well, apart from the fact that I've upped sticks, quit my job, moved to a different part of the country and have nowhere to live, I've just had the most absurd encounter with a crazy woman." She stirred her coffee.

"You've met Ruby Turner then." Bea looked at him in surprise. "She's the only crazy person round here. She thinks she can tell the future."

"She's a fortune teller?" Bea dug her fork into the cake.

"I said she thinks she can tell the future." He took a sip from his own cup, pulling a face when he realised it was cold. "She does readings for people but as far as I know she's never got anything right." He went to the counter to order a fresh cup of tea. "Let me guess." He turned round, leaning back against the counter. "She told you that you'd meet a tall, dark, handsome stranger." With a quick thanks, he grabbed his cup and returned to the table. "Well, here I am."

"She knew my name." Bea was expecting the look of mock horror that crossed his face.

"So do lots of people I should imagine." Eddie was eyeing up her cake. "And if she didn't know it, she probably just took a lucky guess. There's not many names that Bea can be short for."

"You try and guess it then." She pushed the cake over to him, she really wasn't hungry at all.

"It's not Beatrice." He remembered their previous conversation. "Beatie? Bryony? Elizabeth?" He went through as many names as he could think of and each time she shook her head. "Is it just Bea?" His tea was finally cool enough and he took a sip.

"It's Moonbeam." Eddie choked as she spoke, spilling tea everywhere.

"Moonbeam?" He dabbed himself with a napkin where he'd dribbled tea down himself. "Who calls their daughter Moonbeam?"

"My mum was a bit of a hippy in her day." She handed Eddie another napkin. "My brother is called Alabaster and my sister, Emerald."

"Bet that made for interesting Christmas cards." He was mopping up the little spill that had dripped onto his laptop. "It does suit you though." He smirked and she slapped him playfully. "I'm not joking, it does."

"So now you know." Bea watched in disgust as he continued to eat the cake even though it was swimming in tea.

"What?" he said with a mouthful. "I'm a struggling writer."

"I've got to find somewhere to live." She pushed all thoughts of Ruby Turner out of her head and concentrated on the most pressing problem. "Any ideas?"

"We're only a little village so as soon as something comes up, it goes again." He had already demolished the cake. "Most of the people that live here are born and bred but we have a few people that commute into the city."

"That's not very helpful." She put her head in her hands.

"There's always one of the B&Bs." He said helpfully. "It's bound to be cheaper than the hotel and I'm sure a couple of them have taken on long term before."

"But I want a place of my own." Bea didn't mean to sound ungrateful.

"I can take you to a few if you want." He shrugged his shoulders. "We get lots of visitors up here because of Scott and his books, made the place quite famous you know. Bound to be one of them able to give you a good deal."

"Worth a try I suppose." Bea loved the hotel but knew that even at the discounted rate she couldn't stay there more than a week or two. Perhaps if she could just get a room somewhere rather than paying for breakfast every day that would be a start. She could get a microwave and a little fridge, after all she mostly ate convenience foods anyway.

"Shall I meet you in the morning?" Eddie had started packing his laptop away and as Bea looked around she noticed it was starting to get dark outside and the coffee shop was about to close.

"That would be lovely." They walked out of the door. "About ten o clock?"

"Perfect, I'll see you here at ten." He smiled and headed off in the opposite direction to Bea as he had done before.

She didn't feel like going back to the hotel just yet, even though it was dusk she decided a quick walk around the village might sort her head out and help her come up with a solution to her living accommodation. She really couldn't see herself staying in one room for any longer than a few weeks however much she tried to convince herself.

Finding herself back at the little courtyard she plonked down on one of the benches that sat in the centre around a memorial for the village's war dead. She was opposite the general stores which had long closed for the day as had all the other shops. Only the hotel and pub were still open. Deciding to treat herself to a drink in the local pub she headed over the road to the aptly named Inn on the Moor.

It was a beautifully old building inside and out. The huge room was furnished with neatly laid tables and chairs and a small bar with a few seats sat on the left. The owners welcomed her in and the regulars were friendly and talkative. After a couple of glasses of wine she found herself spilling out her problem to the owner's daughter who had just finished clearing the tables after dinner.

"Something will turn up." She laid a reassuring hand on Bea's arm. "It always does."

"Are there any rooms here?" Bea had noticed the B&B sign as she'd walked in.

"I'm sorry they're all being refurbished." The girl shook her head. "We've only just took this place over."

"I'd best get back." Bea stood up and swayed a little, three glasses of wine on an empty stomach had not been a good idea.

"You okay?" The girl had stood up beside her.

"I'll be fine." Bea stood up straighter as if to prove the point. "I've only got to walk to the hotel."

"We'll see you again I'm sure." The girl smiled.

"You will indeed." Bea walked slowly to ensure a straight line. "Night." She remembered to say just before reaching the door.

It was pitch black outside now and Bea fumbled for her phone to turn the torch app on. There were only a few lamps spread sporadically around the village which gave very little light to anyone daft enough to be walking around at night. She turned the torch on just in time to see a piece of broken wall lying on the floor but not in time to stop herself tripping over it.

Landing face downward on the gravel surface of the drive she was glad no one was around to see her and then started to giggle at what she must look like. Flipping herself on to her back she stared up at the night sky. It took her breath away at the brilliance of it. She'd never seen such bright stars or so many. In the city it was hard to see them but here in the middle of the Yorkshire moors with no traffic or light pollution the view was stunning.

She lay there for a few minutes just taking it all in then remembered that she was lying on the drive of a pub car park and really should get up. With very little grace and elegance she got to her feet, sighed when she realised her jeans were ripped and winced at the grazes on her hands, thankful that she had at least saved her face from the same fate.

She swore as she realised her phone must have flown out of her hands as she tripped and hoped it hadn't landed face down otherwise she'd never find it. Luckily it was just a few metres away, shining upwards towards the heavens. She went over to it, reached down to pick it up and screamed as something wet touched her hand.

# CHAPTER 9

Bea stood paralysed for a few seconds before realising that her phone was now lying upside down as she couldn't see any light coming from it at all. There was nothing else to do but kneel on the ground and feel around for it. Tentatively she started to edge her hands out, hoping that whatever had touched her before had gone. She was concentrating so hard that she didn't hear the crunch of tyres on gravel or a car door opening. Only when she found her phone in the bright head lights did she realise someone was there.

"Good evening Bea." The smooth voice of Scott Summers came from behind her. "Can I be of any assistance?"

"Oh, er, hello there Mr. Summers." Bea couldn't believe her luck, of all the people she had to meet it was him. "I dropped my phone, that's all." She stood up with the help of his offered hand and cursed inwardly at what state she must be in. She knew her hands were grazed and was sure her jeans were ripped or at best, filthy.

"You'll soon get used to the dark." There was a tiny clicking sound and Bea found herself illuminated in a torch light. "Always carry one of these around." He was looking at her intently. "You are all messed up aren't you?" Bea looked at herself and realised she was far worse than she thought.

Her hands were trickling with blood and embedded with gravel, her jeans were torn on both knees with small grazes and her clean white shirt was filthy.

"They're just scratches." She started to pick the tiny stones from out of her hands, wincing each time and wishing the ground would just swallow her up. What on earth must he think of her, falling over in the pub car park? "I'll clean them up back at my room." She desperately wanted to get out of this situation before her embarrassment threatened to overcome her.

"You'll do no such thing." Scott walked round the other side of his car and opened the door. "I'll take you back to my house and we'll get you all patched up. You've got a nasty cut by your eye and your hands need a thorough cleansing." Bea reached up to her eye flinching when she realised he was right.

"It's okay really." She was grateful for his help but the thought of prolonging the situation was agony.

"I'm not taking no for an answer Bea." And she knew by his tone that she had no choice. She slipped onto the cold leather seat and stared in awe. She had expected him to drive a big flashy Mercedes but instead she found herself inside a classic Aston Martin. "Beautiful isn't she? Restored her myself."

"Wow." Bea felt the word was totally inadequate but could think of nothing else to say. As they drove off along the country roads she listened intently as he told her all about how he'd found the rusty old shell of the car and worked on her constantly for months until she was like new. "You really didn't have to do this you know, Mr. Summers."

"Scott, please," he insisted. "I wasn't about to leave you covered in blood now was I?"

"Well thank you, it's really very kind." It was amazing how suddenly sober she felt. Nothing like a good dose of humiliation to clear the head.

"Here we are." Bea hadn't noticed that they'd turned off the road and onto a long drive. It was lined with huge old oak trees and she could just glimpse the shimmering of light up ahead. "Welcome to Bloomsdale Manor." Bea gasped in surprise and awe as the house came into view.

"You live here." It was a statement rather than a question but he nodded all the same. The house stood two stories high, Georgian in design and Bea counted five windows across on each side of the door which stood perfectly in the middle. She then counted four windows going back and marvelled at how one man could live in such a big house all on his own. But did he live on his own? She was sure she hadn't read anything about him being married or having children.

"Of course, it's a bit big for me at the moment." He'd answered her question without her even having to ask it. "But one day I hope it will be filled with children." Was she mistaken in the look he just gave her as he pulled the hand brake on?

"It's beautiful." She crumpled under his gaze, then jumped as the car door opened on its own.

"Good evening miss." Bea sighed with relief when she saw a smartly dressed man standing there.

"Evening Johnson." Scott called cheerily, leaning over Bea as he did. "Can you show our guest inside while I pop the car away in the garage?" Johnson nodded and helped Bea out of the car before it drove off around the back of the house.

"This way miss." Bea felt like she had stepped into Pride and Prejudice as she followed Johnson the short distance to the door and then into the hallway. She was mesmerised by her surroundings. Although Georgian on the outside, the inside was very modern and Bea wondered if the building was actually quite as old as it appeared.

Johnson opened a large double door and Bea was rendered speechless, she knew that open plan living was the new 'in thing' but this house took it to the extreme. Apart from the ones on the outside there wasn't a single wall in the whole of the downstairs floor. There were still the obvious rooms set out but there were no physical dividers anywhere and it reminded Bea of Scott's office.

She was ushered towards what Bea would have called the lounge where Johnson indicated to her to sit down on the softest, longest sofa that she had ever seen.

"Would Miss care for a drink?" Bea didn't have time to answer as Scott appeared behind them carrying a green box.

"It's okay Johnson." He placed the box next to her on the sofa. "You get yourself off to bed, we'll be fine."

"Very good sir." And with a bow and a click of his heels Johnson retreated back towards the hallway.

"This place is amazing." Bea hadn't realised Scott was this successful and reminded herself to do better research in future.

"It was just a ruin when I brought it so it was an absolute steal." He knelt down in front of her and opened the box, pulling out lotion and sterile pads. "I'll show you the photos one day but now we need to get these cuts cleaned up."

"Honestly, I'll be fine." But Scott wasn't taking no for an answer and began bathing her grazed knees through the rips in her jeans. Bea grimaced as the antiseptic touched the raw skin.

"It's no good." He suddenly stopped what he was doing. "They're going to have to come off."

"What?" Bea wasn't sure she'd heard him correctly.

"The jeans." He stood up. "I can't get to all the cuts and I'll need to dress them afterwards anyway so you'll have to take them off."

"But…" She cursed her awkwardness yet again. She was supposed to be impressing her new boss but instead he'd found her lying in a pub car park and now she was supposed to strip in front of him.

"I'll just cut them at the knees instead." Bea breathed a sigh of relief then realised this option was far worse as she felt Scott's hand steadying her thigh as he cut her jeans off just above the knee.

then pushed them up a little further, his fingers brushing her skin lightly.

"Have you always been a writer?" She needed to take her mind of what was happening.

"Not always." One knee was now bandaged and he started on the other, repeating the thigh holding again. Bea felt a shiver rush through her. "The publishing came first but writing was always my passion and I've been very lucky to turn my writing into a career but it's the publishing I enjoy the most, helping other writers fulfil their dreams. And I do a lot of volunteer work at the hospital and with the old folks in the community." Both knees were now clean and covered and he started on her hands. "I help out with the homeless when I can and the past few years I've treated some terminally ill children and their families to holidays in Lapland." There was no hint of gloating in his voice.

Was this man too good to be true? Bea asked herself. Not only was he drop dead gorgeous with a body to die for but he spent his life helping others. *Next he'll be telling me he rescues stray animals too.* Bea had never met such a perfect man and found herself drifting off into a daydream involving a church and a huge white dress.

"Then there's the animal shelter and donkey sanctuary." Scott was concentrating on picking out the bits of gravel that were embedded in her hands. "And I'm hoping to visit Africa soon to learn about all the endangered animals there."

"Marry me." Bea hadn't realised she'd spoken out loud until Scott looked up. "I'm so sorry…" She stuttered and stood up. "I'll get myself back to the hotel." She had never been so embarrassed in her life and tried to escape as quickly as possible.

"It's okay." He caught her arm as she made to move past him. She couldn't look at him and tried to free herself gently from his grasp.

"I'm such an idiot." God, what must he think of her? Getting herself drunk, falling over and then proposing to a man she'd just met and not just any man, her new boss.

"Yes." She was still looking at the floor and he put his hand under her chin to lift her eyes to his.

"What do you mean, yes?" she almost whispered, fearing her voice would fail under his gaze.

"Yes, I'll marry you."

# CHAPTER 10

"Beg pardon?" Bea was going to have to get her hearing checked, she definitely didn't just hear him say what she thought she'd heard him say.

"Obviously we'll have to have a few dates first to get to know each other." He led her back to the sofa to sit down and re-started the task of cleaning her hands.

"Well obviously." She didn't really know what to say, surely he was joking?

"I'll tell Johnson in the morning and he can get a room ready for you here." Both hands were now free of dirt and gravel and he had started gently rubbing Savlon into the grazes. "I'll arrange for the vicar to come and see us in the week. How does September sound? I've always wanted to get married in September." Scott turned his attention to the cut by her eye before continuing. "I've got quite a large group of family and friends so we'll need to look at something big enough to accommodate everyone. Oh I do hope they can all come on such short notice. Of course I'll pay for everything so you don't need to worry about that. Do you have a large family?"

"Er…" Bea was speechless.

"You do know I'm winding you up, don't you?" Scott's face spread into a huge smile.

"You were so serious." His smile was infectious and she soon found herself giggling. "I really don't know why I said it."

"Certainly a good way to break the ice with your new boss anyway." He placed a Steri-Strip across her eyebrow. "All done."

"You mean you still want to employ me?" Bea sighed in relief, she didn't relish the thought of going back to her Mum and Carlos.

"Of course." He sat down next to her. "I think we're going to get on just fine, you and me."

The two of them sat on the sofa chatting like old friends and before they knew it, it was 3am.

"We should get to bed." Bea pulled a pretend look of shock at Scott's statement. "You know I don't mean together." He winked provocatively. "Although I'm up for it if you are?" She gave him a playful slap even though she wished he wasn't joking. "You can stop in one of the guest rooms if you like. There'll be a bathrobe and toiletries in there."

"Are you sure?" She really should call a taxi and get back to the hotel, but the thought of waking up and sharing some more time with Scott was far more tempting.

"Of course." He stood up and then helped her to her feet.

"Ouch." Bea had forgotten about her knees which felt a little stiff after sitting down for so long.

"Come on, wounded soldier." He showed her up the stairs and again Bea was mesmerised by the house.

In complete contrast to the open plan layout downstairs, upstairs was a long passageway with countless white doors and further passages leading off on both sides.

"I just love your house." Scott smiled at this.

"Now, I usually have a late breakfast at the weekend; about 10 o clock okay?" She nodded. "I think The Rose Room will suit you. It's the one my sister uses when she comes to visit and she's about your size so there'll be some spare clothes in the wardrobe as well." He opened one of the doors and switched on the light.

"Bloody hell, I can't believe I forgot." Bea had been so wrapped up in everything she'd completely forgotten her meeting with Eddie. "I'm meeting Eddie at 10 in the coffee shop."

"Eddie?" Scott raised his eyebrows quizzically.

"You know Eddie." Bea knew he knew Eddie. "He works for you."

"You mean Edmund." Scott's face darkened a little.

"He's helping me find a place to live." She walked into the room.

"Then we shall have breakfast at 9 and I'll drive you to your date myself." Scott's happy smile had been replaced with a slight frown.

"Oh, it's not a date. He's just a friend." Scott's smile reappeared instantly.

"Then I shall wish you goodnight and see you in the morning." With a quick peck on her cheek he was gone down the hall and she shut the door, leaning against it in disbelief.

"What a night." She spoke out loud to herself as she recalled the events of the evening, and started to examine the room.

It was beautifully furnished with soft floral curtains and bedding. The bed looked enormous, far bigger than Bea's tiny double back home. The triple wardrobe had floor to ceiling mirrors for doors and when she opened them she gasped at the sight of Scott's idea of some spare clothes. From what Bea could see there was an entire department store hanging up in every shade of every colour imaginable with shoes to match. She sighed longingly at a pair of blue suede boots before pulling out a pair of jeans that looked to be her size and a plain white shirt.

She laid them over the chair by the dressing table ready for the morning, thanked the heavens when she found clean pants in one of the drawers then headed into the en-suite bathroom. Here, just as Scott had said, were brand new toiletries. Not mini ones that you got when travelling but brand new, full sized shampoos, conditioners, shower gels, toothpastes and toothbrushes. Bea wondered if all the spare rooms were equipped like this one was.

She decided to set her alarm for 8 o clock which would allow her an hour before breakfast to have a nice soak in the whirlpool bath and use the divine smelling coconut concoctions she'd discovered. After a quick brush of her teeth and wash of her face she dived into the soft bed and was instantly asleep.

"Miss Winters?" Johnson's voice along with an insistent knocking on the door gradually woke Bea up.

"Yes?" She spoke sleepily, trying to stifle a yawn which failed miserably.

"Mr. Summers has asked me to tell you that breakfast is ready." Bea looked at her watch and cursed when she realised it was half past nine. No chance of that long soak she'd been looking forward to.

"Thank you." She leapt out of the bed. "I'll be down in five minutes."

"Very good, miss." Bea assumed Johnson had left as there was no further conversation so she ran into the bathroom, had a quick spruce up and put the borrowed clothes on, rolling the jeans up as they were far too long for her.

"Morning, Sleepyhead." Scott was sitting at a long marble breakfast bar, a newspaper in one hand and a cup in the other. A feast lay before her, white toast, brown toast, jams and marmalades sat in the middle. To the left were plates of bacon, sausage, black pudding, eggs done three ways, tomatoes grilled and fried alongside mushrooms and baked beans. Then to the right were ten different cereals, croissants, crumpets and pancakes.

"I'm so sorry I overslept. I thought I'd set my alarm." She sat down opposite him, her stomach rumbling with hunger. "This surely isn't all for me?"

"No, that would be absurd." He put down his paper and smiled at her, suddenly she wasn't hungry anymore. "I've got a few people coming over to discuss some new projects." As if on cue the doorbell rang. "That'll be them now." He saw her hesitate. "Help yourself to whatever you want then I'll drive you to the coffee shop whenever you're ready."

"But what about your meeting?" She started picking at a pancake. Her stomach was now doing some very strange things as Scott had stood up to greet his guests and she could see his perfectly toned muscles under his tight shirt.

"By the time everyone has eaten and we're actually ready to sit down it will be lunch time so they won't miss me for ten minutes." The kitchen area was suddenly full of men and women dressed in business suits and two men dressed in the same suit Johnson wore had silently appeared to begin serving the new arrivals.

Bea felt underdressed and overwhelmed so she grabbed a slice of toast and headed back up to her room. She sat on the bed flicking through Twitter and Facebook on her phone. It was now quarter past ten and all she could think about was poor Eddie sitting at the coffee shop waiting for her. Why hadn't she given him her number?

"There you are." Scott was standing in the doorway, his arms stretched above his head to rest on the door frame, this stretched his shirt even more and Bea's stomach started doing strange things again. "The Aston is out front waiting."

She grabbed her shredded jeans, top and pants which she had rolled into a kind of parcel and followed him back down the stairs and out onto the driveway. The Aston Martin from last night was indeed waiting and now she could see it was a beautiful shiny silver and looked just like the one from the Bond movies.

Within ten minutes they were drawing up outside the coffee shop, Bea praying that Eddie would still be there.

"I'll see you at the office on Monday morning." Scott pulled the hand brake on. "Remember to set your alarm this time, won't you?" He was smiling as he said this.

"Thank you for everything." She smiled back not wanting to get out of the car but knowing that she had to.

"We'll have to do it again sometime." He placed a hand on her knee and she felt the warmth of his touch through her jeans.

"I'd like that." She reluctantly opened the car door, stepped out and with a roar the car drove off.

"You're late." She turned round to find a very angry-looking Eddie standing in the doorway behind her.

"I am so sorry." Bea seemed to be apologising a lot lately. I had a bit of an accident last night and Scott helped me." She found herself retelling the night's events. "Luckily I was able to borrow some of his sister's clothes because mine are in a right state."

"They're not his sister's clothes. He doesn't even have a sister." He turned to walk into the coffee shop. "They're his wife's."

# CHAPTER 11

"What do you mean, his wife?" Bea was behind him in a flash, surely Eddie was having a laugh? But he didn't look like he was joking.

"Double Espresso please." His voice was curt and his whole stance had an air of anger about it. He didn't even look at Bea as she stood behind him.

"Tea please." She asked the girl behind the counter after Eddie had swiped his cup and headed to his normal table, pulling the chair out with a loud scrape and sitting himself down heavily in it. "What is wrong with you?" Bea was now sitting next to him, in utter shock at the change in the usually mild mannered and quiet Eddie.

"He just pisses me off." He took a sip of the coffee, grimacing at the strength of it. "Swanning around in his flashy cars like he owns the place."

"Well, he is famous you know." The look on Eddie's face made Bea wish she hadn't said that. "So why would he tell me these were his sister's clothes if they were his wife's? I didn't even know he had a wife." She hastily tried to change the direction of the conversation.

"He doesn't. Well not anymore he doesn't." He took another sip of the coffee, grimaced again and pushed it away. "Really should re-think my choice of angry drinks." He smiled at Bea and all of sudden the old Eddie was back. "She left him." Eddie could see that Bea was still waiting for further explanation.

"So why not just tell me that?" Bea was confused. She didn't mind if he had an ex-wife, plenty of people did even at her age.

"Because Mr. Perfect wouldn't want his perfect image tarnished by an ex-wife." Bea was still confused and it must have showed on her face because Eddie continued. "She just up and disappeared one night last year. No one knows where she is or why she left."

"Well, that's just awful." Bea felt her opinion of Scott climbing even higher.

"Awful?" Eddie questioned. "Bloody suspicious if you ask me."

"Suspicious?" Bea was curious as to where this was going.

"One day she's here, walking round the village and the next she's gone. Vanished without a trace." Now Bea really was intrigued. "And he pleads all innocence."

"Why do you automatically assume Scott had something to do with it?" Bea felt the need to defend Scott's honour.

"Scott now is it?" Eddie teased harshly. "Very friendly with the boss all of a sudden aren't we?"

"I just don't see what the problem is?" Bea finished her tea. "He's a successful writer and publisher and let's not mention his charity work."

"Oh no, let's mention his charity work." Eddie placed his head on his hands and his elbows on the table with a look of eager anticipation on his face.

"You're mocking me now." She stood up. "I'll look for my own place, you're obviously not in the mood today."

"I'm sorry Bea." He placed a hand on her arm and she paused. "Let's just agree to disagree on Scott bloody Summers shall we?" She nodded her agreement and arm in arm they headed out into the sunshine.

"Where are we starting then?" Bea looked left and then right.

"I'm taking you to see Sue and Ali first." They turned to the left and started walking. "They own a little B&B called Greenfields. Only have 3 bedrooms but they're the best in the village." They hadn't been walking very long when something caught Bea's eye.

"What's that?" She pointed over the road.

"What's what?" Eddie followed the point of her finger. "I can't see anything."

"Just there." She tilted his head so he was looking in the right direction. "By that hedge." Bea crossed over the road. "Oh, it's you again." The little black dog from her last visit was sitting quite still, panting in the heat. This time he didn't run away when she approached him. He had scruffy fur but was clean and tidy and his eyes were an unusual grey colour. He even wore a smart leather collar with a little silver tag dangling from it.

"It's a dog." Eddie had joined her. "Hello there, little fella." He reached down to stroke him but the dog was too quick and ran off, stopping a few feet away.

"You scared him." Bea didn't know why but she got the impression he was a boy. "I saw him the last time I was here, led me a right merry dance he did and then just disappeared." She took a few tentative steps towards him.

"Well he must belong to someone." Eddie followed slowly behind. "He's very well cared for."

They were right in front of him now but again as Eddie went to stroke him the little dog ran.

"Let me try." Bea walked towards him even slower this time, making reassuring sounds as she did, but yet again as she leant down to touch him the little dog ran off. This continued for what seemed an eternity until Bea realised they were right by Watery Lane. "Why have you brought me here again?" she asked the dog as he trotted down the alley.

"What do you mean?" Eddie was confused. "I've never brought you here."

"Not you." They were nearly at the end of the alleyway now. "The dog."

"Well that makes perfect sense." The dog had once again vanished. "I haven't been here since I was a kid." Eddie seemed to have forgotten Bea was even there as he strolled in the opposite direction to the one Bea had walked in on her last visit. "Blimey!" He almost ran to a beautiful blue boat with flowers on its sides and roof. "I can't believe the *Mavis* is still here." He stepped aboard and knocked on the door.

"How can I help?" A tall man with a white whiskery beard and moustache stepped up through the door. He was wearing a blue sailor's cap and reminded Bea of Captain Birds-Eye. "You were here the other week, weren't you my girl?" He turned to Bea who nodded as she remembered the man waving at her as he sailed past.

"Uncle Joe, it's me." The man gave his full attention to Eddie, looking him up and down.

"Edmund?" He asked. "Young Edmund? Well I never." He grabbed Eddie and gave him a huge hug which Eddie returned with as much force. "How long has it been my lad? Come in, come in, I'll put the kettle on."

Eddie and Bea followed Joe down into the narrow boat. Inside it was old but impeccable clean and tidy. It reminded Bea of a caravan except for its width. Eddie sat down on the wooden corner bench seat with a faded red cushion and Bea sat next to him as they watched the old man place three mugs onto the table next to a sugar bowl, milk jug and an already full tea pot. Not one of the items on the table had the same pattern but this added to the charm.

"Thought you'd finally visit your old Uncle Joe then Edmund?" His voice was teasing and Bea found it strange to hear Eddie referred to by his full name.

"I'm so sorry, I didn't know you'd come back to Bloomsdale." Eddie accepted the mug of tea which Joe had just poured. "How long you been back?"

"Only a few months, my lad, so don't go worrying about not coming to see me." He pushed a mug towards Bea. "Are you going to introduce me to your girlfriend then or not?"

"Oh, I'm not his girlfriend." Bea smiled and held out a hand which Joe shook gently. "I'm Bea, I've just moved here, well sort of moved here."

"How can you sort of move here?" Joe's moustache twitched as he spoke.

"What Bea means is she's starting a new job here on Monday but as yet doesn't have anywhere to live." Eddie explained for her.

"Rents are too high you see and I'm only working part time at the minute so it's really tight." Bea felt she needed to explain further.

"You can say that again." Joe shook his head. "I can't believe how much things have gone up since I was last here, even the mooring has gone through the roof." He shook his head. "I blame that Scott Summers and his books. No one had even heard of this place a few years ago but now…" He shook his head again. "Well, perhaps I can help you out." Joe headed off down the narrow boat while Bea and Eddie exchanged bewildered looks to the sounds of various drawers being opened and closed. "Follow me." Joe had reappeared with a brass key in his hand.

"He's not really my Uncle you know," Eddie whispered to Bea as he helped her back onto the towpath. "It's just what I used to call him because I was down here all the time as a kid."

"I know what you mean." Bea had lost count of the amount of 'Uncles' she had as a child but didn't think Eddie's childhood had been quite like hers.

"My mum brought me here every weekend. We'd sit and watch the boats, feed the ducks and eat ice cream." He smiled as he reminisced. "I haven't been back since she died." The smile faded and he went silent. Bea didn't ask anything although she was curious.

"I'm sorry." This was all she said and squeezed his hand affectionately.

"It's a long time ago now." He squeezed back.

"Here we are." Joe had stopped by an ancient looking narrow boat. The windows were covered in dirt and what little paint was left was peeling and cracked. "She's not much to look at but she's got a solid hull." As if to emphasise this he kicked the steel plate.

"Er…" Bea looked over to Eddie pleading with her eyes to get her out of this situation.

"Uncle Joe, she's perfect." This wasn't what Bea was expecting. "What's she called?" Bea was looking at the side of the boat where the name should be but all she could make out was an A and R.

"*The Wanderer*." Joe had unlocked the door. "Although her wandering days are over." Before she knew it Bea was being shown around the inside. It was damp and cold even though it was so warm outside. There was no furniture whatsoever except for the partition walls that separated the interior into five rooms. She had to admit it was big, as they walked the boat seemed to go on and on.

"Look at the stove." They were right in the middle when Eddie exclaimed in excitement and started examining what looked like a wood burner.

"Now this old girl does all your heating." Joe tapped on the metal. "Runs on coal or wood, either is fine. You've got two bedrooms, a bathroom, kitchen and this is the living area." He could see Bea wasn't impressed. "I know she doesn't look much but with a bit of hard work she'll be as good as new."

"I'll help you." It was Eddie's turn to convince her. "Think how much fun it will be to bring her back to life. We could travel around the country gathering inspiration for our writing."

"Well…about travelling," Joe butted in.

"I can fix the engine." Eddie was full of enthusiasm.

"There is no engine," Joe said sheepishly. "Most of it I've used as spare parts for the *Mavis*."

"Oh well." Eddie shrugged. "It will still be fun."

"How much?" Bea was sure she wouldn't be able to afford it. She didn't have a lot of savings so she wouldn't be able to buy the narrow boat so this could be her get out of jail card.

"I don't want nothing for her." Bea had been about to answer with 'such a shame I haven't got that much' and then didn't know what to say. "Just look after her and do her up for me. I've been meaning to for years but it's never going to happen now. My brother Charles would turn in his grave if he could see how neglected I've let her become." Joe looked around whimsically.

Bea had the feeling that she was going to end up being the owner of a boat she really didn't want.

"It's perfect, Bea." Eddie looked at her earnestly. "It's the answer to everything." Bea didn't agree. "All you need is some coal which is about £10 a week and the mooring fee."

"Mooring fee?" Bea suddenly had hope. "How much will that be?" She tried to look sad but silently she was praying it was extortionate.

"£1200." Joe answered. Bea almost squealed in delight.

"That's amazing." Eddie was beaming from ear to ear. "You've just got to live here Bea, you've just got to."

"Didn't you here what Joe said?" Bea couldn't understand why Eddie was smiling so much. "£1200! I only just about earn that a month and that's before tax, National Insurance and pension."

"£1200 a year Bea, not a month." As Eddie's words sank in Bea started to see a whole different side to living on a narrow boat. The amount of money she'd have left each month would allow her to live comfortably without having to get another job, she'd even be able to save and still have plenty of free time to write.

"I'll take her." Bea shook Joe's hand. It was amazing how quickly she changed her mind when she realised how cheap it would be.

"She's all yours." He handed her the key. "I'll pop some coal round later and show you how to get the stove working."

"I need to get some furniture and a bed." Bea suddenly realised that she had nothing to sit on and nowhere to sleep.

"I'll leave you to it, neighbour." Joe headed out. "If you need anything you know where I am."

"See you later, Uncle Joe." Eddie walked to the door with him. "And thanks again."

"Have I done the right thing?" Bea was suddenly swamped with doubts as she stared at the bare interior of her new home.

"Course you have." She was glad of his enthusiasm. "We'll hit the charity shops and grab you some bits and bobs for now and then we can look at getting this old girl fully kitted out and back to her former glory."

"Then I think we should take a selfie for posterity purposes." Bea pulled out her phone and framed her face next to Eddie's with the empty boat in the background. Switching it back to have a look she noticed a few blurry and dark photos. "When did I take them?"

"Take what?" Eddie peered over her shoulder. "You can't see anything, they're all blurry and dark." As Bea swiped through she realised they had been taken last night.

"Must have been when I dropped my phone." She had deleted all but the very first ones and found herself turning the photo round and zooming in and out. "What do you think that is?" She handed it to Eddie.

"Looks like a nose." And sure enough as they scrolled through the first few photos it became clear that it was indeed a nose. A little black nose attached to a little scruffy black dog with grey eyes.

# CHAPTER 12

"That's the same dog isn't it?" Eddie gave the phone back to Bea. "Looks like you have a new friend."

"But why does he keep turning up and then disappearing again?" She put her phone in her pocket. "It's like he wanted me to come here."

"Don't be silly." Eddie chuckled. "He probably just lives on one of the boats or in one of the houses."

"I'm not convinced." Bea shook her head, she just had a strange feeling about the dog.

"Anyway. Let's go and get some stuff to clean this place up." He looked around. "Can you afford to stay in the hotel till next weekend?"

"I'd budgeted for at least three weeks of staying, but why?" Bea asked. "I thought I was moving in right now?"

"Look around, Bea." Eddie spread his arms out. "It's damp and filthy." He ran a finger along one of the walls then held it up to show her how black it was. "I didn't want to say anything in front of Uncle Joe, didn't want to offend him after he's been so generous but there is no way on this earth you can live here like it is."

"Finally you say something sensible." Although she was starting to get excited about her new home she really hadn't been looking forward to sleeping here in its current state.

"We'd best get moving then." Bea could see Eddie was excited. "You okay to drive us into town?"

"As long as you can direct me?" He nodded.

"We'll have a quick look in the charity shops while we're there and grab anything else you think you'll need." They were back outside now.

"I brought a few bits from home so it's just going to be furniture and stuff like that." She locked the door with a smile, it felt nice to have a home all of her own, even if it was currently an empty shell.

They headed back to the hotel, Bea grabbed the keys from her room and they headed off into the town. Then drove back again after Bea remembered her boot was full of all her stuff from home. After a few trips up the stairs to her room to empty out the car they were on their way again, windows open, singing along to the radio at the top of their voices.

By the time the sun was setting that evening the inside of the boat was spotless. As promised Joe had brought coal and started the stove for them and now the boat was overly hot but they needed to dry everything out after its many years of emptiness.

"That's it for today." Bea arched her back. "I can't do any more."

"I completely agree." Eddie popped his head in from the living area. "The pizza will be here soon anyway." He flopped himself down onto one of the plastic chairs they had picked up in the town and grabbed his can of pop from the coffee table with its chipped sides and scratched glass but at only a pound Bea couldn't refuse it. She'd wanted to get the oak table and matching chairs that she'd seen but as Eddie had pointed out they would be far too big for the narrow room.

The sound of a motor bike followed by a quick tap on the boat door heralded the arrival of their pizzas. Bea paid the girl before carrying the boxes carefully down the steps and placing them on the plastic garden table.

"How much have you ordered?" Bea counted the boxes.

"Not a lot." Eddie was already munching his way through garlic bread whilst opening the other boxes to produce chicken wings, nachos, potato wedges and warm chocolate chip cookies.

"Where's your pizza?" Bea was tucking into a slice of meat feast.

"I don't like pizza." Bea looked at him in surprise. "I don't like cheese."

"Well that's it then." She threw her pizza box down. "We can't be friends anymore." She turned her head away from him. "I can't even look at you." She burst into laughter and picked her pizza up again. "How can you not like pizza? Or cheese for that matter."

"So you like every food there is then?" Eddie asked.

"Pretty much." Bea wasn't lying, there wasn't much she didn't like.

"Damn, I forgot to order the dips." He was rifling through the boxes.

"I don't like sauce." She remembered. "Can't stand ketchup, mayo, BBQ, brown sauce, nothing."

"And you thought I was weird." She chucked a pizza crust at him and they both burst into laughter.

"I've had such a good day today," she said honestly. She hadn't enjoyed herself this much in such a long time. They'd laughed and chatted and sung and even the immense task of cleaning the boat had been a relative pleasure.

"We make a good team." Eddie smiled at her and held her gaze a little longer than was necessary.

"We do indeed." She got up to break the tension that had suddenly filled the room and grabbed a bottle of water. She was starting to get the feeling that Eddie liked her but she couldn't think of him like that. Yes, he was handsome in his own nerdy way but he was five years younger than her and she'd always liked a more mature man. 'Someone like Scott' a little voice in her head whispered. And she had to agree with it. Scott Summers was the perfect man. Now into his early thirties he was successful and kind and so damn sexy.

"Do you want any of these cookies? I'm about full." There was a scratching noise outside. "What's that?" Eddie looked towards the door.

"It's not a rat is it?" Bea lifted one foot off the floor and searched around.

"What are you doing?" Eddie was by the door. "It's not inside and it's certainly not a rat." He opened the door and in waltzed the little black dog. "Well I never." The dog had already curled up on the floor by the stove.

"Come in and make yourself at home." Bea said to the dog who was staring up at her and as if to answer her, he promptly fell asleep. "So what do we do now?" She looked over to Eddie.

"What do you mean?" He was confused.

"We can't leave him here on his own and I'm not throwing him out now he's come to see us." She went over to him and for the first time the dog allowed her to stroke him. She reached down to read his name tag. "He's called Buddy. That really suits him."

"Call the number and his owner can come and get him." Eddie was flattening the pizza boxes ready to take to the bin.

"There isn't one." Bea turned the tag over and over. "Just his name."

"Who owns a dog and doesn't put their phone number on it?" Eddie had to check for himself. "You're right."

"I know I'm right," she stated. "I'll just have to stop the night with him."

"You've got nothing to sleep on." He couldn't believe she was being this silly over a stray dog.

"I'm sure I packed my old sleeping bag. I'll nip back to the hotel and get it." Eddie just stared at her in disbelief.

"You must be out of your mind." But she was already off the boat and running along the tow path.


Bea hadn't slept well that night. The movement of the boat directly underneath her without the cushioning of a bed had made her queasy and numerous times she'd thought she was going to be sick. Buddy hadn't had any trouble at all and she was pretty sure he was in exactly the same position that he'd been in when Eddie had left.

*Poor Eddie* she said to herself. He'd so wanted to stop with her, didn't want her to be on her own but as she explained, this was her home now and she was going to have to be on her own every night once she'd moved in properly. He had eventually admitted defeat and left just after midnight.

Checking her phone she realised it was almost seven o clock so gave up on any more sleep and put the kettle on. Buddy finally stirred and went to the door. Bea opened it for him and he jumped off the boat and onto the towpath. She lifted her face to another gloriously sunny day.

"Morning." She looked in the direction of the voice to find Eddie walking towards her with a paper bag and two cardboard mugs from the coffee shop. Not for the first time Bea wondered how much money and time he actually spent in there. "Breakfast muffins and tea," he stated as he reached the boat. "Rough night?" He noticed the shadows under her eyes and the constant yawning.

"Let's just say I hope it gets better." She went back inside with Eddie following and Buddy soon joined them.

"I even managed to get some food for Buddy here." He pulled a battered old backpack off his back. "Luckily the corner shop opens early." He smiled as he placed a few tins of dog food and biscuits on the table. "And look what Uncle Joe gave me to have a look at." He took out an old photo album. "I passed him on my way down. He says it's full of old photos of this old girl in her prime. Thought it would help us restore her to her former glory."

"Do you think we can do it?" Bea had been puzzling this all night, another of the reasons she'd been awake. "I don't know which end is which or where anything should go and I wouldn't have a clue where to get everything from."

"All sorted." Eddie had already got out his lap top and notebook. "I've researched everything we need. Luckily the outside is solid so it's just a new lick of paint and I can do the name, I've been practising." He showed her a piece of paper with elegant script writing on. "Look."

"Did you actually sleep last night?" Bea had fed Buddy and was now picking bite sized morsels from the deliciously fresh oat and raisin muffins.

"I was too excited to sleep." He showed her another piece of paper which had a long list of items and where to get them. "At least with the photos we'll be able to make her as authentic as possible."

"Let's have a look then." She dragged her chair next to his and they started flicking through the photos. Most of them were black and white and dated in the fifties and sixties. The majority of the photos were of Joe and his brother or their parents on the *Mavis*. Later photos also had a young girl which they assumed was Joe's sister. It wasn't until the photos reached the seventies that *The Wanderer* started to feature.

"Is that definitely this boat?" Eddie was scrutinizing the photos closely.

"Of course it is." Bea was confused. "It's parked right next to the *Mavis* and I'm sure that's Joe's brother at the tiller." She had to admit it was hard to tell as the man in question was quite a distance from the camera. "Joe said it was his brother's boat after all."

"But it's not got the same name." Eddie pointed to the photo. "It's called *Sophie* not *The Wanderer*."

"Are you sure?" Bea took the album out of his hands and stared at the photo before going through all the rest of the album. "Well that's not the only mystery." She handed the album back to Eddie, open at the very last page.

"What do you mean?" But Bea didn't need to give him an answer. Staring back from the very last photo was a little scruffy black dog with grey eyes and the words 'Buddy' written underneath.

# CHAPTER 13

"It can't be him." Eddie looked at the photo, over to Buddy and then back to the photo. "It just can't be."

"Well it bloody looks like him." As if he knew he was being talked about Buddy jumped onto Bea's knees and she stroked him behind his ears as he curled up on her lap.

"This photo was taken thirty or forty years ago." Eddie scrutinized Buddy. "No way he's that old." He looked in the dog's mouth. "Not even a tooth missing. He's still young."

"Just a coincidence then." But Bea wasn't convinced. "And it still doesn't explain why this boat is called *The Wanderer* and the one in the photos is *Sophie*."

"We'll have to go and see Uncle Joe." But there was no need, Joe had already appeared at the door.

"Can I come in, young uns?" He didn't wait for an answer and was already inside the cabin. "I gave you the wrong album, meant to give you the later one. That one's mostly of the *Mavis*." He did a double take when he saw the dog on Bea's lap. "Buddy? Is that you?" The little dog jumped off Bea's lap and started jumping up at Joe who scooped him up in his arms and started crying. "Where have you been, my boy?" He nuzzled his face into his fur.

"Is this your dog?" Eddie spoke first although the same question was on Bea's lips.

"He's my brother's dog." Joe was still crying and in such a state of shock that Eddie got up and helped him sit down. "He ran off the day we buried him and never came back but that was nearly five years ago now." Buddy was busy licking the tears from Joe's face. "Well you've been looked after wherever you've been."

"This may sound a bit silly." Eddie looked at Bea who nodded encouragement. "But it's not the same Buddy as this one is it?" He held up the old photo to show Joe who immediately burst out laughing.

"Don't be daft." He shook his head. "How can it be the same dog? That photo's nearly forty years old. That there is Buddy the Third or to give him his correct title…" Joe paused for effect. "Lord Greyfriar of the Waterways the Third." Joe patted Buddy. "And this is Lord Greyfriar of The Waterways the Sixth."

"Greyfriar?" Bea recognised that name. "As in Greyfriars Bobby?"

"The very same." Joe nodded. "Buddy here is a Skye terrier just like Greyfriars Bobby was."

"Is that the dog that guarded his owner's grave till the day he died?" Eddie had started making tea.

"That's the one. My mother loved that story as a child and when she and my father got married they bought a Skye terrier and his pedigree name was Lord Greyfriar of the Waterways the First but they called him Buddy for short and the name stuck through the generations." He put Buddy down on the floor and stood up. "Don't make me any tea, my lad, I've got to be getting off, just popped in to drop this off for you." He tapped his leg. "Come on Buddy." But Buddy didn't move, instead he curled up at Bea's feet. "Well, looks like you've got a new pet."

"Is that okay?" Bea didn't feel comfortable just taking Buddy, especially as Joe had only just found him again. "Maybe he should go with you for now. After all I'm not staying here yet and I can't keep him at the hotel." But Buddy wouldn't move.

"He looks settled to me." Joe couldn't hide the look of sadness on his face. "He can stay with me when you're not here."

"That sounds like a plan." Joe went to leave but Bea suddenly remembered something else. "Joe?" He turned back round. "Has the boat changed name?" Joe looked at her bewildered. "It's just that we're sure the boat in the early photos is this one but you said it was called *The Wanderer* and the boat in the photos is called *Sophie*."

"I'd completely forgotten." Joe had paused for a few seconds. "She was the *Sophie* for many years but Charles' wife wanted to rename her *The Wanderer*. I told them it was a bad idea, you never change the name of a boat, but she wouldn't listen, said it was just superstitious nonsense." He scoffed. "I never liked her anyway, thought she was too good for us all, making him travel all over the country, hence the name change."

"What happened to her?" Bea was intrigued.

"They got married and settled down, even bought a house but she upped and left him. Kept coming back every few years, in fact I don't even know if they got divorced but it never lasted very long. Very ill matched they were." Joe smiled ironically. "I told them you should never change a boat's name."

Bea shivered a little at his words.

"Tea's ready." Eddie placed two mugs on the table and made Bea jump.

"Just drop Buddy off when you head back to the hotel, I'm sure his old bed is still around somewhere." Joe left Eddie and Bea to their tea and they started discussing their plans for the day before Bea remembered she was starting her new job in the morning. On Eddie's insistence she headed back to the hotel in the afternoon while he continued planning, promising to drop Buddy back to Joe's on his way home. After a hot shower and preparing her clothes and briefcase for the morning she headed into bed and was fast asleep in minutes.

Her first week of work flew by in a blur. She worked late every night only finishing when Scott literally dragged her out of the door. No one had mentioned how far behind the accounts were and Bea was sure it would be a good month before they were completely up to date. Now it was Friday afternoon and she hadn't even been back to the boat or seen Eddie. She'd just have to stay in the hotel for another week.

"There's that name again." She had been trying to match royalty payments with authors, books and amounts but one name kept cropping up time and time again yet she could find no trace of it in the contracts. Even authors with pen names had their real names in the contracts so this made it even more puzzling. Sighing heavily she realised she was going to have to talk to Scott.

Bea climbed the spiral staircase with her ledgers and peeked a head up to check he wasn't busy. Scott was standing admiring the view and Bea took a few seconds to admire the view herself. As normal he was in suit trousers which clung to his tight buttocks and she had to hold onto the rail tighter as her legs started to give way and with a clatter the ledgers fell to the ground.

"You okay there Bea?" Scott turned immediately at the sound.

"I just dropped my books." Bea flushed furiously. "I'll be back up in a second." She was grateful for the excuse to head back down and compose herself.

"How can I help?" He was now sitting behind his desk but this didn't help Bea's composure because although she couldn't really see his lovely body anymore he was now giving her the most charming smile she had ever seen.

"Erm...It's just...I mean..." Why did she turn into a bumbling buffoon when she was around him?

"Tea? Coffee?" He stood up and headed towards a large coffee machine on the back wall.

"I'm okay, thank you." Why was she so nervous? It was her job to ask questions and make sure everything was in order. "I'm just trying to track these royalty payments." Scott was busy adding sugar and stirring his drink. "E Summers? I can't find any trace of an E Summers in the contracts."

"You won't." Scott tapped his spoon on the side of the mug. It echoed loudly in the sudden tense atmosphere. "Oh God Bea. I'm so sorry." He was down on his knees in front of her. "I lied to you the other day and it's been eating me up inside ever since." Bea just stood there in shocked silence, no man had ever got down on his knees in front of her before.

"What do you mean?" She helped him to his feet and they wandered over to the window.

"Last week when I said the room and clothes belonged to my sister?" Bea nodded not trusting her voice all of a sudden. "I lied." He said it quickly and with such emotion that Bea put her ledgers down and hugged him. He burst into uncontrollable tears and she found herself comforting him as you would a child. "They belonged to my wife. I don't know why I didn't just tell you then, perhaps I didn't want to scare you away."

"Why would it scare me away?" Was Bea reading too much into this? Did he have feelings for her? Could this impossibly sexy and successful man really be interested in her?

"Because of all the rumours and stories." He pulled a neatly folded and monographed white handkerchief out of his pocket and patted his eyes. Bea didn't think she'd ever seen a man look so vulnerable and her heart lurched painfully as she realised how deep her feelings for him were. "Eleanor Summers…E Summers is my wife's name. The payments are to her."

"Then she isn't dead?" Bea wished she hadn't said that as Scott's whole demeanour changed and he visibly stiffened.

"I see the rumour mill has already gotten to you." He relaxed again as suddenly as he had tensed. "It's not your fault. You're new here. You're bound to believe the stories."

"I don't believe them." She placed a hand on his shoulder. "I just don't know the truth."

"We married young, Eleanor and I, far too young." He looked out at the countryside but Bea got the impression he wasn't seeing the rolling green moors. "This was her dream to open a publishing house and we put in so many hours to build it up, her more than me but then when I got famous with the books she didn't like it. I was away more and more on book promotions and she was left at home to run this place." He turned back to Bea, tears welling in his eyes once again. "The last straw was when she had a miscarriage. I was in America at the time so I wasn't there for her when she needed me the most. I blame myself. I was selfish and thought she'd be okay instead of getting on the first flight back to comfort her."

"Oh Scott. I'm so sorry." *What a truly awful tale* she thought. *How can anyone think badly of this man*? "Is that why she left?" He just nodded. "Then you know where she is?"

"No." He sighed. "All I have is a bank account number. I've had the police investigating but the money gets transferred into different accounts and withdrawn all over the country. I get texts now and again but the number constantly changes. It's her money as much as mine so I don't begrudge her any of it. We just grew apart." Another sigh and Bea, ever the accountant, made a mental note to change the payments to drawings instead of royalties.

The telephone ringing made them both jump and the spell of intimacy that had weaved itself around them was broken. Scott headed over to his desk and Bea made her excuses.

"Would you have dinner with me tonight?" Had those words really just come out of her mouth?

"I'd love to." He put the phone call on hold. "I'll pick you up from the hotel at 8." She smiled her agreement, still amazed at her brazenness. "Now get yourself home, you've worked far too many hours this week as it is. There's nothing that won't wait till Monday."

"I'll see you at 8 then." She almost skipped down the stairs, quickly tidied her desk and headed off deciding to visit the boat and Buddy on the way.

She walked with such a spring in her step that she reached Watery Lane and the tow path without even realising it. Some of the moorings were empty where boats were out working or travelling. Many of them Bea knew were holiday rentals which added to the constant change of colours and names. She passed the *Mavis* and knew *The Wanderer* was a few boats down from her. She walked past a glorious boat with a blue cabin and beautiful metal jugs of flowers placed in perfect symmetry along its roof.

Bea carried on walking then after five minutes turned around. She couldn't have walked past it could she? After all it was the oldest looking boat there and very easy to spot. She headed back up the tow path and saw Eddie waving eagerly at her. Perhaps he'd moved it? But he couldn't have done, Joe said it didn't have much of an engine left.

A rush of black fur came at her feet and she scooped Buddy up.

"What's going on?" She'd reached Eddie who was beaming from ear to ear. He was dressed in scruffy blue jeans and a faded grey t-shirt. His dark hair and face were speckled with paint.

"I knew it." He started to laugh. "I just knew you would."

"Would what?" She put Buddy down and he ran off onto the blue boat. "Buddy, come back," Bea called after him. "That's not our boat."

"But it is," Eddie said simply.

"What?" Bea looked closer at the beautiful boat and saw *Sophie* neatly painted in gold on the blue cabin. "But…how?"

"Isn't she fantastic?" His voice was full of pride. "Don't look at the other side though, I've not worked out how to do that without getting wet."

"I can't believe it, Eddie, I really can't." She was overwhelmed. "You did all this yourself?"

"Of course not, I called in some favours." He pointed to the gold name again. "Do you mind that I changed her name back?"

"Not at all." Bea shook her head. "It suits her."

"Now, I've not got much done inside." He helped her to step inside. "Just some more cleaning, a working kitchen and a bed."

"I'm speechless." She walked round the now sparkling interior and peeped into the bedroom where a double bed sat against one wall.

"I've got us some nice steaks for dinner and there's a bottle of champagne chilling." He babbled on and didn't see the look that crossed her face. "Thought we could have a little house warming for you."

"Dinner?" How on earth was she to tell him? "Erm...I've sort of made plans for dinner." His face fell instantly. "But I can cancel...I didn't realise, Eddie, I really didn't."

"No worries," he said in a throwaway manner and she knew she'd hurt him. "I should have asked first. You go to dinner. The steaks and champagne will keep till tomorrow."

"Are you sure?" She knew he wasn't but how could she cancel Scott when she'd been the one to ask him? "We'll definitely do it tomorrow night. In fact we'll spend the whole day together. I've had a brilliant idea for a story I want to run past you." She hoped the change of subject would distract him.

They spent the next few hours chatting about work, Bea being very careful not to mention Scott's name in any way. Eddie wasn't quite his usual self but delighted in showing her and telling her all the things that had been done on the boat. He left around five o'clock and at just after six Bea headed back to the hotel, dropping Buddy off to Joe on the way.

"He's done a grand job hasn't he?" Joe was full of praise. "Been there night and day, he has."

"You mean he hasn't been home?" Bea was starting to feel awful.

"Not that I know of. Buddy's been with him all the time as well." He stroked the little dog as Bea handed him over.

"What about work? Has he been to work?" Bea didn't even know if he did work, in fact she was beginning to realise there were lots of things she didn't know about Eddie.

"Like I said. He's been there day and night, all on his own." Bea wasn't sure she'd heard that last bit; well she hoped she hadn't.

"All on his own, you said." Joe nodded. "Well, I'd better be off. I'll see you tomorrow." After a 'goodnight' from Joe she stepped onto the tow path and walked slowly and sadly back to the hotel berating herself as she went.

# CHAPTER 14

Bea couldn't remember ever feeling this bad and there was absolutely nothing she could do about it. She had no idea where Eddie lived and when she'd tried to ring his mobile it had gone straight to answer machine. She didn't want to text him, there was far too much she wanted to say, so she resigned herself to feeling like the most ungrateful person ever, before half-heartedly getting herself ready.

She was downstairs and waiting in the hotel bar by half past seven and ordered a large glass of red wine to drown her sorrows in. By eight o clock the wine had made her feel even more depressed and at ten past eight when she received a text from Scott to say he was running late she ordered a second. When another text announced he wouldn't be coming as he was tied up at work she ordered a third and then a fourth.

"That will teach me," she said, sliding off the bar stool and heading out into the village. "Karma always gets you." She didn't really know where she was going so she just walked and walked. A familiar sounding car drove past and pulled up outside a small house just a few feet in front of her. Bea backed up against a wall and spied on the Aston Martin and its occupants.

Scott stepped out first, dressed in a different suit to the one he had worn to work, walked round to the passenger side and helped the Marilyn Monroe lookalike that Bea had seen at her interview out of the car. She tripped as she stepped out which Bea thought was totally fake but it worked and Scott put an arm around her as they headed into the house.

As soon as the door was shut Bea stood up straight and smoothed down her clothes.

"Work, my arse." She walked unsteadily towards the house and was just about to go up the path when a bark from behind made her turn. "Buddy! What are you doing here?" She scooped him up. "I'm going to have to get you a lead, wandering around the village in the dark—you'll get run over." This was when she realised that was exactly what she was doing, and headed back to the hotel.

"Now, we must be quiet." She spoke loudly making a shushing noise to the dog. "I don't think you're allowed in here but they won't know if we don't make any noise." She stumbled up the stairs, knocking over a lamp on her way into her room without seeing anyone, and fell onto the bed, falling instantly asleep.

"Miss Winters!" Bea could hear someone calling her name but it sounded so far away. "MISS WINTERS!" There it was again only this time much louder. Bea lifted her head and wished she hadn't, it felt like a thousand little men with pick axes were inside tapping away.

"Oh God." She groaned. "I'm going to be sick." She tried to get off the bed, determined to make it to the bathroom but failed.

"Miss Winters, really?" Bea looked up to find the stern face of the receptionist standing over her, she then looked down to find her shoes were covered in sick.

"I am so sorry." Bea was mortified and grabbed the first thing she could find to try and wipe the receptionist's shoes, unfortunately it was the hotel bed sheet.

"Please, Miss Winters, just leave it." The woman took her shoes off gingerly and put them to one side before stepping to the other side of the bed. "It is with regret that the management must ask you to leave this establishment."

"Because I've been sick?" Bea stared at her open mouthed.

"No, Miss Winters." The woman beckoned towards the open door. "Because of this." Andy walked in carrying Buddy. "This creature has had the run of the hotel all night because you left your door open. He has been in the kitchen which now has to be fully sanitised. He has helped himself to food which now has to be thrown away, and left a present in the manager's office."

"You must let me pay for any damage." Bea had to stifle a giggle at the thought of Buddy running round the hotel getting into mischief.

"Don't worry, Miss Winters, the bill has already been prepared and is waiting for you when you check out." Andy put Buddy down, a makeshift lead made from a bit of rope was handed to Bea. "May I suggest you are packed and ready to go in the next ten minutes?" And with that both she and Andy left.

"How rude!" she said to Buddy. "Looks like we need to find somewhere else to stay." She tied him to the bed post and hurriedly packed her clothes and toiletries into the suitcase before dragging it and Buddy to reception.

"Here is your bill, Miss Winters." A tall man with short dark hair and a smarmy smile greeted her. Bea assumed the Irish woman was cleaning her shoes. "It's fully itemised as you can see." He started to point to the various items but Bea was only looking at the final figure.

"How much?" She was quickly adding up her savings and the money she had put by for the hotel.

"That mutt did quite a lot of damage I'm afraid." He pointed at the bill again. "And as you can see we've had to add on the cleaning of your bedroom carpet as well."

"But…" Bea had just enough but it would skint her out completely. "I'll have no money left."

"I can always call the police, Miss Winters." The man was smiling that sickly-sweet smile again. "Criminal damage is taken very seriously here."

"Criminal damage?" Bea couldn't believe how this weekend was turning out. First she'd been the worst friend ever to Eddie, stood up by her new boss, had the fiercest hangover, been thrown out of the hotel and was now skint to boot. "Cash and card okay?"

He nodded and eagerly took the card and cash she handed him.

"Please don't visit us again," he said as she walked down the stairs with Buddy and her suitcase.

"Looks like we're living in the *Sophie* from now on, Bud." She heaved her suitcase into the boot of her car, opened the door and Buddy jumped inside, curling up on the passenger seat. "Who needs a lounge and dining room anyway?" Buddy barked as if in agreement. "We've got a bit of a kitchen, a bed and a bathroom. Everything else will have to wait." She started the engine with a sigh. "Not quite the new life I wanted, eh?"

There was no sign of Eddie all day and Bea couldn't blame him. There wasn't anything to do on the boat now she had no money. Thanks to Eddie's hard work it was as clean as it could be. She put pillows and a duvet on the bed before pegging up a sheet at the window in place of curtains, then after making a cup of tea she grabbed her notebook and pen, lay on top of the boat and started planning the story that had been whirling round her head since she'd seen this place.

Before she knew it she had the characters down, the beginning, the end and the twist. Now all she had to do was actually write it. This was where she usually struggled. She had notebooks filled with first chapters and story ideas but somehow this one felt different and she started chapter one with such enthusiasm that within a few hours she'd written three chapters and knew exactly what chapter four would be about.

"Can I read it?" Bea looked up at the voice and virtually threw herself onto the towpath.

"Eddie!" She flung herself at him and hugged him tightly. "I'm so glad to see you." Then without warning she started crying and couldn't stop.

"What's happened?" And the whole sorry tale came out. "Well I'm not sorry about Scott but I am sorry he hurt you." He put an arm round her. "You have to admit it's a little bit funny though." He started to laugh. "Big city girl like you getting thrown out of a small country hotel." He laughed even louder and Bea found herself laughing with him.

"At least I have somewhere to live." She outstretched her arms to the *Sophie*. "All thanks to you." She hugged him again. "I can't believe you did it all on your own." He went to protest. "Joe told me." He smiled sheepishly. "And you must let me pay you for the bed and the paint. Well when I get paid that is."

"I wouldn't hear of it." He squeezed her hand. "Now I don't know about you but I fancy those steaks and champagne." She squeezed his hand back and smiled, glad he was back to his normal self and promising herself not to hurt him again.

"Sounds like a plan." Bea climbed back onto the roof, grabbed her notebook and slapped it against Eddie's chest. "You can read that while I cook dinner."

"Deal." He nodded.

The evening flew by and after burnt steaks, undercooked chips and half frozen peas, Bea eagerly awaited Eddie's opinion on the first three chapters. He closed the notebook with an air of importance, took a sip of champagne and paused thoughtfully.

"Just tell me, will you," she almost screamed at him in her eagerness but still he paused. "Tell me."

"I love it," he said simply. "I'm not just saying that, it's brilliant."

"Really?" She was practically begging.

"Honestly." He placed his hand over his heart. "I love the setting and the characters. Your writing is so vivid I can see myself there and I'm desperate to read more."

"I can't believe it." Bea shook her head in disbelief. "Really?" She asked again and Eddie nodded. "It felt different to all the other times, it just sort of wrote itself."

"Wish it worked like that for me!" He took another sip of champagne.

"Can I read some of your work?" She topped up both their glasses. "I'd really like to."

"Er..." He stood up, almost knocking his glass over. "Is that the time? I really must go, you know." He was by the door before she knew it. "Thanks for dinner." And without waiting for a reply he was gone.

"What was all that about?" she asked Buddy, who was in his usual spot by the stove. "I only asked if I could read his work." Bea shrugged and started tidying up. After everything was washed and put away she took Buddy out for a quick mooch, locked the door and headed to bed to do some more writing.

She must have fallen asleep because she awoke a few hours later with a stiff neck and a piece of paper stuck to her face. It was still pitch black so she tidied up her notebook and stepped out of bed to go and brush her teeth. The floor was cold and rough and she reached underneath to grab her slippers. A creak from the boat made her freeze.

"Don't be silly." She scolded herself inside her head. "You live on a boat, it moves, it creaks." Then there was another creak—this time it sounded like it was inside the boat. Again she reassured herself but still she didn't move.

"Hey there, Buddy Boy." The unmistakable sound of a male voice and Buddy's excited barking did nothing to alleviate Bea's fears. "Are you looking after our guest?" Bea grabbed the torch by her bed ready to hit whoever it was over the head. She wrenched open the door and shot out into the living room brandishing the torch above her head.

"I'm armed!" she screamed. But as she looked around there was no one there, just a wide-awake Buddy staring at her with his tongue lolling out of one side of his mouth as if he was smiling.

# CHAPTER 15

"What the..." Bea spun round to look behind and then back to look in front of her but there was no one there. She ran to the door but it was locked and bolted just as it had been when she'd gone to bed. "No more champagne for you," she said to herself before checking everywhere once more and heading back to bed, this time taking Buddy with her.

The rest of the night passed by in an uneasy sleep. Bea shot up at every tiny noise or movement of the boat, her eyes wide and frightened and no matter how many times she told herself that she'd imagined it something niggled at her and she couldn't quite believe that she had.

"You must have been asleep still." It was Sunday afternoon and she was in the coffee shop with Eddie. "If everything was locked then no one got in."

"I keep telling myself that." She took a sip of the frothy latte Eddie had treated her to as she now literally had pennies to her name. "The voice was familiar somehow, like I'd heard it before." Eddie was trying not to laugh. "Stop laughing at me. I was really scared."

"I'm not laughing at that." He took a napkin from the table and started dabbing gently just above her mouth. "You suit a milk moustache." She went to take the napkin out of his hand but somehow she misjudged and placed her hand on his instead. Eddie froze and gulped nervously.

"Is it gone?" There was a strange feeling in the pit of her stomach that had never been there before and she wasn't sure she liked it.

"All gone." Eddie pulled his hand away and looked swiftly out of the window. "Beautiful day again isn't it?" Bea nodded eagerly, grateful for the change in conversation. "We should take Buddy for a nice long walk.

"Sounds good to me." She finished her drink. "You can show me round the village properly this time instead of running after Buddy like before."

After grabbing Buddy, his new lead, bowl and plenty of water from the boat they headed off with Eddie leading the way. They walked past the village hall and the bowling green, the old post office which was now a house and three farms.

"And this…" Eddie had stopped by what looked like a house but on closer inspection its windows were too large for a normal house, "…is my old primary school." He said this with such pride that Bea could imagine a little Eddie with curly black hair and grey shorts running around the playground or sitting with his nose in a book.

"You liked school then?" She remembered her own school life with sadness. They'd never really stayed in one place more than a few years so Bea was in and out of different schools all the time.

"I liked this one." He was leaning on the railings of the playground looking out. "This was where I learnt to read and write. Our head teacher Mrs. Young…" He giggled. "…funny name for her that because she was ancient, well she was wonderful. She used to help me with my writing at lunch time and after school. I'd written three novels by the time I'd left this place aged eleven."

"Wow. I haven't even written one and I'm twenty-five." She could sense a sadness in him, as if this school and his writing was an escape for him.

"I said I wrote them, doesn't mean they were any good." He moved away and started walking again. "High school wasn't too bad, I had to get the bus every day which gave me more time for writing but when you come from a little place like this you don't really fit in with the city crowd. I just kept myself to myself and no one bothered me but it was kind of lonely."

"That's possibly one of the saddest things I've ever heard." Bea wanted to put her arms round him and hug him tight. Even with all the schools she'd been to she'd always had friends, okay she was never a popular girl but she always found her place.

"Like I said, it wasn't too bad." He shrugged. "I got even more novels written."

"So when can I read one of them?" He couldn't escape this time, she thought.

"When I write one that's any good." They were at the end of the road now and he turned to her. "Left or right?"

"Well what's left and what's right?" She let him change the conversation but put it at the front of her mind to question him further.

"Left is the church and right is the train station." He knew he'd surprised her by the way she suddenly looked at him. "I take it you didn't know we had a train station."

"Why would a little village like this have a train station?" She couldn't believe it, she'd never seen any signs or heard any noise.

"Well, it's disused at the moment but hopefully one day someone will bring it back into use." Bea didn't know what she wanted to see more, the church or the station, but Buddy decided this for them by pulling so suddenly on his lead that Bea lost her grip and he scarpered off to the left.

"Church it is then." They both hurried after him and found him a few minutes later sitting by the gate of the churchyard. "You've got to stop this, Buddy," she scolded softly and picked up his lead, this time putting the loop round her wrist instead of just holding it and was glad she had, for as soon as they were through the gate Buddy pulled off to the left. "Oh no you don't, boy, no more running off for you today."

"We always came here with the school for Easter and Christmas services, things like that." Eddie walked in front of her on the stone path. "I wonder if it's open." Unfortunately the wooden door was locked so they wandered around the outside, Bea admiring its beautiful stained glass windows and Eddie telling stories of his childhood. "I had my first kiss here." They were at the back of the church now, by the tower. There was an archway carved into the stone and a wooden bench that had seen better days sat in the middle.

"Did you indeed?" Bea raised her eyebrows. "I bet you were a right little charmer."

"I was fourteen and her name was Charlotte." He sat down on the bench and Bea sat next to him, tying Buddy securely to the arm rest. "I'd been in love with her since the first day of infant school. She was so pretty with her dark hair and bright blue eyes but she didn't go to the same high school as me. Her family moved away so she and her sister could go to some fancy school in London but they used to come back now and again to visit family."

"Stop whining, Buddy." Bea shushed the little dog gently who was pulling at his lead. "Go on Eddie." She fished in her pocket for a dog biscuit but he wasn't interested and kept pulling at his lead so she tied it even tighter.

"There'd been a Christmas disco at the village hall and she asked me if I'd like to go for a walk. I remember it being so cold." He shivered a little at the thought. "Well she took my hand and led me here. We just sat for ages holding hands and laughing about school. It was starting to get dark so I said I'd walk her home and that's when it happened. She just turned her face to mine and kissed me."

"That's so sweet." Bea pulled Buddy's lead back again. "What's wrong with him today?"

"He probably wants to get moving." Eddie stood up. "In fact, there's someone I'd like you to meet." Bea untied Buddy and he started pulling again, this time in the same direction that Eddie walked. They went to the end of the church graveyard which led into a further field of gravestones and unmarked mounds.

Bea had a strange fascination with graveyards. She loved to walk through them, reading the names and imagining what sort of people they had been. What did they look like? Where did they live? What did they do for a living? In all the madness of her childhood she always found churches and cemeteries to be a comfort. No matter what city or town she was in, the peacefulness and serenity she found there was like a constant friend.

The headstones closest to the church were as old as the church itself, Eddie told her as they walked. The further away you got the more recent the dates became. Buddy was still pulling eagerly on his lead when Eddie stopped and started looking around.

"What's the matter?" Bea asked. She wasn't sure why they were still here anyway, hadn't Eddie said he wanted her to meet someone?

"I never remember exactly where it is." He started walking along one of the rows. "You go that way will you."

"What am I looking for?" Bea hadn't a clue why she was walking along the graves of people she didn't know.

"You'll know it when you see it," he called back towards her.

"Know what when I see it?" But he was concentrating so hard he didn't hear her and she continued walking down the middle of the rows reading each name as she went. Buddy was almost running on his lead now. "Have you eaten something?" Bea hadn't a clue what was wrong with Buddy today, the constant pulling on his lead was making her arm ache but as she went to switch hands he managed to free himself and run off again. "Buddy!" Bea called after him but he didn't go far. He ran a few rows further down and then just stopped.

"I think it's this row," Eddie shouted.

"I've just got to grab Buddy." She stepped over the rows towards him, apologising to the occupant if she accidentally stepped on a grave. "He's run off again." She sneaked towards him just in case he bolted which luckily he didn't. She picked him up and he licked her face. "Come on, you." He started to wriggle and leapt out of her hands back onto the grass, sitting instantly again at the foot of a grave. "What is wrong with you?" She looked where he was sitting but the gravestone was overgrown with rose bushes and all she could read was Father and Brother.

"I've found it." Bea turned to see Eddie standing in front of a rather ornate looking headstone in the middle of the next row.

"Eddie wants us." She picked him up again, this time holding him tightly even though he wriggled.

"Bea, I'd like you to meet my Mum and Dad. Mum and Dad this is Bea." Eddie was busy cleaning the rather large stone and its angel statue with tissues and a bottle of water. "I haven't been for a while, I know. I'm sorry about that." He turned to Bea. "If I'd known I'd have brought them some flowers."

"But…" Bea was watching as Eddie cleaned the names and she was able to read them properly. "They're called Summers!"

# CHAPTER 16

"**A**re you telling me you're Scott's cousin or something like that?" Bea was still a little taken aback.

"Something like that." Eddie had cleaned the stone as well as he could and took a step back to stand next to her. "He's my brother."

"Your brother!" Of all the relationships she had imagined, brother wasn't one of them. "But you hate him."

"Hate's a strong word." He started walking back the way they had come, Bea still holding a wriggling Buddy. "It wasn't always like that. I idolised him when I was younger but he resented me from day one and you kind of start feeling the same after a few years."

"Why did he resent you?" She clutched Buddy even tighter as they passed by the overgrown grave.

"I'm adopted, you see, so not actually a Summers. Edmund Richards at your service." He did a mock bow in front of her. "He was fourteen when I came along and he'd had everything his own way all those years. Mum and Dad had been older parents when they had Scott and they'd spoilt him. They were in their late fifties when they adopted me and Mum especially doted on me."

"My mum wasn't far off her fifties when she had me." Bea felt a little connection with Eddie. "But she certainly didn't dote on me, I was more of a hindrance I think."

"They'd always wanted a big family but had found it hard even having one so I was probably their last chance." They had reached the bench again. "Shall we break out those sandwiches from the coffee shop?"

"Best thing you've said all day." They sat back down on the bench and broke out the sandwiches that Eddie had had the forethought to purchase earlier. "So do you know anything about your real parents?" She gave Buddy a piece of ham from her sandwich and a bowl of water. He seemed to have given up on his quest to escape and after gobbling down the ham he curled up and went to sleep.

"Not a thing." He shook his head. "I don't even know my real name, Richards is something I started using a few years ago."

"Don't you want to find them?" Bea was sure that under the same circumstances she would want to know.

"Sometimes." He shrugged. "But then I remember that I had a mum and dad who loved me and I feel it betrays their memory somehow."

"They wouldn't mind you finding your birth parents, would they?" *Surely anyone that adopted a child knew that one day that could happen,* she thought.

"We never talked about it and I never got the chance to ask them so it just doesn't feel right." Eddie had finished his sandwich and was busy rifling in the bag for more. "Didn't we put any cake or biscuits in?" He asked, disappointed when he came out empty-handed.

"Only dog biscuits, I'm afraid." Bea pulled a milk bone out of her pocket.

"I'll give it a go." He took it out of her hand and bit into it. "It's a bit dry and not very sweet but it'll do."

"You're mad." She laughed. "So why do you work for him if you don't like him?"

"It's a family business." He looked out into the churchyard. "Scott said it was his wife that wanted me working there which I find very hard to believe because she paid no attention to me growing up. In fact, she used to walk out of the room whenever I came in, suppose that was Scott's influence on her." He turned back to look at Bea. "I think it was Dad really. After we lost Mum and then he became ill himself he must have told Scott that he needed to look after me which in his own way I suppose he does."

"Did you know Scott's wife then?" Bea was fascinated by the family history, so similar yet so different to hers. Her older brother and sister had virtually brought her up and their relationship was so close yet Eddie and Scott's was filled with resentment and pain.

"Not really." He grabbed a bottle of water and took a few long gulps. "Like I said she never really bothered with me even when I was at work. I'm based out of the office most of the time so I didn't really see her."

"So what do you think happened?" Bea didn't know why she was so interested in Scott's relationship, perhaps she wanted to know if he was lying to her about that as well.

"It was no secret that they were having problems." He laughed sadly. "Everyone in the office knew, you can't help knowing in an office like that. When there's no walls everyone hears everything." Bea knew exactly what he meant and now she knew why everyone kind of kept themselves to themselves. Every conversation you had was heard by the rest of the office so you never talked about anything personal. "I just think she'd had enough one day and left."

"You said it was suspicious." Bea couldn't believe his change of heart.

"I was winding you up." He was rewarded with a playful slap.

"Well I believed you." She got up to put the empty wrappers in the bin. "I even said something similar to Scott in the office the other day."

"I'd love to have seen his reaction to that." Eddie's face broke out into the broadest smile that reached his eyes and made them sparkle so much that for the first time Bea noticed how incredibly dark they were. Like rich chocolate that you could just melt away into. "Er. Hello…Earth to Bea, are you receiving me?"

"Sorry?" Bea shook her head to clear the unnerving thoughts that were starting to swirl around her head.

"I said, it looks like it's going to rain." Bea looked up at the sky to see dark clouds rolling in across the fields. How long had she been staring at him for? She was sure those clouds hadn't been there a few seconds ago. "You were away with the fairies for a minute there."

"I was just thinking about Scott." The smile disappeared instantly from his face and she cursed herself. She hadn't been thinking about Scott at all but it was the first words that came out of her mouth.

"I'll get myself back before this storm comes in." He headed off down the path. "You know your way back to the boat, don't you?" Eddie didn't even wait for her to answer and was out of the churchyard in seconds.

"Open your mouth a bit wider Bea and you can fit the other foot in there." She sat back down on the bench so heavily that it made a splintering noise and she shot back up guiltily. "Let's get home, Buddy." She untied his lead and walked slowly down the path and out of the gate. She didn't care that the raindrops had started to fall or that they were getting heavier and heavier. By the time she was back on the *Sophie* she was soaked through.


Bea was dreading seeing Scott on Monday morning, she didn't know why because as far as he was concerned he had only cancelled due to work, he wasn't aware of what she'd seen on Friday night.

"Morning, Bea." Scott's voice was quiet behind her ear. "Sorry about Friday, just couldn't get away."

"No worries," she said with a sudden vision of Scott trying to escape Marilyn's perfectly manicured hands.

"Some other time?" He was in front of her now, leaning on her desk so his biceps stretched through his shirt.

"That would be lovely." She didn't dare look up at him, just seeing those arms was enough to make her voice wobble.

"Mr. Summers." The receptionist that Bea now knew as Lisa called from her desk. "Telephone call for you."

"We'll talk later." As he walked away she finally looked up just in time to see his tight bum and toned legs disappear up the stairs to her office. It was then that she noticed most of the girls and even Giles who worked on covers all staring after Scott as well. Lisa was even pretending to fan herself.

At that exact moment they all seemed to look at each other and burst into laughter.

"How does he even get into those trousers?" Lisa spoke in a loud whisper. "They're practically painted on."

"I swear he buys his shirts two sizes too small on purpose." Giles piped in.

"And those eyes."

"Those cheek bones."

"That ass."

At the sound of Scott coming back down the stairs everyone suddenly picked up a pen or started typing. He must have known something was going on as he looked round the office and raised a quizzical eyebrow at the deathly silence that had suddenly descended.

"Lisa." He spoke in a normal tone but due to the quiet it was like he was shouting. "I have to go out I'm afraid, I'll be gone for the rest of the day and I'm not to be disturbed."

"Yes, Mr. Summers." Lisa nodded and once again they all watched him walk out.

"Tea, anyone?" Giles stood up and headed over to the small staff kitchen area. Bea watched gobsmacked as every single person in the office joined him there. The clatter of cups and spoons mingled with excited chatter about weekends and families, boyfriends, girlfriends and children.

"Come on, Bea." Lisa called her over but still she hesitated. "You heard him, he's gone all day." Bea walked nervously towards them, looking back over her shoulder to check Scott hadn't walked back in.

"Mr. Dictator is fabulous to look at but he's such a miserable boss." Steph who worked with Giles on the cover art and illustrations spoke while reaching for the biscuit tin that was hidden away on the top of the shelves.

"Really?" Bea was surprised. "But he's so nice and kind." She was rewarded with raised eyebrows from everyone.

"You're the new girl." Lisa stated. "Just wait till you've been here a while or someone else starts. He won't even notice you then."

"Why do you think everyone here is under forty?" Bea hadn't noticed this before.

"And not to blow my own trumpet but we are all gorgeous." Giles said this in the campest voice Bea had ever heard.

"But he's not gay?" Surely she'd have picked up on that.

"No, he's not," Giles answered. "But I am and he knows it."

"Mr. Summers wants everyone to focus on him and him alone." Steph was stashing the now empty tin back onto the shelf.

"That's why we're not allowed to talk in case we get to know each other and take the attention off him."

Bea was starting to feel that she didn't know Scott at all and after heading back to her desk she found herself so distracted by the staff's comments and things Eddie had said in the past that she got no work done at all and headed home once Lisa had returned from lunch. Buddy was with Joe for the day as he always was now when Bea worked so she returned to an empty boat, dripping wet for the second day running after yet another summer downpour.

Unlocking the door she placed her bag on the table and switched on the kettle before kicking off her shoes. A clattering noise from the bedroom startled her and she grabbed a knife before heading down the boat. She pushed the door open only to find it empty and exactly how she'd left it that morning except for one thing. Lying on her bed was the photo album Joe had given her and Eddie to look at.

# CHAPTER 17

**B**ea stared at the album for a long time before she finally plucked up the courage to move it. She sat on the bed and began flicking through its pages. The photos were in colour now and featured the *Mavis* and the *Sophie* in various places around the country. Bea even recognised Gas Street in her home town of Birmingham. It wasn't really her home town, she didn't actually know where that was but as it was the longest she'd ever lived anywhere it was as good as.

There was Joe and his Mum and Dad, Joe with some other people and a big gaping hole where a photo was missing and 'The Happy Couple' written at the bottom of the page.

The very last photos were of the newly painted and renamed *Wanderer* as it sailed off down the canal. You could just make out a man and a woman waving but they were so far in the distance that Bea could only presume it was Charles and his new wife. Confirmation of this came when she read the words underneath 'Off on Honeymoon'.

A soaking wet Buddy suddenly leapt on the bed and shook all over her reminding Bea of her own drowned state. She put the album away in a drawer and pushed it shut, consciously seeing herself doing this in case it mysteriously found its way out again. She stripped off and wrapped her dressing gown around herself before grabbing a towel and drying Buddy as she went out to greet Joe.

"Has he been a good boy?" Bea looked up at Joe and almost screamed at the sight of him. He looked like the killer from the 'I Know What You Did Last Summer' films. He was dressed in a yellow fisherman's sou'wester with heavy black boots on and still had his hood up.

"Course he has." Joe pulled down his hood and Bea sighed in relief. "I don't know why he keeps running off with you, never moves from me side."

"He's only done it a couple of times." Bea was a little hurt by Joe's words even though she knew he didn't mean anything by them. "And apart from the graveyard it was always so I'd follow him, like he wanted to show me something."

"The graveyard, you said?" Joe rubbed his beard and Bea nodded. "Perhaps he was trying to find my brother."

"I thought you said he was dead?" Bea realised how daft she was being as soon as she spoke. "You mean his grave."

"Course I mean his grave, you daft beggar." Joe laughed. "I haven't been there since he died and I doubt Ruby's been up there. Bet it's in a right state."

"He was sitting on a very overgrown grave when I caught him." Bea put the now dry Buddy down. "It's one of the newer ones in the second field but I couldn't really read anything through the brambles."

"That's probably it." Joe shook his head. "I can't believe I've not been to see him all these years. What must he think of me?" He pulled his hood back up. "I'll see you tomorrow."

"Wait!" Bea called after him. "Did you say Ruby?" But Joe was gone and she wasn't about to chase after him in her bright pink dressing gown in the pouring rain. "Did he say Ruby?" She was questioning herself now so tucked the thought away to ask Joe or even Eddie next time she saw one of them.

Thinking of Eddie gave her a tight feeling of guilt in her stomach and she promised herself that she would make more of an effort not to mention Scott in front of him. Perhaps she would invite him to the fair that accompanied the classic car show for the bank holiday weekend. But then she didn't want to give him the wrong impression. But if she made it clear it was just as friends?

She turned it over and over in her head as she showered and decided it was probably best not to invite him, she didn't want to give him false hope. She liked him as a friend, he'd been so good to her but she really couldn't think of him in any other way despite the fact that she loved the way his eyes crinkled in the corners when he smiled.

Walking into her bedroom she realised the duvet was damp and muddy from Buddy's paws so she changed her bed clothes, bundling it all up ready for a trip to the laundrette. The rain had stopped so she grabbed her notebook and washing bag, left Buddy fast asleep and walked into the centre of the village.

She hadn't visited the laundrette before, although she'd passed it a few times. It looked so old from the outside that Bea thought she might be hand washing everything but when she stepped in she was pleasantly surprised to find it spotlessly clean with all the modern conveniences.

After changing her money and buying washing powder she commandeered two machines, one for her clothes and one for her bedding. She sat down in front of them, pulled out her notebook and began to write.

There were only two other people in the laundrette and they were both reading papers so the only sound was the methodical whirring of the machines. Bea pondered her next sentence, staring at the washing spinning round as she did.

Something white in the yellow sheets caught her eye and she got up to have a closer look. Now and again she caught sight of what looked like a piece of card and with a sinking feeling Bea realised that the missing photo from Joe's album was currently spinning round at forty degrees.

It was no good, the photo was beyond repair. In fact it was beyond recognition even as a photo. Bea had carefully pulled the sheets out after numerous unsuccessful attempts to stop the machine and had sat watching in despair as the precious memory was washed away. It had disintegrated like a tissue with tiny bits stuck all over her sheets and she picked each one off and placed them to one side.

After tumble drying everything and carefully wrapping the remains of the photo in a tissue she headed home. Eddie was sitting on the boat roof when she got there and she'd never been so happy to see his smiling face. He jumped down off the boat and helped her carry the bags.

Buddy leapt at the pair of them as Bea opened the door so Eddie took him for a quick stroll while she put the washing away and made them both a drink.

"What are you doing?" Eddie enquired when he returned and found Bea trying to dry tiny pieces of paper with a hair dryer.

"It's one of Joe's photos." She said in despair. "The album was on my bed when I came home, even though I hadn't put it there and one must have fallen out and then when Buddy came back he was all wet and so was I so I changed the covers and it must have fallen out and I washed it." Bea finally took a breath.

"Say that again." Eddie unclipped Buddy's lead. "I didn't catch a word of it."

Bea repeated herself, slower this time.

"How am I going to tell Joe?" She slammed her head onto the table, scattering the pieces. "Ow!" She hadn't realised how hard the table was. "That hurt."

"It can't be that bad." Eddie sat down next to her and saw the mush that was once a photo. "Perhaps it is." Bea slammed her head onto the table again. "No, look." Her head shot up again. "There's a bit of a blue jacket here."

"Well I can't exactly give a piece of blue jacket back to Joe now can I?" She brushed the pieces together again and wrapped them back up in the tissue. "I'll just have to tell him the truth and hope he's got another copy somewhere."

"He'll understand." He put a consolatory arm around her. "Perhaps his sister has one."

"Do you know his sister?" Bea was formulating a plan.

"Of course I do," Eddie answered.

"Then we could go and see her and if she has one we could get a copy done before Joe even knows." Bea stood up. "Of course I'll still have to tell him because he'll know it's a modern photo but still…" She nudged Eddie's legs. "Come on then, let's go."

"I'm not sure you'll want to when you know who his sister is?" Bea looked confused. "Ruby Turner is Joe's sister." Bea sat back down. "Thought so."

"That's that then." Bea threw her arms up in the air. "He won't trust me with anything again. He'll probably take the boat back and I'll be homeless."

"I think you're exaggerating a bit." Eddie chuckled. "But speaking of the boat, I've worked out how to turn her round." Bea watched as he took a model barge from his pocket. "This is the *Sophie*." He placed the toy on the table. "And this is the tow path." He put a pen by the side. "Using ropes, we push and pull her, kind of like a three point turn in a car until she's facing the other way round and we can paint the other side."

"You make it sound easy." Bea wasn't convinced.

"It is easy." He put the model away. "Of course we'll have to make sure no one is moored next to us at the time and hope no one comes along as at one point she'll be virtually the whole width of the canal."

"Again, you make it sound easy." She still wasn't convinced so had to watch Eddie demonstrate again. "We can but try." She said after the fourth time of watching the little boat sail around the table.

"It's meant to be nice this weekend so we'll give it a go on Saturday if you want." Bea nodded, she'd have agreed to anything if it meant not having to see Eddie turn a model boat around on a plastic table again.

"You staying for dinner?" Eddie nodded eagerly. "Instant noodle sandwich okay?"

"I'm really going to have to teach you to cook, aren't I?" Eddie shook his head in disbelief and watched as she placed bread and butter on the table before boiling the kettle.

"When you live on your own on a pittance of a wage and work late most nights you tend to live off packet foods." Apart from the disastrous steak she ruined the other night, Bea couldn't think of the last time she'd actually cooked herself a proper meal.

"I live on my own." Eddie stated but Bea noticed no mention of a wage and assumed as she had thought before that he must have a decent amount of money to his name; but he didn't flaunt it if he did.

"There you go." She placed two steaming pots in front of him then sat down and preceded to layer noodles onto a piece of bread before folding it in half and eating it like a sandwich. Eddie did the same but as he bit into his all the noodles fell out down his shirt and some even landed on the floor. "You just don't have the skills." Bea handed him a tissue.

"I don't think I want the skills in eating noodle sandwiches." He wiped his shirt as best as he could before leaning down to clean the floor. "You missed a bit." He held up a piece of the photo that must have fallen off the table when Bea had slammed her head onto it earlier.

"It looks like a pair of eyes." She took the piece from him and looked at it closely. It was indeed a pair of eyes and Bea was sure she'd seen them somewhere before. It fact she knew she'd seen them before. "They look like my mum's."

# CHAPTER 18

"Don't be so silly." Eddie took the tiny piece of screwed up paper from her. "How do you know they're your mum's eyes? I don't think I'd know my own eyes that small, that screwed up and without the rest of my face."

"The colour of the jacket looks familiar as well." Bea went off to the bedroom without further explanation. "That explains that mystery." She was back within a few minutes carrying an open scrap book. "It's my photo that got washed...look." She gave the book to Eddie who could see what appeared to be a family party and a very obvious gap where a photo was missing.

"Is this you as a baby?" Eddie looked at the photos. There was a baby wearing a frilly pink dress being held by a lady that looked like her grandmother. This lady was wearing a very smart pale blue suit. Then there was one of the same baby with a teenage boy and girl both dressed very smartly.

"It's my christening—well, naming day. Mum doesn't do religion." Bea started to point at the photos. "That's me and Mum." She pointed to the lady Eddie had thought was her grandmother. "Me with Al and Em." She continued to explain. "And the one that is missing is the one of Mum with some friends I think."

"Well the jacket is certainly a match." Eddie placed the surviving pieces of washed photo onto the picture of Bea's mum. "And I'd have to agree with you on the eyes so yes, mystery solved." He continued to look through the scrap book. "And of course you know what that means?" Bea looked at him with a blank expression on her face. "It means you didn't wash Joe's

117

photo and you can stop panicking about it." He continued flicking through the pages.

"Thank the lord for that." Bea picked up the bits of photo and threw them in the bin. "He probably took the photo out of the album himself when his brother and wife split up. Lots of people do that. It's like us when we break up with someone, we delete all the photos from our phones like we can delete them from our lives."

"Please tell me this look was a Halloween costume?" Eddie who hadn't been listening to a word of what she was saying was in fits of laughter and holding up the scrap book at a photo of a very sulky teenage Bea dressed in black with long, straight black hair, black lipstick and thick black eyeliner.

"It was my Goth phase." She snatched the book off him and snapped it shut. "Everyone has them."

"I didn't." Eddie was still laughing.

"I look hideous." Bea took another look at the photo. "But the sad thing is I thought I looked good." She sat down next to Eddie and started looking through the rest of the photos.

"There aren't many of you and your mum are there?" Eddie observed. "Mostly you with your brother and sister, and who's this chap?"

"Oh, that's Al's dad." Eddie was pointing to the recurring figure of Bill Davies. "He kind of played dad to me and Em as well. Sends us birthday and Christmas cards signed Dad even now." Bea turned the last page. "And the reason there aren't many photos of me and Mum is because she was never really around. Always gallivanting here, there and everywhere. Dragged me round like a suitcase from place to place. Al got out early but Em didn't leave home till I was 14, she was 30 then but she always told me she'd never leave till I was old enough to cope."

"That sounds like a horrible childhood." The jovial atmosphere had changed.

"It wasn't all bad." Bea shrugged her shoulders. "I had no one telling me what to do or when to be home by. No nagging to tidy my room or do my homework."

"I was always being told off for leaving writing around." Eddie smiled at the memory. "I had that many notebooks lying about with bits of stories in. The worst thing was that if an idea hit me I'd just write it down there and then on whatever was available. A shopping list, a bill. Quite a few times it was something important like a solicitor's letter or something from school."

"I bet you still do that now." Bea had seen ink marks on his hands many times.

"Guilty." He held up his palms to show a few words scribbled on it. "When inspiration hits you've got to write it down." Bea smiled. "Speaking of which, how's your story going?" And that was that. They spent the rest of the evening talking about Bea's characters and plots before Eddie toddled off home about eleven o'clock and Bea turned in for the night.


The banging on the door was bad enough but when the banging moved to the ceiling above her head accompanied with Eddie's shouting of her name, Bea finally gave up and dragged herself out of bed.

"It's seven in the morning." She poked her head outside and immediately shied away from the sunlight.

"I told you I'd be early." He barged past her and headed straight to the cooker, popping the frying pan on to heat.

"But it's Saturday." Bea was very protective about her weekend lie in.

"Exactly." He started placing rashers of bacon in the pan which sizzled instantly. "Need to get the boat turned round before the canal gets too busy. It's a bank holiday weekend and what with the fair and the car show here it will be madness soon."

"Morning young uns." Joe's voice came from outside and Buddy ran out to meet him.

"I had a re-think and we need the *Mavis* to help push *Sophie* about." Eddie answered Bea's enquiring look. "Joe and I have it all planned. It will go like clockwork."

And indeed it did go like clockwork, well most of it anyway. Bea had pushed the pointy end of the boat as she called it despite Eddie constantly telling her it was the bow, away from the edge while Eddie held tight to the rope that they had attached to the stern. Using the barge pole, Bea pushed the *Sophie* as far out as she could before Joe slowly used the *Mavis* to turn her right round.

"Are you sure she won't get stuck?" Bea didn't think the canal was quite wide enough to take the length of the *Sophie*.

"She's only a little one," Eddie had reassured her. "She'll be fine."

"Hold her in a bit more," Joe shouted to Eddie. "Only got inches to spare this end." Bea watched as Eddie pulled hard on the rope. "She's clear." The *Sophie* was now the opposite way round but this was where it started getting tricky. As Joe continued to push the bow out with the *Mavis*, *Sophie*'s stern started to kick out and it was becoming harder for Eddie to hold her.

"Need a bit of help here, Bea." She stood behind him grabbing the rope and together they held the *Sophie* as tight as they could.

"Nearly there," Joe called. "Just a bit more." They held tighter and tighter, pulling back against the boat with all their strength. The *Sophie* was almost straight now so Bea went and grabbed the rope they had attached to the bow. She had to use the hook on the end of the pole as she was still a good few feet away from the tow path.

"A bit more, Joe." Bea reached as far as she could but the rope was just out of reach. The *Sophie* edged closer and closer. "Almost there." The hook of the pole was inches away from the rope now so she edged her foot closer and closer. "Aarghh!" Bea's scream was accompanied by a loud splash as she fell right into the canal. Eddie was there in an instant.

"You okay?" He was trying not to laugh.

"It's not funny you know." She was treading water and splashing.

"It's not deep, you can stand up." He held out a hand to help her out after she realised she could touch the bottom quite easily.

"I didn't know that did I?" She took his hand but instead of helping herself out she pulled him in. "Now we're both wet." She said as he surfaced through the water right in front of her. In fact he was so close their faces were almost touching. She stared into his eyes, then down at his lips then back to his eyes. Their mouths were so close she could feel his breath.

"What are you two playing at?" Joe was alongside the *Sophie* now, chuckling at the state of them. "Get them ropes tied before she floats away." The moment was broken and after helping Bea onto the tow path, Eddie heaved himself onto the boat, throwing the rope over for Bea to catch.

Once she was safely moored Joe chugged away.

"We'd best get dry." It was strange having the boat the other way and Bea was a little disorientated at first. "Do you want a shower?" she asked Eddie, a little flustered still after the episode in the water.

"I've got nothing to change into." Bea thought for a moment.

"If we rinse your clothes off and hang them out they'll be dry in an hour or two on a day like today." She thought again. "You'll have to wear a towel till then I'm afraid." She headed off to the bedroom. "Just chuck them out when you're done and I'll rinse them through while you get showered."

"Are you sure?" Eddie went into the bathroom.

"Perfectly sure." She wasn't sure at all but as it was her fault he was soaking wet and stank of the canal it was the least she could do.

She heard the shower running and picked his jeans and t-shirt off the floor where he had put them. She noticed he hadn't given her his pants and socks and was grateful for that. Underwear washing was a little too familiar.

Stripping off her own wet clothes she wrapped herself in her dressing gown before rinsing everything through and hanging it out on the clothes line Eddie had rigged up for her the other day. The boat looked awful from this side, so old and unloved and she couldn't wait to get it painted.

The shower had stopped when she went back in so she waited till she heard him go into the bedroom before heading into the shower herself. The water was lovely and soon the smell of the canal was washed away. She reluctantly turned the shower off after a few minutes and reached for a towel only to find the towel ring empty.

"Bugger." She'd forgotten to bring one in and Eddie must have used the other one. Dripping wet she wiped her feet on the bath mat, grabbed her dressing gown and dashed into her bedroom. "Oh!" Eddie was standing there, a towel wrapped round his waist and a wet one in his hand.

"I...Er...I came back for the wet towel." Bea had forgotten she was naked, she was far too busy wondering where Eddie had been hiding his tightly toned chest.

"You have a tattoo." It was a statement rather than a question as she noticed a small quill tattoo peeking out above the towel just on his hip bone.

"So have you." Bea hadn't noticed that Eddie had stepped closer.

"What?" How could he know that unless he could see it? Bea suddenly realised Eddie could see it. She tried to cover herself up with her dressing gown but her hands wouldn't obey her and she stood frozen to the spot as Eddie lightly brushed her stomach just by her belly button.

"Why wings?" He traced the outline with his finger.

"It's my guardian angel." Her voice didn't sound like hers, it had a much deeper tone than usual.

"Mine's obvious." He smiled wryly as he reached a hand up to her face and smoothed her cheek with his palm. His touch was so soft that she felt like floating away. "Can I kiss you?" She saw the hesitation in his eyes, the indecision and the uncertainty.

She wanted nothing more than for him to kiss her and when she didn't say no, kiss her he did. So gently at first that she hardly felt it but gradually the kiss deepened. She reached her hands round his neck as his went round her back, pulling her into his embrace and onto the bed behind.

# CHAPTER 19

Bea woke up a little confused. It was broad daylight outside but she didn't have a clue what time it was, what day it was and for a few seconds even where she was. She lay staring at the ceiling till her mind woke up properly then sat bolt upright when she remembered who was lying next to her.

She stole a tentative look at the sleeping Eddie and half smiled, half groaned when she recalled what had happened. He looked even younger than twenty in his sleep and without his glasses on. His hair was now dry but extremely messy, with the odd curl stuck to his forehead. His chest rose and fell evenly in time with his breathing and she found her eyes once again wandering to the tattoo on his hip bone.

Shaking the thoughts out of her head she checked the time on her phone, tutted when she realised it was gone noon and then reached down for her dressing gown.

"What time is it?" a drowsy Eddie's voice whispered in her ear before she felt a line of kisses run down her neck. Despite herself she shivered.

"After twelve." She turned her head to catch his lips with hers. "And this isn't getting the boat painted." Bea stood up and Eddie fell back onto the bed in mock annoyance.

"More fun than getting the boat painted though." He raised his eyebrows in a 'come to bed' look and she climbed back onto the bed to kiss him once more. "Sorry we didn't get to...you know...finish." He looked embarrassed and Bea kissed him reassuringly.

"So you don't carry condoms." She shrugged her shoulders. "Makes me think more of you in a way. Like you're not expecting anything and that you don't go in for one-night stands." She got off the bed again and pulled on her dressing gown and turned towards the door. "It was still nice."

"Nice?" There goes that foot again Bea thought and turned back to look at him. "Nice?"

"You know what I mean." She didn't know Eddie well enough yet to know if he did. "It was lovely."

"That's even worse." He shot over the bed and knelt down in front of her.

"Eddie don't be daft, you're taking everything far too serious...oh!" But the last word was lost as he started kissing her inner thighs.

"Lovely! I'll show you bloody lovely!"


"Well, Mr. Richards, we've done a fine job even if I say so myself." Bea stepped back to admire the now gleaming blue paint-work just as Eddie was finishing off the E in *Sophie*.

"She looks superb." He ended his brush stroke with a flourish. "Just the inside to get finished off now."

"There's no hurry on that." Bea clicked the lid back on the paint pots and wrapped the brushes in plastic bags to clean later on. "She's perfectly habitable the way she is."

"We're not leaving her half done." He joined her on the tow path. "She's beautiful on the outside now and her inside needs to match." He reached into the back pocket of his jeans. "I sketched a quick plan the other day and I've been meaning to show it to you." He unfolded a piece of A4 and held it up for her to see, miraculously still legible after its earlier dip in the canal.

"This is a quick plan?" Bea stared at the intricately drawn and labelled diagram.

"I'm a perfectionist, what can I say?" He started pointing to the various parts and explaining them to Bea. "When you walk in from the bow you walk into the dining area, bench seats both sides and a fold away table. The step up to the bow has a removable cushion so it can be a wraparound lounge area for watching TV." He could see Bea was very impressed so far. "Knowing how much you like to cook, I thought the kitchen on one side with another bench seat opposite so if you have friends round they can sit and chat with you while you make noodle sandwiches or fire up the microwave."

"Oi! I can cook, I just choose not to." She feigned a haughty look. "There's a difference, you know."

"You'll have to show me sometime."

"When I have a fully fitted kitchen I promise that the first meal I make in it will be for you." She really shouldn't make promises she couldn't keep. She'd never cooked a proper meal in her life, egg and chips was as far as her skills in the kitchen went.

"I'll hold you to that." The look in his eyes told her he wasn't just thinking about food. "Now at the tiller end I've got big plans to maximise the space. Instead of having the bathroom and bedroom separate and on one side I thought about making it en-suite and having the bedroom open up onto the stern, like a private balcony sort of thing."

"You can't do that on a tiny boat like this?" Bea was questioning the bedroom plan. "Nowhere near enough space."

"You'll be surprised." Eddie took out his phone and showed her a picture on the internet.

"That is amazing." The whole back end of the boat was taken up as the bedroom with fitted wardrobes and drawers and a small spiral staircase leading out to the tiller.

"Because it's just you and one bedroom what's the point of cramping everything into a tiny space." He put his phone and the plan away. "Open it all out I say, make the most of it."

"It's going to cost a bit though isn't it?" Not that it mattered really. She could do it bit by bit.

"Not as much as you think." They started walking back inside. "With planning and knowing where to look." Bea put the kettle on for what felt like the tenth time that day. "Most of the cost will be in the kitchen and bathroom followed by the wood for the shells of everything. Then it will just be your soft furnishings."

"You make it sound so easy." She popped tea bags into the cups and reached for the biscuit tin. Buddy, who had been sunning himself on the roof all afternoon, came running in at the sound.

"It is." He came up behind and hugged her, resting his chin on her shoulder. "I can't wait to get started. I love restoring things." A simultaneous beeping made them both reach for their phones.

"Giles." Bea held up her phone.

"And me." Eddie showed her his. "It will be to remind me about the fair tonight and invite you if he hasn't already done so. It's a bit of a Summers Day tradition." He opened the text and Bea did the same.

"Meet at seven by the big wheel. Colour this year is pink." Bea read hers aloud. "What does that mean?"

"Giles always picks a colour that we have to wear." He texted as he spoke. "The person wearing the most pink things wins this little gold trophy and the person wearing the least has to do a forfeit."

"Thanks for the notice." Bea started racking her brain for anything pink she had.

"No one will have had any notice." Eddie locked his phone. "That's the fun of it. Giles only gives two hours' notice including to himself. He does a live video on Twitter where he picks a colour out of a hat. I completely forgot to watch it."

"Blimey. Bit over the top isn't it?" Bea hated anything that made her stand out from the crowd. "I don't think I'll bother."

"Oh come on, you have to go," Eddie begged. "We have such a laugh." She still wasn't convinced. "I'll buy you some candy floss."

"If I must." She couldn't resist his smile any longer.

"Then I shall get off home, get changed and meet you under the big wheel at seven." He gave her a lingering kiss before he left.

"Well then Buddy Boy. Looks like you're off to Uncle Joe's for the night." Buddy barked in reply and she gave him a bit of ginger biscuit before heading into her room to find anything pink.


At five minutes to seven Bea was standing by the Big Wheel with nearly all the staff from Summers Day press, some with their respective partners some without, but all wearing varying shades of pink, and Bea was pretty sure that her pink t-shirt, socks and an old plastic bangle she'd found would not be anywhere near enough to win the contest. It was pretty obvious that this year's winner was Giles.

He was dressed from head to toe in bright neon pink. He wore pink socks over pink tights over pink pants. A pink waistcoat over a pink shirt with a pink tie. He'd even found a pink cape and dyed his hair pink with clip on pink earrings and comic pink glasses.

Eddie arrived bang on seven and was declared joint loser with Bea as all he could find was boxer shorts, socks and a tie.

"And the winner is…" Giles left a dramatic pause. "Me!" Everyone cheered and clapped and last year's winner Stacey handed him a tiny gold cup on a plastic stand. "I want to thank my publicist, my agent and of course all of you." He blew kisses before collapsing into laughter.

Everyone headed onto the big wheel and Bea realised she hadn't even said hello to Eddie. He'd been hijacked by Lisa and was now several carriages away so Bea headed onto the wheel with Giles' boyfriend Richard.

This continued for most of the evening. As soon as they got to a ride Lisa or Stacey would almost fight over Eddie and he was too nice to say no so Bea shared rides with nearly every member of staff after an apologetic smile from Eddie.

"Are you and Eddie an item?" She was on the ghost train with Giles and was slightly taken aback by this question.

"Don't be silly." Bea was glad they were in the dark as she could feel her cheeks going red. "We're just friends."

"Trust me, the way he looks at you is not as a friend." Giles suddenly screamed as a skeleton dropped down in front of them. "It's nice to see him happy. We've all noticed a change in him since you came." Another scream as a ghost flew across the ceiling. "Even Mr. Summers doesn't seem to upset him anymore." A final scream as a werewolf popped up before they headed back into the light.

"Forfeit time!" Steph had already grabbed Eddie and was dragging him off as Lisa took Bea's arm and followed. "Time to have your fortune told." Bea had been worrying about the forfeit so her relief was obvious when they found themselves standing outside an old red and green gypsy caravan with a gaudily written plaque announcing *Mystic Rosa – knows all – sees all.*

"I'm game if you are?" Eddie stretched out his hand to hold hers which was immediately accompanied by wolf whistles and cheers. "Don't worry about them, we're just the new office gossip, it'll blow over." But Bea did worry about it, she wasn't sure she was ready for the world to know about her and Eddie—in fact she didn't even know if there was a her and Eddie. It had all happened so quickly that she was struggling to comprehend the day's events.

"Come in my dearies, come in." A voice from inside beckoned them forward. It was just how Bea had expected it to be.

A woman dressed all in black with a black veil sat behind a round table that held a large crystal ball. The room was dimly lit with soft red lights and smelt strongly of incense.

Eddie and Bea sat down opposite the woman, trying not to giggle. The woman started to wave her hands over the ball but she didn't speak.

"Who's going first do you think?" Eddie whispered to Bea.

"Edmund Richards!" The voice was familiar to Bea. "I see your future."

"How does she know your name?" Bea was in shock.

"One of the gang have told her, of course." He leaned forward. "What do you see, Mystic Rosa?"

"I see a great many things, a great future for you, but wait…" She waved her hands faster. "The mists are clearing." Eddie gave Bea a smirky smile. "A face from the past emerges."

"Interesting," he said. "I was expecting a tall, dark stranger but that will do."

"What do you see for me?" Bea was enjoying this little bit of fun.

"I see many things, my dear." She stopped waving her hands over the crystal ball and reached for Bea's palm. She grabbed it tightly, so tightly that Bea wanted to pull away but the strength in the woman was surprising. "Moonbeam Winters." Bea went cold, there was no way the gang had told them her name.

"Did you tell her?" she mouthed at Eddie but from the look of shock on his face she knew he hadn't.

"His sorrowful search has ended but still he cannot rest." Her voice was soft and Bea instantly recognised it, it was Ruby Turner. "Not until the truth is known by all will he finally be at peace." She suddenly let go of her hand. "Now then dearies, cross old Rosa's palm with gold." Eddie threw a fiver onto the table before rushing out after Bea who had left as soon as Ruby had let go of her hand.

"You okay?" Eddie could see that she wasn't, she was visibly shaking and he steered her away out of sight before the others came back.

"What the hell, Eddie? What the hell?" Bea didn't know what else to say. "How does she know my name? What does it mean? What does any of it mean?"

"Eddie?" A woman's voice interrupted them. "Eddie Richards!" This time she almost screamed in delight and flung herself at him. "Oh my God! It's so good to see you." And from the way he was hugging her and smiling it was obvious to Bea that Eddie felt exactly the same way.

# CHAPTER 20

"I'm so sorry, Bea." Eddie finally remembered that she was standing there. "This is Charlotte, Charlotte this is Bea."

"Lovely to meet you." Charlotte held out a perfectly manicured hand and smiled with perfectly straight white teeth.

"Likewise." Bea shook her hand lightly and felt a strange sensation in her stomach as she was once again forgotten.

When Eddie had been telling her about his first kiss she hadn't imagined Charlotte like this. She thought she'd look a bit nerdy like Eddie did but here she was, a virtual goddess with perfect ash blonde hair, bright blue eyes and a body to die for with legs that went on for ever in skin-tight jeans. Even her make-up was perfect, just light enough to look natural. Bea's make up consisted of mascara, the green cream that tones down rosy cheeks and the same deep purple lipstick she'd been wearing since she was sixteen, in fact it was probably the very same stick.

"Did you hear what I said?" Eddie was looking at her now as was Charlotte although she was looking at Bea as if someone had just shoved a rotten fish under her nose. "Honestly Charlotte, she's off in a world of her own, that's writers for you." He turned back to look at Charlotte and Bea watched her face change in an instant.

"I remember you being the same." There was that feeling in Bea's stomach again as Charlotte touched him lightly on the arm.

"I'm going to find the others." Bea was already walking away.

"But I just said that." He shook his head. "I'm going with Charlotte for a few minutes to say hi to her sister and her parents then I'll be back."

"Oh, okay then." But Charlotte was already leading him away and without a backward glance he was gone. She had no intention of meeting up with the others. She was going to buy a nice bottle of wine or two or maybe even three, go home and get very drunk and forget all about Ruby Turner.

*Maybe she was a clairvoyant though*, Bea thought to herself. After all hadn't she predicted a face from the past for Eddie, and lo and behold up pops Charlotte as soon as they left the caravan. But what on earth did she mean by sorrowful searches and finding peace? None of it made any sense to Bea and two hours and four large glasses of wine later it still wasn't making any sense, but now at least she didn't care.

She weaved her way to bed feeling quite sure that the boat was rocking more than it usually did. She was feeling a little homesick for Al and Em so took out her photo albums, sat cross-legged on the bed and promptly fell fast asleep in a heap.

*"You can't take her from me."* Bea could hear the upset in the man's voice. *"Not again."*

*"I can't stay."* This time it was a female voice that spoke. *"It isn't working."*

*"I thought we were happy."* The man was getting desperate now. *"I thought you wanted a house and a family."* Bea could hear the couple but she couldn't see them. She was in a room she didn't recognise with a small suitcase at her feet. She felt like she was a child again, a really young child.

*"I can't stay,"* the female repeated. *"She's my daughter and she belongs with me."* All of sudden the door swung open and Bea felt herself being dragged away, down a long dimly lit hallway.

*"She's my daughter too." She felt a hand try to grab her but the woman was too fast.*

*"Don't try and stop me or you'll never see her again." The man dropped to his knees and as Bea looked back all she could see was his dark hair and tears streaming from his eyes.*

*"I love you." He mouthed before she was dragged out of the door and into the night.*

Bea woke up with a pounding headache, a mouth as dry as the Sahara desert and full recollection of last night's strange dream. She told herself it was all because she'd been looking at old photos before she fell asleep and it was just her brain sorting things out but it had felt so real. The man had seemed known to her in the dream but when she tried to recall his face it was that of a stranger.

The woman on the other hand was another matter. In the dream she was sure it was her mother but she never saw her face and the voice had been that of Ruby Turner. Again Bea consoled herself with the fact that it was just her brain going over the day's events but she still shivered as she remembered Ruby's words in the caravan.

Shaking her head to bring herself round she dragged herself out of bed and into the kitchen, holding onto the sides of the boat as she went. She drank a large glass of water, swallowed two paracetamols and headed into the shower.

Half an hour later and some semblance of normality had returned although her head still felt like it had bricks in it. She'd forced down a slice of toast while checking her phone. There were three missed calls, two voicemails and countless texts from Giles but not a thing off Eddie which gave her that horrible feeling in her stomach again. She was just about to text Giles when he called.

"You'd better be dead, young lady." His voice was a mix of anger and relief. "The gang's been worried sick. We went to the hotel but you weren't there and the snotty manager gave us a right mouthful for banging on the door at half past midnight. No one knew where you lived and Eddie had disappeared with that gorgeous blonde and he wasn't answering his phone either." There was that stab again.

"I came home after that fortune teller and got a bit drunk." So Eddie had gone home with Charlotte had he? So much for the lovely innocent young man she thought him to be. "I'm so sorry Giles, I really am."

"Well, as long as you're okay." He was calming down. "Now don't forget it's the classic car festival thingy today and tomorrow and Mr. Summers expects us all to attend in our Sunday best, just think summer wedding."

"What?" This was the first Bea had heard about this.

"We have a stand and everything." Giles hadn't noticed the panic in her voice. "Mr. Summers brings all his cars and trust me there are quite a few and we usually get to have a drive as well. He uses it as a bit of an advertising event for his books and for the publishing house but really we all think he just likes to show off." Giles sniggered.

"And you're telling me this now?" Bea was mentally rummaging through her wardrobe. "At ten o clock in the morning with a raging hangover."

"Goodness me, is it ten o clock already?" She could hear Giles grabbing keys. "We have to be at the church for half past. I'll see you there." He was gone before Bea could even say goodbye.

"Shit! Shit! And double shit!" She raced into her room and pulled out the only thing that was vaguely suitably for a wedding. It was a knee length baby blue, lace overlay, off the shoulder dress and thankfully she'd brought the matching shoes. In ten minutes she was fully dressed after snagging two pairs of tights and deciding to go bare legged. She didn't have time to dry her hair so it fell in soft curls around her shoulders and her mascara had been so hastily applied that she'd got more on her eye lids than lashes so she'd wiped it all off and decided on the natural look.

Pinning a note to the door for Joe she started to run, thought better of it in her heels and the morning heat so took a fast walk instead, arriving out of breath, red faced but just on time as the church clock chimed once for half past the hour. Giles was waiting for her by the door, a manic expression on his face.

"Where...Are...All...The...Cars?" she asked, bent over double trying to catch her breath.

"Never mind that." Giles was ushering her inside. "Mr. Summers has been going crazy wondering where you are. Stand up. Smile." Bea straightened up even though the stitch in her side was hurting and plastered a smile on her face. Scott turned round from his place in the front pew and beckoned for her to join him. He was dressed in a long grey frock coat with a baby blue waistcoat and matching cravat. Bea felt her knees buckle and she leant on Giles for support. "Yes, he has that effect on everyone." Giles patted her hand reassuringly. "I'll see you after the service."

Bea was left to walk the last steps on her own as Giles had taken his place in the third pew on the left. It was only then that she noticed how incredibly quiet the church was and how incredibly full. Her heels clicked noisily as she walked and she felt the eyes of the entire congregation on her. She resisted the urge to walk slowly and quietly, opting instead to clatter towards Scott and sat down just as the vicar walked out onto the altar and everyone stood up.

It was the most painful hour of Bea's life. She was unnervingly aware of Scott's presence next to her throughout the entire service and had lost count of the times she'd brushed against him as they stood up and down and shared a hymn book. He had a rich deep singing voice that made her tingle and despite all the other things she knew about him she still couldn't help thinking how beautiful he was as she risked a quick glance at his perfect face from beneath her lashes.

"Finally I'd like to thank you all for coming." Bea sighed in relief that it was over at last. "And I'll hand you over to our most famous resident and generous benefactor, Scott Summers." Now Bea was in a dilemma. She knew she had to move to allow Scott to get past but did she do the knees to one side or full stand? In the end she went for the full stand wishing she hadn't as she felt his hard chest brush against her and his hands on her hips as he moved past her in the very small space of the pew.

"It's wonderful to see so many of you here today." Scott's voice was full of warmth and confidence but this was the last she heard of his actual words. She found herself day dreaming as she stared at him standing behind the pulpit, the sun shining in from the window behind him and making him look like an angel.

"Are you coming with us or are you just going to sit there catching flies with your mouth?" Bea hadn't even seen Eddie in the church so his voice behind her was a shock.

"Of course I'm coming." She said harshly, standing up and waltzing past him to catch up with Giles and Richard, linking her arms between the two of them. "So what happens now then?" She asked Giles, completely in the dark about the day's events. "And where are all the bloody cars?"

"Weren't you listening?" Giles shook his head at her. "Of course you weren't. You were too busy gawping."

"I was not gawping." Bea was indignant then slapped Richard as he did an impression of her with her mouth wide open. "Was I that obvious?" He nodded and she hung her head in shame.

"It's okay though," he reassured her. "Most of the congregation were the same." They were outside now and the heat hit them hard after the coolness of the church.

"Nice job on the dress by the way," Giles complimented her. "Perfect match to Mr. Summers and you look stunning in it. Eddie can't keep his eyes off you." And indeed when she stole a glance at Eddie he was looking at her but it was a glare and she looked away instantly.

"Why are you and Eddie and Scott dressed the same?" This was the first time Bea had noticed the identical suits although Giles' waistcoat and cravat were navy blue and Eddie's were a deep red.

"It's a publicity thing." Richard explained. "Scott wanted the girls all dressed the same as well but they refused."

"How many times, Richard?" Giles scolded. "Mr. Summers."

"He's not my boss, Giles, I'll call him what I like." He smiled. "And I often do." The smile turned into a dirty laugh.

"So are you going to tell me what the rest of the weekend involves or shall I just walk round like a headless chicken?" Bea looked towards Eddie again who was talking animatedly with Scott. The tension between them obvious to everyone.

"The cars are here." Steph had joined them now along with the rest of the gang. "I love this weekend." She squealed with excitement. Bea wished she could share her enthusiasm but as she had no idea what was going on she was finding it increasingly difficult to even smile.

"Where's your overnight bag?" Lisa, who was dressed in gorgeous green silk asked Bea.

"My what?" She looked at Giles accusingly.

"Whoops." Giles grabbed Richard's arm and scarpered off down the path towards the fleet of waiting cars. There were old Jaguars, Daimlers, Rolls Royces and Aston Martins and then towards the back Bea could see some vintage double decker buses.

"Come on, we get first choice." Lisa grabbed her arm.

"Is everyone from the village going?" Bea looked round at what appeared to be hundreds of people milling around and getting into the various vehicles.

"Anyone that wants to." She was making her way to the black Daimler parked by the gate that Steph had already got into. "Mr. Summers lays on transport for everyone to the hotel and because we work for him we get first choice." She stepped elegantly into the car, tucking her long dress underneath her.

"But I haven't got a change of clothes or anything." Bea was almost desperate now. She felt out of her depth, ill prepared and extremely confused by it all.

"I'll take you home first." Her knight in shining armour had arrived and she turned to smile at Eddie.

"I'll drive Miss Winters to fetch her things, Edmund." Scott was by her side and the use of her full name made it sound like an order. "You're needed at the hotel before everyone else gets there. Shall we?" Bea placed her hand on his proffered arm and allowed him to move her away. She risked a look back at Eddie but he was already storming off towards a British racing green Mini. She pretended to drop something so she could buy some time and try and catch his eye but it was too late. The Mini was driving off and from the noise and speed it was going she knew the driver was angry, very angry indeed.

# CHAPTER 21

"Wow." The word was totally inadequate for the sight that met Bea's eyes as Scott turned the old Jaguar E-Type into a very unassuming drive that transformed into what would have been a carriageway years ago. Bea imagined huge black horses pulling a pristine carriage with its occupants dressed for a country ball trotting down. How on earth the horses had got up the hills in this county she had no idea. She'd been surprised that the little Jaguar had managed it and was immensely worried about the people on the buses.

"We do it all the time," Scott had reassured her as they had approached one particularly steep hill with a sheer drop on the left hand side. He'd dropped into second gear and climbed slowly before racing down the other side. "If you live in Yorkshire you've got to expect a few hills. And sheep." He added, slowing down suddenly to let a small flock walk by on the other side. "Why a canal boat?" Scott asked as he waited for the sheep to pass.

"Only thing I could afford round here." She thought back to when Scott had pulled up outside Watery Lane. He had opened the car door for her and was about to accompany her when his phone rang. "Five minutes." He'd mouthed to her and she instantly knew that meant she had five minutes to grab her stuff not he would be five minutes so she kicked off her heels and ran to the boat.

"I suppose a roof is a roof." He drove off as the last sheep passed by with a sharp bleat.

Bea hadn't talked much on the journey, she was too busy thinking about Eddie and trying not to think about the little car careering off the side and smashing down the rocks especially after Scott had answered her question about a lane of sand that just seemed to be lying there for no reason at the bottom of what felt like an almost vertical hill.

"That's if your brakes fail on the way down," he said calmly while Bea stared at him in disbelief. "You just drive into it and it stops the car." This had only added to her fears and she had closed her eyes at every hill from then on.

She wished she could have stopped thinking about Eddie as well, the look on his face when Scott had told him he'd drive her had been one full of hate. Mind you, the glare he had given her earlier hadn't been much nicer. Why had she ignored him? Why had she allowed petty jealousy of a girl he'd shared his first kiss with to get in the way? She resolved to find him first thing as soon as they got to the hotel.

"Wow," Bea uttered again as the hotel came into sight.

"Breath-taking isn't it?" Scott stopped the car for a few minutes. "It always gets me, every single time." He stared at the building. "I used it as the setting for one of my novels, you know."

"Well, I can see why." The hotel was a mixture between a huge country manor and a castle. It was made of yellow and grey banded limestone with pointed turrets and gothic archways. Long arched windows, some with stained glass gave it a church-like feel. "I just want to grab my notebook and write an historical romance here and now."

"Why don't you?" He started the engine again with a roar.

"I couldn't do all that research." Bea shook her head. "Give me a modern day story or a fantasy world I can build myself and I'm happy."

"How is the writing coming along, by the way?" They were now outside the hotel. The buses and cars were all parked up along the driveway in what could only be described as show formation. People were milling around and various stalls had been set up selling local produce and handicrafts.

"Really good." She watched him park the Jaguar right by the front doors. "This one just seems to be flowing."

"You'll have to let me take a look when it's done." He stepped out of the car and walked round to her door. "Perhaps we'll be able to publish it." He flashed her a smile as she took his hand to help her out of the car.

"Thank you." She felt herself blushing as his eyes travelled down the length of her.

"You look absolutely beautiful, by the way," he whispered in her ear as he leant past her to shut the door.

"Thank you." Why was she repeating herself so much today?

"I know I shouldn't say that as your boss." He grabbed their bags from the boot. "But you really do."

"Thank you." Bea kicked herself internally as she used the same phrase once again.

"Shall we get checked in?" He smiled at her again and she smiled back not trusting her brain to say anything other than 'thank you'.

Bea resisted the urge to say 'wow' again as they went in. The inside was even more impressive than the outside with sweeping staircases, marble floors and huge crystal chandeliers. The walls were lined with oil paintings and the furnishings were rich and elegant. The reception desk was a beautiful shiny mahogany with an impeccably dressed young lady standing behind it, her tongue almost hanging out when she caught sight of Scott.

"You're in the King's Chamber on the third floor." The receptionist was oblivious to Bea and only had eyes for Scott as they signed their check-in cards. "We've put Miss Winters in the Queen Suite as requested and Mr. Richards has the Junior Suite next door." Bea was sure she felt Scott tense next to her as the receptionist said Richards.

"Could you tell the manager I'll be down in about half an hour and we'll get things officially started?" The receptionist nodded, trying to catch his eye as she handed them their keys but it was no use, he was already thundering away towards the staircase.

"Everything alright?" Bea knew Scott well enough by now to know he was annoyed about something and it didn't take long for her to find out why.

"Bloody Richards." He bumped his case up the stairs. "How many times do I have to tell him?" Bea wasn't sure he was actually talking to her so she walked a few steps behind. "He should be grateful he's a Summers. Using that ridiculous name all the time." He continued his rant. "Edmund Summers he was christened and Edmund Summers he is not Eddie bloody Richards." He stopped suddenly and turned to Bea. "I suppose he uses that name with you as well?"

"He explained to me about being adopted." Bea didn't really know how to answer that but she felt she needed to defend Eddie. "Perhaps that's why he doesn't feel he has the right to use it, because it's not his name."

"Of course it's his name." Scott carried on up the stairs. "What else would it be?" But this was a rhetorical question as they reached the landing of the third floor and with a curt thirty minutes he'd unlocked his room and slammed the door behind him.

"What on earth was all that about?" Bea said to herself, opening her door. The room was stunning. A queen-sized bed stood under a huge window with a chaise longue at the bottom. It was decorated in cream and peach with velvet curtains at the windows and velvet cushions on the bed. She desperately wanted to explore but she needed to see Eddie more so she dumped her bag on the bed and quickly unpacked before checking her watch to see that she had fifteen minutes left. Grabbing her key and her phone she headed out onto the landing and knocked quietly on the door marked 'Junior Suite' in elaborate lettering.

"What do you want?" Eddie leaned sulkily against the door. He'd taken off his jacket and loosened his cravat with the top buttons of his shirt undone.

"Can I come in?" He didn't answer, just beckoned for her to enter. His room was very similar to hers only without the chaise longue, instead he had two high backed chairs and it was decorated in red. "Sorry." She turned to look at him standing against the now closed door with his arms folded.

"For?" Bea didn't know what she was actually sorry for, it had just seemed the right word to say at the time.

"For being an idiot." That seemed to do the trick and he smiled.

"I'm sorry too." He uncrossed his arms and stepped towards her. "I was such a jerk. You were upset and I just left you to go off with Charlotte." Bea hadn't expected him to apologise. "It was just such a shock to see her and then she wanted me to spend some time with her and her family, I couldn't find you, and my phone was dead and..." She stopped him with a kiss. "You forgive me then?"

"We were both jerks." He kissed her and walked her backwards towards the bed. "We haven't got time," she said as Eddie reached behind her dress for the zip but didn't try and stop him.

"There's always time." His shirt was already lying on the floor as they fell onto the bed.

"Ow!" There was something pointy sticking in her head. "Presumptuous?" She pulled a brand new box of condoms out from under the pile of clothes that were on his bed.

"I prefer the word hopeful." He grinned sheepishly, his arms either side of her.

"Seeing as you brought a box of twenty-four I'd say very hopeful." She reached up to kiss him then froze when someone knocked loudly at the door.

"Edmund." Scott's voice and more knocking made them both leap up.

"Quick, behind the door." He ushered Bea towards the door throwing her dress and shoes at her before opening the door just a fraction of an inch and showed only his head and shoulders. "It's not half past yet, Scott."

"Don't use that tone with me." Bea could feel the anger radiating from Scott. "You're half dressed, what have you been doing?" Bea shoved her dress in her mouth to stifle a giggle then felt Eddie's hand stroke her stomach. Well two could play that game she thought to herself and ran her fingers lightly up his arm and down the side of his torso. He tensed immediately at her touch.

"I wasn't using any tone." He sounded out of breath as Bea moved her hands further down. "I was just saying it wasn't time to go."

"Downstairs in two minutes." Bea heard Scott march off and then knock on her door. "Bea?"

"Shit!" Now what was she going to do.

"I think I heard her go down a few minutes ago." Bea sighed in relief at Eddie's quick thinking.

"Two minutes." Scott repeated as Eddie shut the door.

"That was close." Bea was pulling her dress back on and tidying her hair as Eddie reached for her again. "You heard him, two minutes." She slapped his hands away playfully.

"We can be quick." He was kissing her neck.

"No, Eddie." It took all her willpower to push him away. "The first time is not going to be a quick fumble."

"I'm not a virgin you know." He seemed quite offended by her comment. "I'll have you know I've slept with two women since Charlotte." Bea tried not to giggle at his bragging then realised what he'd said, so Charlotte had been his first. She had to swallow the jealousy in her stomach back down.

"I mean our first time." She kissed him gently on the lips. "Later." She slipped on her shoes and opened the door checking the landing was empty. "Now get dressed and get downstairs. I haven't got a clue what's going on or what I have to do so I'm going to need some help."

"I'll see you down there." He caught her hand before she left and pressed his lips to the back of it. "Until tonight." She shivered at the promise in his words and walked rather unsteadily towards the stairs.

Standing at the top she tried to compose herself before going down. She brushed her hands through her hair and smoothed her dress. Thank goodness she hadn't worn make up or it would have been smudged to high heaven. A coldness crept over her all of a sudden and she got the feeling that someone was watching her but when she turned around no one was there. As she walked down the stairs she felt sure she heard a door closing quietly.

# CHAPTER 22

"Where have you been?" Bea had never seen Giles in such a panic. "Oh, I see." Eddie was walking down the stairs tidying his cravat and he couldn't help catching her eye and grinning at her like a Cheshire Cat. "You're playing with fire, you are."

"I have absolutely no idea what you are talking about." She feigned innocence.

"You've got your dress on back to front." Bea looked instantly down before realising he was pulling her leg. "Then why would you think your dress was on backwards if it hadn't been off recently?"

"I was going to change then decided not to." She knew he didn't believe her.

"Just watch you don't get caught." Giles warned. "Mr. Summers doesn't like office relations especially when he wants to be the one doing the relations if you get my meaning. Nudge, nudge, wink, wink."

"Giles!" Scott called from across the room.

"I've found her, Mr. Summers." He grabbed Bea's arm and dragged her through the busy room. "I was just filling her in on her job for today." He handed her a clipboard from a nearby desk marked 'book sales' before dashing off with a quick wink at Bea.

"You'll be next to me in the morning room." He started to walk and she assumed she had to follow. "I'm doing a meet and greet for the next hour or so then heading outside to the cars. I need you on book sales and crowd control."

"Crowd control?" Bea was sure she hadn't heard him correctly but when they turned down the hallway there was a huge line of people, young and old that stretched as far as the eye could see and round the corner to the morning room. Every pair of eyes turned to watch them as they went past.

"I've asked Richard to help." They were now inside the exquisite morning room with its soft green sofas and the afternoon sun streaming in from the windows that stretched from floor to ceiling. "Not strictly an employee I know but he did such a good job of it last year when we had that awful cock up with tickets and three ladies had to be thrown out for fighting."

"Yoo hoo! Over here." Bea could hear Richard but all she could see was a hand waving above the small crowd of women standing at least ten deep.

"Excuse me, ladies." It was like the parting of the Red Sea as the women magically melted away. "Thank you all so much for coming. Lovely to see you again Jenny. Hello Maggie." Bea followed behind in awe and admiration.

"Thank the Lord." Richard looked flustered. "I can't cope with all these fans," he whispered to Bea as she took the empty seat next to him and Scott made his way towards a desk that had been set up on the opposite side of the room with a life size cut-out of himself behind.

"What do I do?" she whispered to him, a little overcome by all the different perfumes mingling together in the already stuffily hot room.

"All the books are £10 which goes in here." He pointed to a blue cash box. "We've got some of the older ones in a box under the desk, they're all £5 but most of them are diehard fans so they've already got his back catalogue." He placed his hands on a pile of raffle tickets. "Now anyone wanting their book signed needs to pay £5 and gets one of these raffle tickets. The money goes in the black box and the corresponding ticket goes in the tombola over there."

"Slow down." Bea's head was hurting and she could see the women getting impatient.

"You'll get the hang of it." He was already handing over a book and a raffle ticket depositing the money in the corresponding boxes.

"Have you got any photos?" The woman standing in front of Bea was as old as her mother but dressed far more sensibly.

"Er..." Richard came to her rescue and handed her a pile of immaculately dressed Scotts beaming back at her.

"£5 if brought with a book, £10 without. Yes, my darling." He was already serving someone else.

"With or without a book?" Bea put a smile on her face and did her best to cope with what felt like a never-ending queue. After an hour Richard's phone started vibrating and singing 'Girls just wanna have fun'.

"Sorry ladies and gentlemen but the next five people will be the last for today." There was a collective groan of disappointment from around the room. "We'll be here again tomorrow." They served the next five people and Bea started tidying away while Richard placated the next few people in line with the promise they'd be first in the queue tomorrow.

"That was horrendous." Bea watched as the last few paid fans joined the queue to meet Scott while the ones that had missed out filtered slowly away with backward glances at him. "I can't believe he charges people for signatures." Richard was locking up the two cash boxes.

"Oh, he doesn't." He pulled some empty boxes out from under the table and started filling them with raffle tickets, photos and unsold books.

"Er...haven't I just been selling his signature?" Bea was a little confused.

"Well he does, but it goes to charity." Bea felt awful for thinking badly of him. "He donates it to the local hospice that helped his mum when she was dying." Now she felt really bad.

"That's the last one." Scott was beside them, his life-size cut-out tucked under his arm. "Make sure this gets locked away Richard, you know what happened to the last one."

"Will do Mr. Scott sir." Richard saluted.

"Now put this lot away and get yourselves a drink. I'm heading outside to the cars and I'll need you to relieve the others for their breaks." Richard saluted again and Scott smiled as he walked out.

"Come on Sexy." He grabbed the cut out and kissed it full on the lips. "And you Miss Bea, there's work to be done."


Bea was exhausted. She'd never known a day like it in her life. She'd flitted from stall to stall, run errands and fetched drinks and snacks. As the newbie she was expected to watch and learn and help where needed. Everyone else seemed calm and collected as they explained things about the publishing house or showed people around the cars. It felt like the whole of Yorkshire was crammed into the hotel and its grounds and she couldn't wait for them all to go home so she could take off her shoes and sleep for a week.

It was starting to get dark and the crowds were beginning to leave. The buses and limos had already departed taking the villagers with them and soon the only people left were the Summers Day gang and their families.

"Well done guys, I think that was our best yet." Scott was still high on the euphoria of the day. "Dinner and drinks on me." There was a huge cheer as everyone headed inside and towards the dining room. It was set out as if there was a wedding with crisp white table cloths laid over round tables set with eight places.

Bea sat with Giles, Richard, Lisa, her husband David and their six-year-old daughter Daisy. Scott was on a table with some people Bea didn't recognise but Giles explained they were potential investors in some new scheme he was planning.

"He'll be here." Giles spoke reassuringly. "You don't need to keep looking every time the door opens, you know."

"What?" Bea hadn't realised she had in fact been doing this very thing and gulped down her now filled glass of wine before pouring another.

"Slow down girl." Richard took the bottle off her. "You've not eaten since lunch, it'll go straight to your head." He was right. Within five minutes she was starting to feel tipsy and giggly.

"Stop watching the door," Giles told her again. "Eddie won't be sitting with us anyway, he has to sit with Scott."

"I don't know what you mean." She finished the second glass.

"Bea!" Lisa scolded. "Slow down!"

"Shan't!" She grabbed Richard's glass and downed it before he could take it back.

The waiters appeared with starters for everyone and Bea made a big deal of blowing her soup to cool it. The door opened again and this time it was Eddie who came in, he smiled over at Bea before heading to Scott's table as Giles said he would.

"We're having sex tonight," she slurred, dunking a chunk of bread into the soup and watching him walk by.

"Oh dear Lord." Giles put his head in his hands, Richard laughed out loud and Lisa choked on her bread as David tried to cover his daughter's ears.

"Could we get a coffee over here please?" Richard asked a passing waitress. "A really strong one." It arrived within a minute. "Drink it now." Bea made a face as she took a sip and pushed it away. "Drink it!" he warned and she did as she was told as everyone moved their glasses out of her reach.

After being force-fed a further two coffees, a jug of water, steak and chips and a huge piece of chocolate cake, Bea was feeling more like herself.

"My head is pounding." She leant down on the table. "I need to go to bed."

"Yes, we heard." Richard tried not to laugh.

"Oh God!" She tried to lift her head from the table as she realised what she'd said. "I'm so sorry," she apologised to Lisa and David, shame filling her face. "I have got to stop drinking."

"You think?" The sarcasm in Giles' voice was clear. "If you'd been sitting with anyone else?" Bea shivered at the thought.

Music filled the air and tables were pushed back as a DJ Bea hadn't even noticed started playing. Steph was dragging Lisa onto the newly cleared dance floor as Richard grabbed Giles' hand.

"I'd better get this one off to sleep." David picked Daisy up who had been nodding off in her chair which left Bea alone, her head once again on the table.

"Not dancing?" She hadn't noticed Eddie had sat down next to her.

"No." She groaned. "I just need my bed."

"There's an offer I can't refuse." Bea didn't even have the energy to answer him back. "Are you okay?" Eddie's voice was full of concern.

"Come on, Eddie." Steph was beckoning him from the dance floor.

"In a minute," he shouted back. "What's wrong Bea?" He placed a hand on her back.

"I've made an idiot of myself." She still didn't lift her head up and he had to lean down to hear her over the music. "I told the whole table we were going to have sex tonight."

"You did what?" He clearly wasn't sure whether to laugh or be angry but laughter won in the end. "I suppose they'll find out eventually anyway." He shrugged and she finally lifted her head off the table. "Yikes!" Her hair was sticking up and her eyes were red.

"Do I look that bad?" She tried to smooth her hair down.

"You look beautiful." He squeezed her hand.

"Liar." She smiled. "But thank you."

"Now off to bed." He stood up and then helped her do the same.

"Aren't you coming with me?" She gave him what she hoped was a coy look.

"That would get the tongues wagging, wouldn't it?" He looked genuinely disappointed. "And I've still got work to do with these suits Scott invited. I'll see you in the morning." He touched her tenderly on the arm before heading back to Scott and the businessmen.

Bea's head started to clear as soon as she left the noise of the dining room. She trudged wearily up the stairs, cursing herself at her foolishness before fumbling with her key and dropping it just as she reached the landing of the third floor.

"There you go, miss." She hadn't noticed the elderly gentleman until he picked up her key and handed it to her.

"Thank you." She looked at his face, it looked familiar. "Have we met?" She was sure she'd seen those grey eyes before.

"I don't think so." He shook his head but she wasn't convinced.

"I'm sure we have." Bea racked her fuddled brain. "You've helped me before." It was like a light bulb had gone off in her head. "Back in Brum, we bumped into each other and you helped me pick up my papers."

"You must have me mistaken, miss." The man left hurriedly and Bea watched him leave, one hundred percent convinced that she wasn't mistaken, that it was indeed the very same man, but what on earth was he doing in Yorkshire?

# CHAPTER 23

"Thank goodness that's over." Steph leaned back into the coolness of the limousine. "I love this weekend but loathe it all at the same time." It was late on Monday evening and after a second busy day everyone was shattered. "I'm so glad we've got tomorrow off."

"I know exactly what you mean," Giles agreed. "I'm sure there were twice as many people as last year."

"The cars this year were superb," Richard piped in.

"Did you see that Cadillac?" Steph was flicking through the photos on her phone.

"Saw it, heard it, drove it," Giles screamed excitedly.

"You never did." Steph was jealous. "How an earth did you manage that? I spent a good hour sweet talking the owner and fluttering my eye lashes for a drive."

"When you've got it, you've got it." Bea started to zone out of the conversation. Her head was throbbing, had been since the wine incident the previous night. Sleep had invaded her and the unwavering heat and constant crowds of the day had done nothing to help. She hadn't seen Eddie since breakfast and was desperate to talk to him about the man she'd met but as she was constantly reminded by Giles he was permanently with Scott.

Luckily she was the first to be dropped off and after numerous goodbyes and air kisses she left the delightfully air conditioned car and stepped out into the still stifling heat. More waves as the limo drove off then a short walk to collect Buddy and she was back in the peace and quiet of the *Sophie*.

It took all of her energy just to remove her shoes. Her feet ached from two solid days of heels and she felt so drained that she couldn't even make it to her bed and just slumped down in the plastic chair.

"Anyone in?" Eddie's voice was accompanied by a light knock but he didn't wait for a reply. "You look knackered." He headed straight to the kettle.

"I feel like death." She looked at him. He looked clean and fresh. His eyes were bright and his hair was its usual tidy mess of curls. "How?"

"How what?" He was busy washing mugs she'd forgotten to do in the rush of the previous morning.

"How do you look like you've just stepped onto a film set and I look and feel like I've done ten rounds with Mike Tyson." Against her better judgement she'd worn make up today and she knew it had now melted on her face and mascara would be smudged all around her eyes.

"When you've done as many of these things as I have you get used to it." He placed a cup of tea on the table and she groaned at the noise. "I know what you need." He took the tea away. "A long soak in a nice bath."

"That sounds divine." She stood up then remembered she was on a narrow boat and sat back down. "Small problem."

"No problem at all." He took her bag into her room and after some shuffling noises and drawers opening he emerged with the same bag. "Come on." He clipped Buddy's lead on and grabbed his bowl and food.

"Come on where?" She was in no mood to go anywhere. "I'll just stay here."

"You're coming to mine for the night." He pulled her up with his free arm. "And I'm not taking no for an answer.

He half dragged her to the Mini and literally had to shove her into the passenger seat. Buddy leapt straight onto the back seat, excited by the new adventure. Bea was half asleep as they drove through the village, past the church and took a turn down a road she'd never seen before.

"Here we are." Eddie had parked outside what appeared to be the back of a stone cottage. It was hard to see details in the dark but it was perfectly square with a window either side of the door and two windows on the top floor like a house a child would draw. "Let's get you inside and I'll run you that bath."

Bea followed behind as Eddie switched lights on and ran up the stairs. Buddy darted round the place finding new smells and settled himself down on a brown leather sofa opposite a brick fireplace. She had a distinct feeling of deja vu as she looked round the cottage. It was like a tiny version of the manor that Scott lived in. Completely open plan but in total keeping with the feel of the outside. Unlike the manor though it felt like home.

She was drawn to a desk that sat under a window and could imagine Eddie sitting here writing. His laptop sat neatly on the top and notebooks and numerous pens lay underneath and to the sides. There was a book case full of reference books and novels and she noted with a wry smile that he had the entire series of Robin Sparrow books.

"They are brothers after all, I suppose," she said to Buddy who was already asleep.

"It's nearly done." Eddie came back down the stairs. "I've put your bag in the bathroom and a nice clean towel so you get yourself up there and I'll fix us something to eat."

"Thank you." She gave him a soft kiss as she passed by on her way upstairs. The bathroom was the only room in the house with a door but surely there would have been at least two bedrooms up here originally. Now there was just a large bedroom, masculine in style with not a flower in sight. Bea couldn't help wandering around.

Another desk almost identical to the one downstairs sat under the window and Bea was positive it was directly above the one downstairs. She took a peek out of the window and although it was pitch black she was sure she could see the canal just a few feet away and what looked like a massive ditch running alongside it.

There was a photo of a very young Eddie with who Bea could only assume was his mum and dad. They were considerably older, and she would have said they were his grandparents if she hadn't known better.

"I can still hear the taps Bea, you need to turn them off before it overflows." Bea ran guiltily into the bathroom not wanting to be caught snooping as Eddie shouted up.

"Sorry," she called back down the stairs. The roll-top bath sat in the middle of the room and was virtually full with luscious coconut smelling bubbles and she quickly turned the taps off before stripping and stepping in to the welcoming water. She sighed with complete contentment as every muscle in her body relaxed and just lay there for ages thinking about nothing other than how good it felt.

"You'll get all wrinkly." Obviously a door meant nothing to Eddie as he sauntered in.

"Eddie!" She was suddenly embarrassed even though she was completely covered by bubbles.

"You're not going shy on me are you?" He sat down on the blanket box under the window. "Not after Saturday." He winked provocatively at her.

"Well…no…" When he put it like that she couldn't really say anything.

"I've come to give you a nice relaxing massage." He rolled the sleeves up on his shirt as he knelt down behind her. Today his colour scheme had been pale blue which suited his dark hair, but the cravat and jacket had long been abandoned.

His hands felt sublime as he rubbed her neck and shoulders and she felt sure his hands would wander but he was the perfect gentleman and after twenty minutes dried his hands, kissed her head and went back downstairs to check on the food.

Waiting for her when she came down was a delicious meal of spaghetti bolognese followed by apple pie and custard.

"Have you just made this?" Bea was on her second helping of pie.

"I told you I could cook." He poured another glass of water and although Bea would have loved a nice glass of wine she was grateful he hadn't served any.

"You certainly can." She resisted the urge to lick the bowl, opting instead to help him clear the table and load the dishwasher.

"And now to bed." Eddie was turning off lights and checking doors were locked. "You coming, Buddy?" Buddy opened an eye, looked at him then decided he was comfortable enough where he was and curled up even tighter. "Rejected by a dog." He shook his head. "Bea?" He held out a hand towards her and she took it allowing him to lead her upstairs. "You get in, I'll be five minutes."

She didn't need telling twice and was in the bed before he had even got in the bathroom. Feeling suddenly nervous she lay back on the pillow and pulled the covers under her chin. She heard him brushing his teeth and closed her eyes for just a second.

The sound of a canal boat chugging along woke Bea the next morning. The sun was streaming in from the curtains and she felt refreshed after what was possible the best night's sleep she'd ever had. Stretching lazily, she stopped suddenly when her arm brushed against Eddie's chest. Turning on her side she stared at him.

As before she was amazed at how young and innocent he looked when he was asleep. An odd curl had fallen across his face and he'd kicked the covers off in the night revealing tight white boxer shorts. She traced the outline of his tattoo with one finger and he stirred a little but didn't wake so she let him sleep and headed downstairs.

"Morning Buddy." She ruffled the fur on his head. "I bet you need to go out." Having remembered that the back of the house was completely open she hoped the front would be enclosed and safe for Buddy to have a wander around. She was right.

At the front of the house was a delightfully enclosed courtyard with a patio table and chairs and sweet-smelling roses in stone pots. The canal was closer than she had thought last night but what intrigued Bea the most was that the house appeared to be on a train platform. She opened the gate, being careful to shut Buddy safely behind her and stepped into the past.

Visions of steam trains flooded her mind as she walked along the cracked platform. The large ditch she had seen from the bedroom window was where the train tracks would once have stood but now it was overgrown with brambles and weeds. She looked back to the house and realised it must have been the old ticket office.

"I see you've found my little station." Eddie was by the gate still only wearing his boxer shorts.

"You said it was disused." She was standing back in front of him now.

"The station is." He opened the gate for her. "But not the house." They headed back inside where the kettle was already boiling and toast already grilling. "Breakfast on the terrace?" He started laying a tray with orange juice, plates, glasses, butter and marmalade.

"Sounds divine." She piled the now popped toast onto a plate as he made a pot of tea. "Sorry about last night."

"What is there to be sorry about?" He placed the teapot and cups onto another tray.

"You know what." She tried to convey what she wanted to say through a look but it didn't work. "That we didn't have...you know...sex." She said the last word with such embarrassment that Eddie laughed.

"Oh Bea." He picked up the heavier tray leaving her the lighter one. "You do make me laugh sometimes." They went back into the garden and sat in the sun. "So what if we didn't have sex. I had as much fun just cuddling you all night." She raised her eyebrows disbelievingly. "Well not quite as much fun but you know what I mean."

"I still haven't told you have I?" Bea completely changed the subject and went into a full on explanation of the strange encounter with the man in the hotel.

"So now you're seeing strange men as well as hearing them." Eddie bit into a slice of toast with a crunch.

"I'm serious, Eddie." She wagged the butter knife at him. "I swear to you it was the same man I saw in Brum a few weeks ago, he helped me pick up some papers I'd dropped."

"It could be the same chap I suppose." Eddie was thoughtful. "But it's highly unlikely."

"There just seems to be some very strange things going on round here." She sat back in her chair. "And all centred on me."

"You're being paranoid now." He poured her another cup of tea. "I think you're still tired from the weekend."

"I know you're probably right but I just can't shake the feeling that I've seen him before." Buddy came rushing out of the house all of a sudden and barked and barked at the gate. "What's the matter boy?" He barked and pawed at the gate but Bea wasn't about to let him out. She could hear a canal boat approaching, an older man at the tiller.

"Good morning," he called. Buddy's barking was almost high pitched now and he was digging at the paved ground in desperation.

"Good morning, beautiful day." Eddie called back as the man and his boat drove past. Buddy had stopped barking and was now whining softly. "So what do you want to do today?" He grabbed another slice of toast and began to butter it. "We could go for a walk, head into town and grab something to eat." He realised Bea wasn't speaking in fact she wasn't even moving. She had gone deathly white and seemed frozen to the spot, staring out at the canal. "Bea?"

"I'm sure that was him," she whispered.

"Who was him?" Eddie could hardly hear her and leaned closer.

"The man from the hotel." Bea's voice was scared. "He just went by on the boat."

# CHAPTER 24

"Well that explains it all then." Eddie relaxed back into his chair. "That's Charlie."

"I don't care who it is." Bea was still whispering. "Why is he following me?"

"He's not following you." Eddie laughed kindly. "I've seen him round here a few times."

"That still doesn't explain why he's following me." Bea didn't seem to be able to make Eddie understand.

"For the last time, he's not following you." He started clearing up the breakfast things. "He was obviously here for the car show and now he's heading back to the Midlands by the look of it."

"It still doesn't explain how I saw him in Birmingham." Bea still wasn't convinced. "And why he denied it."

"Perhaps you did see him, perhaps he forgot." Eddie picked up the trays and headed back into the house. "I don't remember strangers I've said hello to in the street before." He gave her a quick kiss on top of the head as he passed by.

"I suppose you're right." Bea sipped her tea and stared into the distance. What Eddie said did make sense, it made perfect sense but she just couldn't shake the feeling that there was something weird about it all.

"So?" Eddie almost bounced back into the courtyard. "Have you decided what we're doing today?"

"Do you know what I'd really like to do?" Eddie shook his head. "I know we can't do it on the *Sophie* but I'd really like to have a cruise round the canal. Do you think we could rent a boat for the day?"

"I don't see why not." Eddie ran in the house and came out seconds later with his phone and began searching the internet. A distant ringing from the house made them both look round.

"It must be mine." Bea got up. "I've no idea where I left it." She followed the noise inside and upstairs to her bag. It had stopped ringing but there was a voicemail from Em.

*'Mum's in hospital, think it's her heart.'* Em sounded so distressed. *'Al's on holiday in Dubai and I'm leaving now to drive to Birmingham.'* There was a pause. *'She's in The Queen Elizabeth by the way.'* The message clicked off to be replaced by the computer-generated voice.

She rang Em back straight away but it kept going to voicemail so Bea assumed she was already driving. She got dressed hurriedly and started shoving everything into her bag.

"Good news." Eddie was at the door. "What's the matter?" He could see from the look on her face that something terrible had happened.

"That was Em." Bea was trying to hold back tears. "Mum's been taken into hospital."

"Oh, that's awful." He covered the space between them in seconds and hugged her tightly. Bea couldn't hold them back any longer and burst into tears.

"I know we're not that close." She hiccupped through sobs. "But she's still my mum."

"Of course she is." He held her even tighter and stroked her hair. "Do you want me to drive you?"

"I don't know how long I'll be gone for." She looked up at him with a tear stained face. "Can you just look after Buddy for me?" He nodded.

"I'll drive you back to the boat so you can get your things and I'll grab some stuff for Buddy." He threw on a shirt and jeans and after locking the house with a none-too-pleased Buddy inside they drove back to the *Sophie*.

"I'm so sorry our day's been ruined." They were back on the boat and Bea was busy packing a small suitcase.

"Don't even think about it." He had Buddy's bed under his arm. "Are you sure you don't want me to drive you?"

"I'll be fine, honestly." She shoved more things in the case. "You get back home." She could tell he was reluctant to leave. "Honestly, I'll be fine." She kissed him to emphasise the point.

"Well okay then." He shuffled slowly away to the door. "Are you sure?"

"Yes, Eddie, I'm sure." She blew him a kiss.

"Phone me when you get there." He blew her a kiss back and then was gone.

Bea took a breath as she tried to concentrate on anything else she might need, remembered underwear from the bedroom and almost ran back down the passageway spending five minutes in her room deciding how many pairs of pants she might need. The noise of someone coming down the stairs of the boat made her smile.

"Honestly, I'm going to be…" She looked up expecting to see Eddie but instead bumped into the hard chest of Scott. "Hi." She smoothed her hair then realised she had pants dangling from her fingers.

"I came to see if you fancied a drive out?" He smiled at her then noticed the underwear and case. "Are you going somewhere?"

"I've got to drive back to Birmingham." She shoved the pants in the case and hastily zipped it up. "My mum's been taken ill." The tears started again. "She's in hospital, they think it's her heart. I was going to phone you when I got there to say I wouldn't be in tomorrow." The words were a babbling mess but Scott got the gist of them.

"Hey, don't worry about work." He grabbed her bag. "Have you got everything?" She nodded. "Then I'll take you."

"I can't ask you to do that." Bea was making a mental check list in her head of everything she'd packed. "I'll be absolutely fine."

"I won't take no for an answer." He was already out of the door with her bag and she followed him. "You're in no fit state to drive anywhere." Bea really didn't know what else to say. She knew he was right, driving all that way when she kept bursting into tears was a recipe for disaster. Perhaps she should have let Eddie drive her after all, but then who would look after Buddy?

Bea's phone rang again as they walked along the towpath. It was Al. She explained to him what little she knew and that she was on her way to the hospital and that she'd let him know what was going on as soon as she got there.

"What if she dies?" They were at Scott's Aston Martin now and he'd just put the case in the boot. Bea couldn't imagine life without her crazy mother and at this she broke down into more tears.

"Hey." Scott put his arms round her and rubbed her back. "There's no point worrying about things like that." She sobbed on his shoulder. "Let's just get you there and then you'll know what's going on." She nodded and got in the car unaware that Eddie had been watching the whole time.


"This isn't the way to Birmingham." Bea watched as they drove past the turning for the M1. She didn't know a lot about directions but she did know they were now travelling the opposite way.

"Trust me." He said it so sincerely that Bea couldn't not and five minutes later they were pulling up at a private airfield where a helicopter was sitting on the tarmac. "I know a much quicker way." He parked the car, helped her out, then got the bag and walked her over to the helicopter. "This is James." Scott introduced her to a smartly dressed man with headphones on. "He can't land at the hospital but there's an airfield not too far out and I'll arrange for a car to pick you up." He put her case in the helicopter and helped her inside.

"But…" Bea was a little bewildered. She thought he was going with her—but then she should have known better than that by now, she said to herself as he closed the door and waved as the helicopter took off.

It was a rather strange experience for Bea, totally different to flying in a plane but she rather enjoyed being able to see everything as they flew over the congested motorways and was grateful to Scott that she would arrive much quicker this way.

It didn't seem very long at all till they were landing and after a thank you to James she was soon speeding to the hospital in a black Mercedes.

"Kathleen Winters?" She asked after her mother at the reception desk and was directed to the cardiology ward. "Kathleen Winters?" She repeated to the ward sister and was directed to bed 11. Bea didn't know what she was expecting to find when she got there, her mum lying on her death bed with machines beeping perhaps but she certainly didn't expect to find her mum sitting up in bed drinking tea looking like she hadn't a care in the world.

"Bea?" Her mum seemed surprised to see her. "What on earth are you doing here?"

"Em called." Bea sat down in the chair. "She said you'd been taken into hospital and it was something to do with your heart."

"Oh, that girl never listens." Her mum put down her tea. "I told her I had to come in for some tests on the old ticker." She tapped her chest where Bea noticed she was hooked up to an ECG machine. "Nothing to be worried about."

"What!" Bea realised she was on a ward of sick patients and lowered her voice. "Em's on her way up from London. Al's worried sick and I've dashed here from Bloomsdale."

"Well there really was no need." She started flicking through a magazine. "Carlos is picking me up later and we're off out on the town." Bea didn't know what she was more annoyed about, the fact that there was nothing wrong with her mum or her flippant attitude about it.

"You just don't care do you?" Bea shouted quietly. "All three of us run round after you and you don't give a damn how that affects our lives. In all these weeks you haven't once asked how my new job is or where I'm living."

"Fine." She closed the magazine. "How's the new job and where are you living?" She looked at Bea with pretend interest.

"The job is brilliant." Bea answered her in a monotone fashion, she knew her mum wasn't really interested. "It gives me plenty of time to write and I'm living on a canal boat called the *Sophie*." The line on the ECG machine started speeding up.

"You're living where, dear?" Her mum seemed to have turned a funny colour.

"On a canal boat." The ECG machine was going crazy. "Mum, are you okay?"

"Just feel a little funny, dear." Her mum suddenly grabbed her chest in pain and Bea ran for the nurse.

"If you could just give us some space please." There were doctors and nurses all round and the curtains were drawn hastily as Bea stepped out into the corridor.

"What's going on?" Em was running down the ward. "Is she okay?"

"She was." Bea looked at her sister. "She was absolutely fine, said she was only in for tests then suddenly the ECG machine went bonkers, she grabbed her chest and then this." She opened her hands outwards to show Em the hive of activity that was now going on inside the curtains.

"What do you mean she was only in for tests?" Em looked worried but she still wanted to know what was going on.

"Exactly that." They backed up towards some chairs and sat down. "She said you'd misheard her and she was only in for tests. She's going out with Carlos later." Bea and Em both looked up as another doctor headed into the cubicle.

"Well she must have been having problems if she's in for tests." Em took Bea's hand. "She'll be alright you know. She's a tough old bird." They sat like that for what felt like an hour before one of the doctors came out to speak to them.

"Are you Mrs. Winters' daughters?" They both nodded, it seemed strange to Bea to hear her mum addressed as Mrs. She'd never been married but she supposed the doctor just assumed she had been at some time in her life. "I'm very sorry but your mum suffered a massive cardiac arrest. We did everything we could but we just couldn't get her back."

"You mean she's dead?" Em asked, her voice shaky and the doctor nodded.

"We'll get the tubes and machines off and then you can go and see her." He placed a reassuring hand on top of their closed ones then headed off.

"She can't be dead." Bea stood up and went to the cubicle before Em stopped her.

"She's gone, Bea." Em pulled her back down. "She's really gone."

# CHAPTER 25

The next two weeks passed by in a blur. Al flew back from Dubai on the next available flight and along with Em they stayed at Bea's house for a few days. Carlos had done a runner as soon as he'd heard and Bea was sure he'd taken some of her mum's jewellery and probably some of her money as well but she was too numb to care. Scott had been amazing. He'd sent flowers and texts every day assuring her that everything was fine and to take as much time off as she needed. Eddie on the other hand was nowhere to be seen.

She'd called him and sent messages but there was no reply. His phone clicked to answer machine almost instantly each time she rang and the messages although the iPhone told her they were delivered were never marked as read.

Giles and Richard had turned up unannounced on the middle Saturday bearing the largest bouquet Bea had ever seen. They didn't have a clue where the house was and had phoned her from New Street Station asking for directions.

It was a relief to have a tiny slice of normality back for just a few hours. Giles and Richard asked how she was and how the rest of the family were. Was she sleeping? Eating? She had answered yes to both but they knew she was lying. Dark shadows under her eyes gave the most obvious clue and the fact that there was little more than off milk and mouldy bread in the house when they checked her fridge gave the second.

Richard had immediately tutted and left for the small supermarket he'd seen on their way in. This left Giles and Bea alone.

"How's Eddie?" Bea had been dying to ask this question.

"No one's seem him." Giles sipped the black tea with disgust then pushed it away. "I'll wait till Richard brings some milk."

"What do you mean no one's seen him?" Bea was a little worried that something awful had happened to him.

"Well, I don't mean no one's seen him." Giles stumbled over his words. "Just that he's been in the office once in the past week, he went straight upstairs to hand something over to Mr. Summers, came straight back down and left without a word to anyone."

"I don't understand." Bea was confused. "We had such a nice time on Monday night." Giles raised his eyebrows provocatively. "No, not like that." She slapped him. "Then all this happened and I haven't heard a peep out of him." She sighed into her cup before taking a sip and pushing it away exactly like Giles had done. "He does know my mum died, doesn't he?"

"We all do, so I presume so." Giles took her hands in his. "Don't worry about him for now." He said raising her hands to his lips for a kiss. "You just concentrate on what needs to be done. I'll go and see Eddie when we get home."

"Will you make sure Buddy's okay for me?" Bea asked. She was missing him like crazy.

"Buddy's fine." Richard had reappeared with two heaving bags of shopping. "I saw him with Eddie and that girl from the fair…" His voice trailed off at the sharp look from Giles and the crestfallen look from Bea. "I'm sure it doesn't mean anything."

"It's fine." She got up and made fresh tea for everyone. "It's not like we're going out or anything." But she was far from fine and they knew it.

It was now Sunday and Bea was packing to drive back to Bloomsdale in the car Scott had sent for her. The funeral had been on Friday and as their mother hadn't left a will they had decided to have her cremated and to scatter her ashes in the sea so she could continue her travels even after death. They knew she would never have wanted to stay in one place so Al, Em and Bea had arranged for the funeral director to keep her ashes safe until they could all come back together.

Remembering the papers she had printed out the previous evening she scooped them up into a folder smiling as she stroked what was now her finished manuscript. She had thrown herself into her writing the past fortnight. It was the only way she could forget about the guilt she felt over her mum's passing and Eddie.

A tight pain pulled in her chest at his name but she ignored it. Instead she packed all her belongings up from the house, putting anything she needed into her car and the rest for charity or rubbish. Tackling her mum's belongings was another matter. She didn't feel even vaguely strong enough for that right now so she boxed everything up and put them in a local storage unit on her way.

The only thing she took with her was a beautifully carved box that Bea had never seen before. It was about the size of an A4 folder and had been hidden amongst her mum's clothes. She had tried to look inside it but she could find no way of opening it. It appeared to be completely sealed but when she shook it, Bea could hear what sounded like papers rattling around.

She had been sad to say goodbye to the house and to Birmingham. She'd lived there since her university days and it held such good memories but her life was in Yorkshire now. She didn't know why but she felt she belonged there, more than she had ever done in any other place.

The *Sophie* was waiting for her, gleaming and shining in the now autumn sunshine. With the help of Sean the driver, the car was soon empty and the little boat full of Bea's worldly possessions. She really was going to have to down-size even more she thought, as the *Sophie* seemed to almost groan under the pressure of bags and boxes.

"Right then." Bea summoned all the courage she could muster. "Off to get Buddy." She walked to Eddie's house, driving would have got her there far too quickly and she still needed time to think about what exactly she was going to say to him. Did she play it casual? Did she shout at him? The way she was feeling she thought she'd probably just end up sobbing in front of him. But in the end all her thinking and planning was futile as no one answered.

She decided to sit and wait for a few minutes, perhaps he'd taken Buddy for a walk—so she walked round to the front and sat down on the chair that less than two weeks ago she'd sat in sharing breakfast with him. She thought back to that day, going over and over the morning's events thinking of anything that could have happened to change Eddie in this way but nothing came to mind so she just sat there and stared out at the canal.

"What the devil are you doing here?" a female voice called. Bea turned to look at the house and saw a bare shouldered Charlotte leaning out of the bedroom window.

"I've come to get my dog." Charlotte didn't reply, she just slammed the window shut then emerged a few moments later by the door hastily tying a very short silk night gown around her perfectly proportioned body. She thrust a few things of Buddy's at her then shut the door again. Bea stood there a little shocked for a few moments before knocking loudly. "Where's my dog?" She asked far more politely than she felt after Charlotte had eventually opened the door again. "And where's Eddie? I'd like to see him."

"Your dog is back with that Joe person." She looked as if the words were hurting her to speak them. "As for Eddie he doesn't want to see you." She went to slam the door but Bea was too quick for her and jammed her foot between the door and its frame. "Kindly remove your foot."

"What do you mean Eddie doesn't want to see me?" Bea didn't believe a word that came out of her mouth. She'd thought she was pretty the first time she'd seen her but now with her face twisted and angry Bea thought she was one of the ugliest people she'd ever seen.

"Exactly that." Bea still didn't remove her foot even though Charlotte kept slamming the door against it.

"I'd like to hear it from him if you don't mind." Bea was stronger than Charlotte and pushed the door open, barging past her into the house.

"He isn't here." Bea wasn't convinced especially when she heard a creak from upstairs but after running up the stairs calling his name all she found was an unmade bed and evidence of Charlotte everywhere. "I did tell you." Bea trudged back down, past Charlotte and out of the house. "And next time you want someone to look after your dog while you go swanning off don't ask us."

Bea didn't have the strength to reply in fact she didn't even really hear what she said. She walked out of the courtyard, taking a last look back at the house before closing the gate. Charlotte was standing at the door, her arms folded across her chest, a smug smile on her face, but when Bea looked upstairs she was sure she saw a figure move hastily away from the bedroom window. She sighed as she realised Eddie had been there all the time and as he'd obviously moved on she vowed not to waste another minute thinking about him.


Everyone was so kind to her at work on Monday morning that she cried. The place seemed far more relaxed than usual and she discovered this was because Scott was out for the morning. The pile of work on her desk was huge and she busied herself sorting it into piles of urgency. Luckily she had another week before the wages and royalty payments had to be processed so it was mostly bills and emails that needed sorting.

The chatter in the office stopped abruptly at half eleven after Giles had heard Scott's car pull up and a few minutes later he sauntered in making a bee line for her desk.

"It's so lovely to have you back." He stood in front of her, his smile genuine and warm. "We've missed you." He handed her a bunch of white roses from behind his back and there was a collective sigh from around the room. Scott turned round quickly and there was a sudden clattering as everyone shot back down in their seats. "Pop up and see me before your lunch and we'll have a chat." He gave her a little wink before heading upstairs.

"Thank you," Bea shouted after him, suddenly remembering she hadn't yet spoken a word to him.

"Wow." Lisa was the first over quickly followed by Steph, Giles and the rest of the office.

"You are so lucky."

"He's never brought flowers for ANYONE before."

"He must really like you."

The door behind opened and everyone turned to see Eddie walk in. Bea's heart flipped at the sight of him. He had a folder tucked under his arm but he paid no attention to anyone and walked straight past them all and up to Scott's office.

"That's all we get now." Everyone except Giles had gone back to their desks. "He never smiles anymore, just looks stern and waltzes past us like we're not even here."

"He's got a new girlfriend." Bea's tone was childish and she knew it. "Perfect bloody Charlotte.

"I'm sorry, Bea." Giles was full of sympathy. "We didn't know how to tell you but they've been seen round the village together."

"After what happened yesterday I really couldn't care." Bea put her nose to the roses inhaling their sweet smell.

"What happened yesterday?" Giles was all ears.

"I went to pick Buddy up and that Charlotte was there." Bea explained. "They'd obviously been having sex because she was naked and the bed was unmade." Giles was looking at her a little perplexed. "He didn't even have the guts to show his face. Must have hidden in the wardrobe or something." Giles was still looking confused. "He's an absolute coward if you ask me. Can't tell me himself so he sends Little Miss Perfect to do his dirty work."

"If you didn't see him, how do you know he was there?" Giles was looking at her most oddly.

"Because when I looked back I saw him move away from the window." Bea wasn't sure why Giles was acting strange all of a sudden.

"So you didn't actually see him." Giles wanted to be absolutely sure.

"Not actually, physically see him, no." Now it was Bea's turn to be confused. "But I know he was there."

"He can't have been there, Bea," Giles stated.

"You don't need to soften the blow Giles." Bea was grateful for his tact. "I'm a big girl now, I can handle it."

"I'm not trying to soften the blow," he said. "It's just you can't have seen Eddie."

"I told you I didn't see him." Bea was getting fed up of the conversation. "But I know he was there."

"He can't have been there, Bea." Giles shook his head. "He was in London for the weekend and judging by how stressed he looked when he just walked in I'd say he's only just got back."

# CHAPTER 26

"How do you know he was in London?" Bea folded her arms and leaned back in the chair. "If he's not talking to anyone then you can't possible know where he was."

"Well that's where you're wrong Miss Know It All." Giles wagged a finger at her. "Friday morning in here was like World War 3 had started. Mr. Summers was shouting, Eddie was shouting, very uncharacteristically of him I must say." Giles added this bit as if to make a point. "After a few minutes they both storm down the stairs and Mr. Summers hands Eddie train tickets and says 'You're going and that's that.' Eddie grabs them and walks out."

"But how did you know when they were for?" Bea needed absolute proof. "Could have been for next week or even next month."

"Because, Clever Clogs, Lisa had only picked them up this morning for Mr. Summers to go to London so that's how we know." Giles stuck his tongue out playfully.

"So who was in the house with Charlotte then?" Bea was intrigued. "I definitely saw someone there. I wonder if Eddie knows."

"Well whoever it was it wasn't Eddie so you can stop blaming him for that." Giles was about to head back to his desk. "And no one has actually seen them kissing or even holding hands you know. Perhaps they are just friends."

"Perhaps." Bea knew Giles was trying to make her feel better. "Still doesn't excuse his behaviour over my mum though."

"True." Giles shrugged his shoulders then hurried back to his desk as he heard footsteps coming down the stairs. It was Eddie. He handed something to Beth in the editing department and without a glance in Bea's direction or a word to anyone else he walked out in exactly the same way he had walked in.

A few days later and Bea had finally plucked up the courage to hand her manuscript to Scott to see if it was suitable for publishing. *After all* she said to herself, *if you work for a publisher you may as well get some benefit from it.* Even if it was rubbish at least she'd know.

"Here I go guys." She stood up and grabbed the folder from her drawer. Everyone gave her the thumbs up. She'd only told Giles and Giles had made no secret of telling everyone else but it was nice to have everyone's support. "May I have a word Mr. Summers?"

He was sitting at his desk, his head bowed over some paperwork. He looked up at Bea's voice.

"Mr. Summers is it?" He smiled quizzically. "You haven't called me Mr. Summers for a long time." He beckoned her forwards and she sat nervously down on the chair in front of his desk.

"Sorry." She gulped, her mouth dry. "Do you remember at the interview when we talked about me being a writer?" He nodded. "Well I've actually finished my very first manuscript and I wondered if you'd give me your professional opinion on it?" She placed the folder on his desk and he immediately picked it up and started flicking through.

"You don't have a title?" He raised an eyebrow.

"Everything I could think of is already a book title." She'd spent hours trawling Amazon to check.

"No worries on that." He put it back down. "I'll have a read over the weekend and let you know. If it's good enough I'm sure someone here will think of a title."

"Thank you, Scott. Thank you." She knew one of the hardest things in publishing was actually getting someone to read your finished work so feeling the happiest she'd felt for a few weeks she walked back down to her desk flashing a smile and returning the thumbs up back to everyone.

It was still warm when she finished work, the September sun streaming through the trees as she walked home. She collected Buddy from Joe and decided to go for a walk. It had been a strange week and she needed a breath of fresh air to collect her thoughts. She hadn't allowed herself to think about Eddie since Monday morning and now she'd finished her first book she was keen to start another.

Buddy walked eagerly and before she knew it she found herself at the church. Her subconscious must have taken her there and as soon as she walked through the gate she felt the peace engulf her. She headed to the back of the church intending to sit on the bench for a while but it was already occupied by a man who was bending over looking in a bag. Bea continued walking past.

"There's room for two you know?" The voice was familiar to her and she almost froze in shock. "Oh, hello again," he said as she turned round. "I saw you at the hotel the other week."

"Er...hello." Bea started to back away but Buddy was going ballistic and pulled towards the man.

"Hello Buddy Boy." Buddy was already on the man's lap, licking his face.

"How do you know his name?" Bea was starting to feel a little scared now.

"It's on his tag." The man smiled at her. "The name's Charles by the way." He held out a hand and Bea shook it tentatively.

"Bea," she said simply.

"Well Bea, it's a pleasure to meet you properly." He'd taken out a sandwich box from his bag and opened it to reveal chocolate chip shortbread. "Biscuit?"

"No, thank you." She shook her head even though they were her absolute favourites. Buddy was still going crazy running up and down the bench and on and off the man's lap.

"It was you in Birmingham, wasn't it?" Now that Bea could see him up close she was positive it was the same man. He had the same grey eyes and when he smiled little crinkles appeared at the sides.

"Yes, I think it was." He munched on a biscuit. "We crashed into each other if I remember correctly and you dropped your folders." Bea nodded. "Are you sure you don't want a biscuit? They're homemade." She took one and bit into it. It melted in her mouth and Bea had a feeling of recognition, like she'd tasted them before.

"Is there something in these?" Bea sat down feeling suddenly at ease in the man's presence.

"My secret recipe." He tapped the side of his nose with his finger. "Everything okay?" Bea nodded again. "Sorry, I didn't mean to pry. You just look like you have the weight of the world on your shoulders."

And then for some reason Bea found herself telling him all about the past few weeks. All about Eddie and how she didn't know what had happened and then all about her mum and how guilty she felt over her death. She was sobbing by the end but it felt so good to unburden herself to someone that wouldn't judge or criticise.

"But your mum always had a heart problem." Bea must have misheard him as she dabbed her eyes with a ripped tissue she'd found screwed up in her pocket. "I mean if she was having tests then there must have been something wrong to start with. Doctors don't run tests on healthy people."

"That's what Al and Em tried to tell me but if I hadn't started talking about this place and the boat then maybe she'd still be here." Bea blew her nose loudly. "I just don't understand why it would cause her to get upset. She'd never really been interested in my life before and I know she only asked because I made her."

"Your mum sounds like a very complicated woman." He pulled out a packet of tissues and handed them to her. "I'm sure she loved you in her own way. It's just some people find it really hard to express their emotions."

"I suppose you're right." She blew her nose again feeling a bit better. "So do you live here?" It was only right to ask about him after she'd talked about herself for so long.

"Some of the time, I live on a barge." He gave Buddy's ears a stroke idly as he spoke. "It allows me the freedom to come and go as I please."

"I live on a boat too." She smiled at him. "More from necessity than choice though."

"Wouldn't live anywhere else." Charles smiled back.

"So have you always lived on the canal?" Bea reached for another biscuit.

"Since I was born." He nodded. "I did try living in a house once but it wasn't for me."

"What wasn't?" Bea was interested in his story.

"Living in one place." He took another biscuit and snapped it in half. "When you've lived on the canals all your life and can travel where you want when you want it's very hard to live in a house. Even sleeping in a normal bed was strange."

"It was like that for me when I slept back at the house." Bea agreed. "I sleep so soundly on the *Sophie* now it's like you're floating."

"You called her the *Sophie*?" Bea was sure she heard his voice falter. "What a lovely name."

181

"She's a bit run down still." She devoured another biscuit as she spoke. "All of the inside needs doing but she's beautiful to me."

"Maybe I could help you." She was sure his eyes were glistening, perhaps he had something in them. "I've made a bit of a business for myself these past few years doing up run down boats."

"That would be great." She pulled out her phone and flicked to the photos that she'd taken of the plans Eddie had made. Charles looked at them with interest.

"I've never tackled anything so modern but I like a challenge." He gave her back the phone. "If she's in dry dock it will be easier."

"She doesn't have an engine," Bea stated. "And I still need to live on her."

"Oh yes, I forgot that." A cold breeze blew round the corner of the church and Bea shivered. "It's getting late." They both looked up. The sun was starting to set, streaking the sky with red and orange.

"We'd best get back." She stood up and Buddy stretched. "It was lovely to meet you."

"And you." He delved back in his bag and pulled out a business card. "Just give me a ring if you want any help with the boat."

"I will do." Bea took the card without looking at it and tucked it away in her pocket. Charles stayed sitting down as she walked back round the corner and down the side of the church. But the extendable lead came to a halt. She tugged and tugged but Buddy wouldn't move. "Buddy, come on boy, it's time to get home." She walked back towards the bench ready to share a laugh with Charles but he had gone.

Bea looked to the left of the church, down to the right and over into the graveyard but there was no sign of him. *Well he couldn't have just vanished*, she thought to herself. Buddy was sitting there looking completely innocent. She sat down on the bench for a minute. She couldn't have imagined him could she? Then she remembered the business card. She patted her pockets trying to find it but they were all empty.

# CHAPTER 27

"How can someone just disappear?" Buddy cocked his head to one side as if listening. "He was here, I know he was." She licked her lips. "I can still taste the biscuits." She slouched back onto the bench not caring that it was almost dark now and the autumn warmth had left the day leaving a slight chill in the air. "Come on, Buddy Boy." She stood up then froze at her own words.

She'd heard that phrase before. Charles had said it earlier when they'd first met but she'd heard it before then. She knew she had. As she walked down the path and out of the gate it suddenly hit her.

"That night on the boat," she told Buddy who was happily trotting along beside her. "When I heard that voice and you were barking." The little dog looked back at her. "He called you Buddy Boy and now I think about it, the voice was the same. It was Charles on the boat that night." She shook her head in disbelief. "Now I'm just being silly. No one was on my boat that night. It was all locked up."

Bea reached for her phone to ring Eddie then remembered sadly that Eddie was no longer in her life. She'd have to sort this out on her own. By the time they were back at the *Sophie* Bea had come to two conclusions. She was either stark raving bonkers or Charles was a ghost.

Deciding that being bonkers was probably the more likely of the two she set about making her and Buddy some tea before settling in front of the TV for the evening. She was running a little low on coal now the nights were getting cooler so decided on an early night rather than stoking the fire up. Buddy came with her and curled up at her feet as she pulled out her notebook and started planning another book. Charles might be a figment of her imagination but it had given her a brilliant idea for a story.


It was Monday afternoon and Bea was just about to finish for the day when Scott came bounding down the stairs with the biggest smile on his face and plonked her manuscript rather unceremoniously on her desk.

"I love it!" He said simply.

"What?" Bea was in shock.

"I absolutely love it." He looked like the cat that had got the cream. "The characters are so real I couldn't put it down. Just finished it now."

"I can't believe it." Bea was sure he was going to say he was joking anytime now. You didn't get your first book published just like that. It took months if not years of querying and rejections.

"It needs a bit of tweaking here and there but I'm sure Mandy and Beth our fabulous editors will work all that out." He was still smiling. "Now, let me take you out to dinner tonight and we'll discuss everything and I'll get a contract drawn up for you to sign."

"You really mean it, Scott?" She wanted to throw her arms around him but as they were in the office and already attracting a lot of attention she refrained.

"I've even thought of a title and a cover." He turned to go. "I'll pick you up at seven."

"Wow." Bea sat back in her chair and was immediately flooded by congratulations and questions from everyone.

"What are you going to wear tonight?" the ever fashion-conscious Giles asked after questions about the book had been exhausted.

"I don't know." She had to admit she hadn't even thought about that, she was too busy smiling about her book. "Skirt and top probably."

"No!" The look of horror on his face was priceless. "Do you know where he's taking you?"

"Of course I don't." Giles almost ran over to her desk.

"Well I do and it's not a skirt and top affair." He started faffing with her hair, pulling it this way and that. "Definitely hair up, Steph, don't you think." Before she knew it, most of the office were standing in front and behind her talking about hair styles, make up and clothes.

"Ah Hum." She coughed. "I am here, you know."

"Sorry, Bea," Lisa apologised. "It's just The Crooked Spoon is a big deal."

"The Crooked Spoon?" Bea laughed. "You're pulling my leg." But when she looked at the serious faces all around her she knew they weren't.

"Why is she laughing?" Steph asked Giles.

"The Crooked Spoon is the poshest restaurant this side of York." Giles pulled out his phone and scrolled through some pictures before thrusting it under Bea's nose. "Look at the website."

"Oh!" The restaurant was an old Tudor house with black beams and a white façade.

"Carry on scrolling through," Giles told her.

Inside, the restaurant was amazing. Richly decorated with intimate candlelit tables for two, gleaming silverware and staff dressed identically in black and white. The head chef and sous chef were pictured in their pristine kitchen holding a plaque with three Michelin stars on.

"But how do you know he's taking me there?" Bea was sure Scott wouldn't be taking her to such a romantic place.

"Trust me, that's where you're going." Giles was certain. "Go and ask him." Bea stood up, smoothed down her skirt and headed upstairs.

"Erm…Scott?" He looked at her as she walked up the stairs and into his office. "Could you tell me where we're going tonight please?" He raised an eyebrow at her. "Just so I know what to wear."

"My old friend owns a restaurant called The Crooked Spoon, we'll be going there." He put his head back down to his work. "Just wear something like the blue dress you wore the other weekend."

"Okay, thank you." She came back down the stairs in turmoil. She only had the blue dress, she could wear the blue dress but no, Scott had something like the blue dress. "I've got to go shopping." She grabbed her things off the desk and with a quick wave was gone.

At half past five she was staring at herself in the mirror in despair. Her make up wouldn't go right and her hair kept kinking out every time she tied it up. Her newly acquired pale pink dress had cost almost a week's wages as she'd had to buy matching shoes and a bag as well. But it was going to be useless if she couldn't get her face and hair right.

"Anyone aboard?" Giles' voice accompanied by footsteps made Bea walk out of the bedroom to find Giles, Lisa and Steph armed with hairdryers, straighteners and the biggest make up bag Bea had ever seen. "Makeover time."

An hour and thirty minutes later and Bea was ready. She didn't recognise the elegant woman in the mirror and as she stepped out of the bedroom for the others to see they just gasped.

"You look amazing." Steph was almost crying.

"Thank you so much, all of you." Bea hugged each of them in turn then at a beep on her phone she squeaked. "He's here."

"Where?" Giles looked around.

"He's at the end of the lane by the car." She grabbed her bag. "I've got to go and meet him there."

"Such a gentleman," Lisa tutted.

"Buddy!" Bea screamed. "I haven't picked him up from Joe."

"Don't worry," Lisa soothed. "I'll get him and take him back to ours for the night. Daisy will love that. She's been pestering us for a dog." Bea hugged Lisa again. "Just tell me which boat it is."

"Thank you, Lisa." Bea slipped her shoes on. "It's the *Mavis* just a few moorings up."

"You'd best go." Steph smiled and they all piled out of the boat, leaving her to continue alone as they reached the *Mavis*.

"No red wine," Giles shouted after her and she waved back in acknowledgement.

Scott was leaning against the car, another Aston Martin, but this was a modern DB9, its sleek lines shining under the lamp light. Scott was dressed in a dark suit and he smiled when he saw her and opened the door, helping her in with an outstretched hand.

"You look beautiful," he whispered to her as she passed by him into the car, and she was sure she heard him inhale as if smelling her perfume. "And you smell beautiful too." She gave a silent 'thank you' to the borrowed Dior perfume that Steph had hastily sprayed on her when she had emerged with her empty bottle of Calvin Klein.

It was around a twenty-minute drive to the restaurant and Bea could feel herself getting hotter and hotter as she lost count of the times that Scott's hand had brushed her knee. Was he really taking her to dinner to discuss her book?

Scott handed the car keys to the impeccably dressed valet and with her hand on his arm they walked in. Bea immediately felt like a fish out of water. The place was even posher than it had looked on the website and she was immensely grateful that she at least outwardly looked like she belonged there. But on the inside she was telling herself to walk gracefully and slowly in her new heels.

Every table in the restaurant was full and as they walked through to their table all eyes turned to look at Scott. Bea always forgot he was a local celebrity and felt uneasy at the scrutiny. Their table was in a little alcove at the back of the restaurant. Scott pulled the chair out for her and she managed to sit down without embarrassing herself.

"So far so good." She hadn't realised she'd spoken out loud.

"Pardon?" Bea quickly picked up a menu and was alarmed that it was all written in French.

"I said it looks good." He nodded his head in agreement.

"Everything is good here." He opened his menu. "The fish is superb, fresh from Whitby this morning."

"Then I'll have that." She closed her menu.

"Which one?" He looked at her. "There's at least ten different ones."

"What do you recommend?" The only French she knew was from school.

"Shall I translate?" So he spoke French as well, God he was perfect, Bea thought to herself.

In the end she chose scallops to start followed by sea bass and a delightful desert called La Bombe where you poured hot chocolate sauce over a sugar cup to reveal a delicate vanilla mousse. The food was delicious but Bea wondered why it was all so small. She'd had three tiny scallops and a bit of green stuff as a starter. The sea bass fillet was about two inches long and served with four chips neatly placed in perfect symmetry to the fish.

"Does *a la carte* mean small?" Scott laughed and poured her another glass of wine and water for himself. She had lost count of how many she'd had but as it was white she knew she was safe. She never got drunk on white wine.

"Oh, Bea." He took her hands in his. "You do make me laugh." The meal had been wonderful. Scott was amazing company, telling her all about his charity work and his latest adventure that he was planning to research for his next novel. They had talked about her book and he'd handed her a contract which she'd signed without hesitation, happily trusting Scott with her first novel.

Bea had also discovered that he was an outrageous flirt, touching her hand and stroking her arm at every opportunity. She found it a little disconcerting to start with but as the evening wore on she found herself doing the same to him. At one point she even ran her hand down his thigh then blushed at her brazenness.

"Shall I get the bill?" She nodded, not trusting herself to speak after what she'd just done. God, what must he think of her?

When she stood up the world spun, dear lord how much had she drunk? She leaned on Scott as they walked out. The valet had already brought the car round and this time it was he who helped Bea into the car as Scott hopped in the other side. With a roar the car sped off and Bea found herself staring at Scott all the way home in what she hoped was an alluring way.

He parked the car and she stumbled as she stepped out but Scott caught her and as she looked up she found his lips close to hers, so close she could just reach up and kiss him. In almost slow motion she wound her hand round his neck and pulled his head closer to hers till their lips touched but he pulled away all too soon.

"Let's get you to bed shall we." He lifted her up and carried her to the boat.

"Why Mr. Summers!" She said in mock disgust. "I'm not that sort of girl." She nuzzled her head into his neck, kissing him as they walked.

"Which one's yours?" Scott asked, looking up and down the towpath.

"The *Sophie*. Down there." Bea flung her arm to the right.

Scott put her down when they reached the boat before fumbling in her bag for the keys. He unlocked the door and carried her into her bedroom, laying her down on the bed. She reached up to kiss him again but this time he didn't pull away and matched her kiss for kiss.

A loud and insistent banging the next morning woke Bea. She shot up then held her head at the pain in it. Looking at her phone she was alarmed to see it read eight thirty.

"Shit!" She threw back the covers. "I'm going to be late for work." The banging came again. "Who on earth?" She didn't know who she was expecting to be behind the door when she opened it but it certainly wasn't Eddie.

"Oh my God!" He looked tired and his eyes were red as if he'd been crying. "I've just heard." He hugged her tightly. "I'm so sorry. I didn't know." He held her face in his heads. "Richard just told me off for being an arse when your mum had died." He kissed her hard. "Bea I didn't know."

"Morning Edmund." A dripping wet Scott clad only in a towel came sauntering down the passageway. Eddie virtually threw her away from him. "Morning Bea." Scott planted a kiss on the top of her head. "Any breakfast going, I'm starving after last night."

Eddie didn't wait for an explanation he looked at Bea with such a look of disgust that she felt dirty.

"Do you know what?" He didn't wait for a reply. "I am sorry your mum died but I'm not sorry for anything else." And with that he turned on his heel and was gone.

"Always was one for the dramatics." He came up behind Bea and cuddled her. "Now, how about that breakfast?"

# CHAPTER 28

"They're here, they're here." Giles came running into the office brandishing a stack of A4 posters in his hands. "I cannot wait for this." It was the first week of October and until this very moment the entire office had been depressed. Summer had officially gone, leaving dark nights and chilly mornings.

"Let me see." Everyone except Bea rushed to Giles and there were 'oohs' and 'ahs' of excitement.

"What's the theme this year then?" Bea was half listening to the conversation and half trying to figure out how her life had become such a mess.

She'd moved here hoping to start over and initially it had been wonderful but since that fateful day back in August it had taken a turn for the worse. No matter how many times everyone told her it wasn't her fault she still blamed herself for her mother's death. She'd lost Eddie, a fact that hit her hard every time she remembered it, and somehow she'd managed to get herself into a relationship with her boss.

The only good thing on the horizon was the fact that her book was almost ready. Scott had pushed it to the top of the pile and after extensive editing and cover design he had informed her that it was almost ready to be published. She hadn't seen it since the day she gave him the copy and was eagerly awaiting the finished article when finally she would see her name in print.

"Can you believe it, Bea?" Steph was standing in front of her. "Labyrinth!" She squealed then went back to her desk. Bea had absolutely no idea what she was talking about but as the whole office was buzzing all of a sudden she got up to investigate.

"Look, Bea." Giles held up a poster of the late David Bowie in his role of Jareth in the 1980s movie Labyrinth.

"Halloween Masquerade Ball." Bea began to read. "In aid of Cancer Research." Bea looked up at Giles. "At Bloomsdale Manor?" Giles nodded.

"Oh, it's so exciting." He rolled up the poster and put it with the others. "We didn't have one last year because of Mrs. Summers disappearing but my word it's coming back with a bang this year. Labyrinth!"

"I won't be going." Bea had never been one for fancy dress, she felt enough of an idiot most of the time without wearing a costume to make her look like one as well.

"Oh yes you will." He sounded like a pantomime audience. "You'll be Mr. Summers' partner." It was no secret in the office that Scott and Bea were seeing each other, a fact that Bea hated.

"Don't be daft." Bea was sure he wouldn't be making their relationship public knowledge. "It's only been a few weeks he's not going to be announcing it to the world."

"I wouldn't be too sure of that." He smiled wryly. "He's smitten with you."

"Oh God!" Bea shook her head and went back to her desk. Sitting heavily down in her chair she pondered on her life once again. There was nothing she could do about her mum or Eddie but how on earth had things with Scott got so far?

Bea thought back to the night of their first date, as Scott liked to call it now. She still remembered Eddie's face the next morning, in fact she didn't think she'd ever forget it. The look in his eyes when he realised what she'd done was like she'd shot him through the heart. She hadn't even slept with Scott that night, she'd passed out on the bed and the next thing she remembered was waking up to Eddie banging on the door.

She knew Scott had been acting the attentive boyfriend purely for Eddie's benefit but how could she explain that to him if he wouldn't take her calls or answer her messages? Even though they hadn't actually had sex it would still have looked bad to Eddie. There he was apologising to her and out walks the person he hates most in the world scantily clad in just a towel. Bea had to admit Eddie had every right to feel the way he did.

But that still didn't explain how she'd let her and Scott's relationship develop further. She could have easily passed the night off as a drunken mistake but she'd allowed him to take her out again and again. If she was honest with herself she knew it was because he was her boss. I mean how did you turn down your boss?

Yes, he was attractive and sexy but there was a harshness about him that she really didn't like. She was also starting to see that he was conceited and completely up his own arse. He loved to show off and receive attention and Bea was finding this a complete contrast to the man who spent his life giving to charity.

The office went quiet as the man himself walked down.

"I'll see you tonight, Bea." He winked at her as he went past then headed out of the office telling Lisa to forward any calls to his answer machine as he'd be unobtainable for the rest of the day.

"Where you off to tonight then?" Steph asked peeking over her desk.

"I have no idea." Bea tried to sound happy but failed miserably.

"What's up?" Lisa, Steph and Giles were in front of her desk in seconds.

"Don't mind me." She waved her hand in front of them as if to wave them away. "It's just all happening a little fast, that's all."

"So have you slept together yet?" Giles had never been one for tact.

"No we haven't," Bea said indignantly. Even if they had she wouldn't have told them. There were some things you didn't share with your work mates, especially when it involved the boss. "We've come close a few times." That was as much information as she was prepared to give. Come close didn't even cover it. It was the same routine every time. Scott would kiss her, grab her boob then try and shove his hand down her pants.

There was no romance, no wooing and certainly no feelings on Bea's side. He was a good kisser but that was as far as it went. She thought back to the gentle, caring touches she had shared with Eddie.

"Look at the smile on her face." Bea immediately stopped smiling, but let them think it was because of Scott. They continued to tease her for the rest of the morning but she didn't take any of it to heart, she was just glad she could go home after lunch.

When she walked into work the following Friday morning it was to find everyone up in Scott's office. She walked up the steps to find the Marilyn Monroe look alike standing next to Scott in front of a covered up pin board and a cardboard box on his desk.

"Finally she's here." Scott beckoned for her to come to the front. Everyone started clapping and cheering and she had no idea why. "So, you all know why we're here today." Well everyone except Bea clearly did. "Our very own Bea has written a marvellous book which we've been working really hard on to get finished so we can release it at the Halloween ball. It gives me the greatest pleasure to reveal it to you all first." He pulled the cover off the clip board and everyone clapped and cheered again.

Bea stared in horror. That wasn't her book, please God that wasn't her book. But as everyone started shaking her hand and congratulating her she realised it was. She stared at the poster in all its horrific glory.

A busty blonde haired woman with garish red lipstick dressed in a red bikini top, tight denim shorts and red high heels stood at the tiller of a canal boat. The name on the boat was also the name of the book – *The Saucy Sue* – and the author's name wasn't Bea Winters but Tanya Mounts.

"Now Tanya here has kindly given her agreement to be the face of the author in this instance and I hope you'll all take a copy home and read it over the weekend." Everyone grabbed a copy out of the box and headed back downstairs. Bea was still standing staring at the poster in shock. "Good, isn't it?"

"No." She couldn't lie.

"What do you mean, no?" His previously happy demeanour changed. "Giles worked really hard on the cover and the editing work that's been done has been phenomenal."

"I don't mean to sound ungrateful." She really didn't but she had never imagined it looking that way. "And why aren't I named as the author?"

"Well that was in the contract." Scott said matter of factly. "I've been looking for something to merge with Tanya's work and when I read your little story it fitted in perfectly with her, shall we say, sexier stuff." He threw an arm round Tanya who smiled prettily at him. "It's going to be a huge hit."

"But it's my book." Bea was getting worked up. "It should have my name on it." Not that she wanted her name anywhere near such a cover. She'd imagined soft pastels and a nice subtle title not this in-your-face picture with its blinding colours and suggestive boat name.

"Technically it's mostly Tanya's book actually." Scott kissed her on the cheek and she once again smiled at him. Did this woman actually speak? Bea thought angrily to herself.

"But you said my book was good." Bea couldn't believe what was happening.

"It is, but it just needed a little extra to spice it up." He handed her a copy. "Have a read over the weekend you'll feel much better about it then." Bea knew she was being dismissed. "And I've got to cancel tonight I'm afraid. So much work to do."

Bea walked despondently down the stairs and to her desk in silence. Only one good thing had come out of it and that was the fact that she didn't have to go out with Scott that night. In fact now Tanya was firmly on the scene she was hoping she'd never have to go out with Scott again.

She was wrong!


"The costumes have arrived." It was an hour later and Bea still hadn't got over the shock of the morning's earlier events. Mandy and Jess came in the door pushing a clothes rail full of black dress bags on hangers.

There was a collective scream of excitement from around the room except from Bea who was busy flicking through the pages of The Saucy Sue and despairing at how her story of love and heartbreak had turned into soft porn.

"Bea!" Scott had joined them and even though the boss was in the room no one could contain their excitement. "Bea!" He called again. Tanya had thankfully left over half an hour ago so she looked over at him. "Come and see our costumes, they're fabulous." There was that 'we' word again. She groaned inwardly.

The rail was empty now except for one bag that hung on its own. The name Edmund Summers written in the clear plastic pocket. Bea's heart fell into her stomach at the thought of him but she put a smile on her face instead and took the bag Scott gave her.

She almost collapsed under the weight of it. What on earth was inside? A suit of armour perhaps? But it didn't feel hard in fact it felt incredibly soft.

"Right everyone." Giles shouted above the noisy chatter. "Let's go try them on."

It took almost twenty minutes for everyone to get changed into their costumes but when they did it was just like the ballroom scene from the film had been recreated in the office. The girls all wore huge ball gowns in different colours and Giles had a frock coat and breeches. Even the masks had been made in perfect homage to the film with a slightly scary feel about them.

"Come on, Bea," Beth shouted. "We want to see yours." She had no desire to dress up, really wasn't in the mood but didn't want to disappoint them all so she headed into the toilets to change.

She unzipped the bag to reveal a white and silver ball gown with the widest skirt and puffiest sleeves Bea had ever seen and she knew instantly it was the gown that Jennifer Connelly wore in her role as Sarah. She sighed knowing that if she was wearing this, Scott would be dressed as Jareth and she was right.

As she wiggled her way out of the toilet and back into the office there were audible sighs and gasps. Then the attention was taken off her immediately as Scott came down in a high collared sparkly dark blue frock coat with matching trousers and boots. It was an exact replica of the one from the film. He even had a wig on and Bea could imagine if he'd had time he would have done the eye make-up as well.

He looked good and he knew it. Everyone was in awe especially when he held out his hand for Bea to join him. She walked over to him feeling so embarrassed that she thought her cheeks must be on fire. He twirled her round and round until she was dizzy. Someone had even fired up the song 'As the world falls down' on their phone as they danced.

"Well I'm glad to see you've all been working hard in my absence." The room went silent as they all turned to see a tall, smartly dressed woman in her early thirties saunter in. Bea had never seen anyone so beautiful. If Scott was Adonis then she was Aphrodite. She walked straight through the staff, looked Bea up and down with a withering smile then turned to Scott. "A word, if you don't mind." Scott gulped and followed her up the stairs.

"Well." Giles stared open mouthed. "The shit really is going to hit the fan." Everyone took their masks off, the mood suddenly sombre.

"Who is it?" Bea hadn't a clue who the elegant lady was.

"That, my dear, is Eleanor Summers." The name instantly rang a bell in Bea's head but in case she didn't know Giles spelled it out for her. "His wife."

"Oh." Giles was right, the shit certainly was going to hit the fan.

# CHAPTER 29

It was Friday, the day of the Halloween ball, and everyone had been allowed to finish early to give them enough time to get ready. The office was a completely different place now that Mrs. Summers was back. It was like Scott had never been the boss, as if he'd just been holding the fort while she was away.

She shared the office with him upstairs but now it had become very feminine in appearance with fresh flowers and floral cushions. Everyone worked just as hard but there was a more relaxed atmosphere as if they knew they wouldn't be shouted at if they had a conversation whilst working.

This applied to everyone except Bea. Mrs. Summers spent a lot of time with the staff, talking about various books but not once had she spoken to Bea. Even when Bea had had the monthly finance meeting with her and Scott she hadn't said a word. She'd just sat there staring at Bea which made her so uncomfortable she fluffed her words, stuttered and stumbled over figures and continually dropped her notes. When she had left she had heard Mrs. Summers say 'Where on earth did you find her from?' and Scott hadn't said a word in her defence.

It was the change in Scott that had been most significant. He had gone from being arrogant and strict to meek and mild. It seemed to change his appearance as well. Before his attitude gave him a confident and assured look making him seem sexy, now he was like a little mouse and his once handsome features appeared almost weasel-like.

Mrs. Summers had given no explanation for her absence and no one asked, which Bea found strange to say the least. There had been nothing in the local paper to say she had returned and Bea could only assume that her disappearance had been kept as quiet as possible or had been completely and utterly planned.

Deciding on the latter Bea vowed to keep her eyes and ears open. She'd escaped one nasty woman and she really didn't want to have to start dealing with another. She'd go and have it out with her before things went too far. The office was empty now but Bea had dawdled. Looking braver than she felt she started up the stairs to talk to Mrs. Summers then stopped dead halfway up.

"He needs to know." Mrs. Summers' voice was stern.

"Why?" Bea could imagine Scott shrugging his shoulders.

"Because it's time." Bea heard footsteps and assumed Mrs. Summers was walking up and down. "I've spent a lot of time thinking about this and I know your parents thought it was for the best and at the time I suppose it was but now…" She trailed off.

"Now you want to ruin his entire life." Scott spoke in a harsh whisper as if he was right in front of her. "Do you think telling him will change anything? He'll still hate me, probably hate me even more. I don't know how he feels about you but you tell him this and he'll hate you as well." Scott must have sat down as Bea heard a chair scrape on the floor. She was rooted to the spot not daring to move in case they heard her yet not wanting to move either.

"But it would answer so much for him." This was the first time Bea had heard Mrs. Summers speaking softly and Bea could tell she was upset.

"No, Eleanor." This was the Scott Bea knew. "You swan back in here after all these months and take over the office as if you've never been away."

"It is my office," Mrs. Summers interrupted him.

"It might be your office in name but who's kept it going while you've been sunning yourself in the Caribbean?" Scott accused, and Bea realised then that her absence had been planned. "Whose books bring the most money in?"

"Not yours!" Mrs. Summers screamed at him.

"They've got my name on," Scott shouted back. *What on earth does that mean?* Bea asked herself.

"Only because you hoodwinked the poor author just like you did with that poor girl out there." Bea became even more alert at this. "What did you have to do to get her to sign that ludicrous contract you gave her?"

"She's besotted by me." Bea had to stifle a rather rude retort.

"You are deluded." Mrs. Summers was getting her confidence back. "She's no more besotted by you than I am. From the first time I saw her I could see it. She's like a deer caught in the headlights, scared stiff of upsetting you because you're her boss."

"What rubbish," Scott scoffed.

"Prove me wrong then." The sound of footsteps coming towards the staircase made Bea leap onto the floor and back to her desk.

"Still here?" These were the first words Mrs. Summers had ever spoken to her.

"Just going now, Mrs. Summers." Bea hastily shoved papers into her briefcase not even knowing what she was putting in there. "Erm...Mrs. Summers?"

"Yes?" She raised her eyebrows in a questioning manner.

"Its...just..." Why did she feel so intimidated by this woman? "Well...erm..."

"Spit it out girl, I haven't got all day." She tapped her foot impatiently.

"I just wanted to ask if you still wanted your monthly payment going into the same bank account." The blank look on

Mrs. Summers face was unexpected. "It's due to go out next week so I'll need to change it with the bank on Monday if you do."

"Monthly payment?" Mrs. Summers laughed. "I own the company, do you think I need a monthly payment?" And with that she walked out of the office leaving Bea staring after her.

"Ah, Bea, glad you're still here." She hadn't noticed Scott appear. "About the ball tonight. Obviously I can't take you now my wife has decided to reappear and it wouldn't be appropriate for you to wear 'The Sarah Dress'." He made quotation marks with his fingers. "So as Tanya is the face of the book she'll be wearing it. Hope you don't mind." He didn't give her chance to answer and headed back upstairs.

"Where are you?" Giles screamed down the phone at her. "We're all waiting for you. There's only half an hour till the taxi comes."

"I'm not coming," she said simply.

"What do you mean, you're not coming?" Giles wasn't impressed.

"I haven't got a costume." Bea replied. "Tanya's wearing it." *Thank goodness for Tanya,* Bea thought to herself. She'd been dreading wearing that dress from the moment she'd seen it.

"Get yourself over here right now Missy," Giles insisted.

"Did you hear what I said? I haven't got a costume." She shouted at him in case he hadn't.

"There's a spare one here," Giles answered. "There's always spares. Now get in a taxi and get your cute little ass over here." He clicked the phone off without a goodbye.

"Well that's me told," she said to Buddy who cocked his head. "Looks like you're off to Uncle Joe's again." Buddy spent more time with Joe than with her but it suited everyone perfectly. Buddy was always happy to see Joe just as he was when he saw

Bea. She clipped on his lead, grabbed her bag and locked the door to the boat before jumping onto the towpath.

"I'm so sorry." She apologised profusely to the person she'd just bumped into.

"This is becoming a bit of a habit." Bea stood stock still at the familiar voice.

"Charles!" It was really him and definitely not a ghost as this time she had literally bashed into him and he was quite definitely a solid, real person.

"Off somewhere nice?" He had knelt down to fuss Buddy who as usual in his presence was going crazy.

"Work Halloween party." She didn't say this with much enthusiasm.

"The charity one at the manor?" Bea nodded. "You'd best hurry up then, it starts soon doesn't it?" Bea nodded again.

"I've just got to drop Buddy off to Joe then I'm away." Bea started to walk. "I'm so sorry to rush off." She waved as best she could with a bag in one hand and dragging Buddy in the other. "I just hope Joe's back."

"No worries." Charlie walked in the opposite direction. "I saw the *Mavis* on my way down."

"Thanks." Bea walked as fast as she could, tugging at Buddy's lead till she gave up and carried him instead. It wasn't until she reached the *Mavis* that she realised. Turning to look down the tow path she shouted. "How did you know Joe lived on the *Mavis*?" But Charles was nowhere to be seen.


Bea looked at herself in the mirror and thanked Tanya once again for not having to wear the white dress that would have made her stand out like a sore thumb. Instead she was wearing a lilac dress with huge puffed sleeves and a mask that covered almost all of her face. She was even more grateful for this. No one would know her and she could for once just enjoy herself without worrying about falling over or making a fool of herself.

The manor was already busy with people when they arrived and after much pushing and pulling they had all managed to get out of the taxi and through the door. Bea looked around and couldn't believe the transformation. The entire downstairs had been cleared of furniture, the floor was now covered in a springy dance floor and the walls had been draped with glossy curtains.

There was an array of costumes. Some people had opted for traditional Halloween vampires, witches and mummies. Then there were some who hadn't worn a costume at all but were still elegantly dressed in ball gowns and tuxedos. A few had got the theme wrong and were dressed as 'Pan's Labyrinth' and one chap had decided to come as the singer 'Labyrinth'.

She could see Scott straight away, everyone could see Scott straight away. He was the vision of David Bowie's Jareth even down to the eye makeup and hair. On his arm was Tanya who looked absurd in the pure white dress. It clashed with her red lipstick and her boobs were threatening to spill out but she looked entirely at ease with herself and Bea envied her that.

Then she saw it. A huge poster of 'The Saucy Sue' dangling from ceiling to floor at the back of the room with a cardboard cut-out of Tanya next to it. She felt suddenly sick and dashed upstairs. She headed straight to the room she'd stayed in that night after Scott had rescued her and shut the door, leaning her head against it.

It was then she remembered that this was Mrs. Summers' room but as she went to open the door she heard a familiar voice and she froze, instantly rooted to the spot.

"Charlotte, don't be like that." Eddie must have been right outside the door.

"I don't understand you, Eddie." Charlotte's voice was whiny. "I thought we were getting somewhere."

"I can't help how I feel." His voice was soft and Bea could see the apologetic look on his face even though there was a door between them. "I love her." Bea held her breath, was he talking about her?

"But she slept with your brother." Yes, he was talking about her. Bea's heart grew wings and flew out of her chest.

"Don't you think I know that?" Bea's heart returned to her chest with a thump and sank to the bottom of her stomach. "Not a second goes by when I don't think of his hands on her or him kissing her but I can't help loving her still."

"Then you're a fool, Edmund Summers." Bea knew how much he hated that name and she could feel Eddie's anger rising in him.

"Don't call me that." She could tell he was trying to keep his voice even. "Don't ever call me that."

"Why?" Charlotte was teasing him now. "It's your name after all."

"I think you should move out." Bea hadn't realised things had moved so fast between them.

"Oh, don't be so dramatic, Eddie." Charlotte's voice had turned nasty. "It's not like we're sleeping together is it?" Bea smiled as she heard this. "It's not like I haven't tried, but you're too wrapped up in that little harlot."

"Don't call her that." Bea felt his fist slam against the door and she jumped back in shock. "You don't know what he's like, what he's said. Look what he's done to her book!"

"I can't believe you're defending her." Bea was smiling inside, hope suddenly returning to her. "You saw it with your own eyes."

"I know what I saw, Charlotte," Eddie spat. "That image is burned on my brain for life."

"Then forget her and have me." There was silence for a few seconds and Bea knew she was kissing him.

"No." It sounded like he had pushed away.

"You're no match for your brother anyway." Bea knew Charlotte had said completely the wrong thing.

"What do you mean by that?" Eddie questioned.

"We've been sleeping together." Charlotte had nothing to lose now. "In fact, I was sleeping with him when we were together." Bea knew she wanted to hurt him. "And he's twice the man you'll ever be." And with that Bea heard her footsteps as she disappeared down the stairs.

There was a crumpling sound as Eddie fell down the wall into a heap on the floor. Bea was desperate to go to him but how could she? She was probably the last person he wanted to see. But what if she explained everything? Told him they hadn't slept together, explained about how Scott had duped her over the book.

"What's happened?" Another voice full of concern and warmth spoke and although Bea had never heard her speak in this way she knew it was Mrs. Summers. Oh God! What if she came in her room? Bea panicked and looked for somewhere to hide but she needn't have worried as the next thing she heard was two sets of footsteps heading further down the landing.

"Where have you been?" Giles scolded as she finally re-emerged downstairs. "Mr. Summers has done the book presentation and everything. He's fuming." Bea couldn't care less. Her head was pounding and her heart was aching for the hurt and turmoil that she'd caused Eddie and now he had Charlotte's betrayal on top, his first love sleeping with his brother.

"I need to go home." She looked up at Giles.

"You look awful." He hugged her reassuringly. "I'll call you a taxi and don't you worry about Mr. Summers, I'll cover for you."

Luckily the taxi didn't take long and Bea was grateful to be back by the peacefulness of the canal. She hadn't realised how late it was or how cold it had become and she certainly hadn't thought about how she was actually going to get through the door in the huge skirt. She couldn't even step up onto the boat without the weight of the dress pulling her backwards.

"Bugger." There was only one thing to do and that was get undressed. She scanned the tow path both ways before unlacing what felt like hundreds of layers and finally being able to get inside. She didn't even bother turning the lights on and headed straight to her room, flinging herself on her bed. "Ouch." She'd hit her head on something hard. "What on earth?" She turned on the light and stared at her bed. The carved box belonging to her mum was sitting on the bed. "How did you get there?"

Bea picked up the box, she hadn't touched it since the day she'd come back from Birmingham. She'd popped it away in a drawer as she couldn't open it and hadn't even thought about it. She looked at it closely. It looked a little different to last time, like the carvings had changed.

"Is that a button?" Bea pressed what was now a raised piece in the wood and instantly a drawer slid open revealing envelopes all addressed to Miss Moonbeam Winters.

# CHAPTER 30

Bea looked at the pile of cards, all were written in the same unfamiliar handwriting with a variety of different addresses which Bea recognised as some of the many places she'd lived in as a child. Every single one was unopened, a few had clearly been hand delivered but most had been posted. There was even one that had been redirected to a different address.

She looked at the date stamps and picked one of the older ones to open first.

"Happy Birthday, Daughter." Bea read the words on the card in total confusion before reading the inside. "All my love, Daddy." Her hand flew to her mouth in shock. She opened another and another, they were all the same. Birthday and Christmas cards to her from her dad for almost every year of her life. She was in utter shock that her mum had kept these from her. She had to speak to Em.

"Hello?" A groggy-sounding Em answered the phone.

"Did I wake you?" Bea had forgotten it was late.

"It's okay." Bea could imagine her sister's face. "We've had thirty kids here for a Halloween party that's all."

"Sounds fun," Bea lied.

"Well you didn't phone me to discuss a kid's party." Em knew Bea better than that. "What's up?

And Bea spilled the story of the box and the cards.

"Mum said he never contacted me." Bea had started crying. "And now I found out he's sent a card for nearly every birthday and Christmas. Why would she have hidden them from me?"

"You know what she was like." Em tried to comfort her. "She always did what she thought was right at the time." Bea was unconvinced. "She loved us all in her own way, she just wasn't cut out for motherhood."

"You can say that again." Em and Al had had more time to come to terms with their mum's strange ways, Bea still found it hard, especially now after finding out she'd lied about her dad.

"Any return addresses?" Em asked.

"I wish." This had been the first thing she'd looked for.

"Don't think too badly of Mum," Em had said just before saying goodbye, but how could she not? All these years she'd thought her dad didn't want to know her, maybe didn't even know she existed but now...Bea smiled at the thought. Somewhere out there was her dad and she was going to try and find him.

After returning the dress to Giles the next morning and a lengthy discussion about Eddie, Scott and her newly discovered dad with him and Richard she picked up Buddy and decided to take a walk round the churchyard to try and calm her thoughts.

November had arrived with a brilliantly sunny day but a slight chill in the air and Bea had dug out her winter coat for the first time. Buddy didn't seem to mind the change in temperature and toddled along happily, stopping now and again to sniff at a lamp post or tree.

There were a few people pottering around the graveyard, tidying graves, laying flowers or simply staring at the headstones. Bea wandered aimlessly up and down the rows, reading the odd one here and there whilst she mulled over the current situation in her head. What on earth was she going to do about Eddie and

Scott? And how did she even begin looking for her dad? The only person who knew him was dead.

"Hello Bea." The voice that greeted her was sad and as she looked up the last person she had expected to see stood in front of her.

"Eddie!" He was in front of his parents' grave, probably talking to them, she thought. "How are you?" What else did she say?

"Shit!" He looked like he hadn't slept and his eyes behind his glasses were red. "What happened, Bea?"

"I don't know." And that was the truth, plain and simple. She didn't know. "Scott and I were never really together." He looked at her confused. "If you know what I mean." It took a few seconds but his face seemed to brighten a little when he realised what she was trying to say. "I'm so sorry Eddie, I never meant to hurt you."

"It's okay." He stared back at the grave. "I know how manipulative he can be."

"Have you seen what happened to my book?" She tried to lighten the mood. "Susan's been turned into a prostitute." He laughed at this, not his normal deep chested laugh but a laugh all the same. "It's not how I imagined my first novel."

"Didn't you read the contract?" She shook her head. "Don't worry about it. Eleanor's on the case."

"Mrs. Summers?" Eddie nodded. "Why is Mrs. Summers on the case? What case?"

"You'll see." He smiled. "I wish they were still here." He nodded in the direction of his parents' names. "None of this would have happened. Scott always listened to them, he didn't like it sometimes but he always listened."

"Do you want to get a coffee?" Bea was starting to feel the cold just standing still but she didn't want to part company with Eddie, not now they were talking again.

"I can't, I'm afraid." He looked genuinely sorry. "I've got to drive Charlotte to the station."

"Oh, is she leaving?" Bea feigned surprise.

"She's going back home," he said. "Turns out she's not suited to village life anymore."

"Another time then?" she asked hopefully.

"Another time," he agreed, and she knew not to push him for an exact date and to just be content with the tiny olive branch that had been offered.

Eddie headed off back to the church and was soon out of view.

"Come on boy, let's get home and have some dinner shall we?" Buddy stretched lazily then barked suddenly, his tail wagging like crazy.

"Afternoon." It was Charles. "What are you two doing here?"

"Just having a walk." Bea wanted to ask him the same thing, he had a sudden habit of turning up where she was lately.

"I'm just visiting an old friend." He had a bunch of yellow roses in his hands.

"Oh, I see." Bea felt guilty for thinking badly of him. He wasn't some crazed stalker, she told herself, just an old man visiting an old friend. That's probably why he was here the other week when they'd sat chatting on the bench.

"He's been gone a few years now and not a day goes by when I don't miss him." Now Bea felt twice as guilty.

"Have you got another business card?" she changed the subject. "I couldn't find the other one you gave me and I so want to get the boat finished."

"Here you go." He took off a glove, fished around in his pockets and handed one to her.

"Charles Winters," she read. "That's my name."

"Small world." He put his glove back on.

"I don't think I've met another Winters before." Bea was sure she would have remembered it.

"Really?" Charles raised an eyebrow. "It's not particularly uncommon." He leant down to fuss Buddy.

"Perhaps we're related?" Bea joked.

"Perhaps we are." He smiled up at her. "This little chap loves a fuss doesn't he?" Buddy was on his back, his tongue lolling out of his mouth and his leg kicking out in pure ecstasy.

"He seems to like you." Bea had never seen Buddy act this way with anyone, not even her or Joe.

"Well, I'd best be off." He stood up. "Just give me a ring when you want me to pop over and see the boat. I'm free most of next week."

Bea watched him walk off towards the overgrown grave she had found Buddy on that day with Eddie. He stopped in front of it and Bea could see it was no longer overgrown, Joe had obviously been there to tidy it up like he said he would. So Charles must have known Joe's brother.

She watched as he placed the roses in the little vase and then headed off back towards the church. Bea was intrigued, she had to go and see the grave for herself. Buddy was more than happy to follow her. The stone was pristine, all the bushes cut back to reveal the name written in black on grey.

"It can't be." Bea looked up towards the very distant figure of Charles Winters and then back to the head stone. "Charles Winters." Bea read it out loud as if to convince herself of what she was actually seeing. "Father, Brother, Husband, Friend."

# CHAPTER 31

"What the hell?" Bea stared at the writing, her mind in turmoil. "But he's dead?" She looked up again to where Charles had been but he'd either walked out of sight or vanished into thin air like a ghost. She shivered. "Let's get home, Buddy." She kept checking behind her as they walked back to the *Sophie*, her brain working overtime.

After feeding Buddy and making a cup of tea for herself she pulled out her laptop and started searching for anything she could find on Charles Winters. She was rewarded instantly by a local newspaper article dated nearly five years ago.

"Local man dies in tragic accident." She read the headline out loud. The article told how on a particularly wet and foggy night Charles Winters had been driving his sister Ruby Taylor home. "It is believed Mr. Winters lost control of the vehicle on a tight corner and plunged down the hill and into the river. Mrs. Turner was found the next morning with a severe head injury on the bank of the river but rescue workers have still not found the body of Mr. Winters."

Bea sat back in the chair, *so maybe he wasn't dead after all. If they never found his body*, she questioned herself. But he had a grave. *How can you have a grave without a body?* She searched the internet a bit more until she came across an article dated a few months after the first.

"Local man's body found." She started reading. "The badly decomposed body of Charles Winters was finally recovered from the River Dale today. Mr. Winters, who has been missing for several months, can finally be laid to rest by his family." Bea looked at Buddy who was sitting by her feet. "Well that explains that then." She picked him up and cuddled him. "But it doesn't explain how I keep seeing a dead man."

A knock on the door made her jump and she was over the moon to find Eddie standing there.

"Can I come in?" The sight of him made her heart melt.

"Of course." She put Buddy down who ran immediately to Eddie for a fuss. "Tea?" He nodded and sat down at the table as she got up.

"Why are you looking at stuff about Joe's brother?" He flicked through the article on the screen. "Such a tragedy. Ruby's never been the same since."

"Look at this though." Bea sat next to him, careful not to touch him, she didn't think she could handle accidently brushing against him and him flinching at her touch. "Recognise him?" She'd pulled up the original article.

"It's Charlie!" Eddie exclaimed. "I'd forgotten they were called Winters." He looked at Bea. "That's your name."

"So please tell me why a dead man with my surname has been following me around?" She finally spoke her fears out loud. It was so good to be able to talk to Eddie again.

"More importantly." Eddie took a sip of tea. "Why doesn't Joe know his brother is alive?"

"Maybe he's not alive." Eddie looked at her over the rim of his glasses. "He could be a ghost."

"I don't think ghosts drive boats and walk around." He laughed out loud, then stopped at the serious look on her face. "You don't honestly believe he's a ghost, do you?"

"Yes. No. I don't know." She threw her hands up. "It would explain how he got on a locked boat in the middle of the night and how he seems to just disappear every time I see him."

"When was he on your boat?" Eddie switched into protective mode.

"I told you about it." She loved how easy the conversation was flowing, it was just how it used to be. "When I heard that man's voice on the boat, he called Buddy 'Buddy Boy', and Charles does that all the time."

"Well, I don't really know what to say." Bea looked at him.

"And that's not everything I've discovered lately either." She fetched the box full of cards from her room and showed them to Eddie. They spent the next few hours chatting and discussing everything except the one thing that both of them wanted to talk about.

"I'd best get home." Eddie looked at his watch and realised it was almost midnight.

"Do you have to?" He looked at her in a strange way. "I mean…it's just…" What did she say? She couldn't help it but she started crying.

"Bea, don't." She wanted nothing more than for him to wrap his arms round her and tell her everything would be okay, that she wasn't seeing ghosts, that her mum's death wasn't her fault and that above all else he could forgive her.

"I'm just being silly." She wiped her eyes with her sleeve but the tears wouldn't stop. It was like she'd finally been able to unburden herself. "Will you stay the night?" The look he gave her was one of turmoil. "Not like that, just as a friend. I really don't want to be on my own that's all."

"This is tearing me up inside." He placed his head in his hands.

"I'm so sorry, Eddie." She tentatively put her hand on his back and when he didn't flinch she placed her arm round him. "I didn't mean for any of this to happen I really didn't." She inched herself closer to him. "It's all gone so wrong since that morning back at your house. I moved here to get away from my crap life and I've just ended up with different crap."

"I saw you get in his car." He looked up at her, his eyes glistening with unshed tears.

"Whose car? What car?" Bea was confused.

"It's all my fault." He put his head back in his hands. "I should have driven you, I should have insisted, instead I let him be your knight in shining armour."

"I don't understand." He lifted his head and now she could see the tears rolling down his cheeks.

"When I left you on the boat I felt so bad for leaving you that I came back but then I saw him and I thought you were lying to me. I thought you wanted to spend the day with him. Then Charlotte said you were just using me as a dog sitter." It all came spilling out, how Charlotte had played on his fears and put ideas in his head. How his issues with Scott had clouded his judgement and how he hadn't even known her mum had died till Richard had told him. "Can you forgive me?"

"Me forgive you?" She couldn't believe what she was hearing. "There's nothing to forgive." She placed the tip of her fingers under his chin and drew his mouth to hers. The kiss was soft and hesitant at first before all the feelings of anger and guilt melted away.


"Morning." Bea walked into the bedroom carrying tea and toast on a tray. She was still in shock that last night had actually happened.

"Morning yourself." Eddie stretched lazily in the bed and hitched himself up on the pillows. "Feeling better?" He smiled knowingly at her.

"Much better." She put the tray down on the chest of drawers and crawled into bed beside him.

"Any idea where my glasses are?" He felt around on the bed.

"Did they fall down the side?" She leant over and stuffed her hand between the side of the bed and the wall of the boat. "What's this?" She pulled out what appeared to be a small piece of paper and threw it on the bed before shoving her hand back down. "Here they are." She pulled out Eddie's glasses which were miraculously still intact.

"Er...Bea?" Eddie was looking at the paper in his hand. "Remember the photo that was missing from your album?" Bea nodded looking at him peculiarly. "Is this it?" He turned the piece of paper round to show a man and woman standing outside a church clearly having just been married.

"That's the church here isn't it?" Eddie nodded. "And that's my mum." Bea recognised the blue suit. "And is that...?" Bea couldn't bring herself to say the name.

"The man in the picture that your mum has just married is Charles Winters and if I'm not mistaken Charles Winters is your newly discovered ghost, Charlie." Bea took the photo off him.

"How didn't we recognise Charlie before?" She stared at the photo.

"Because all the photos we saw of Charles were either when he was much younger or he was in the distance." Eddie looked at her in disbelief. "More to the point...do you know what this means?" Bea shook her head. "This means that Charlie, Charles Winters, is your dad."

"Don't be silly." Bea looked at the photo again then suddenly realised what Eddie was saying was true. "He's my dad!" She continued to stare at the photo. "And he was married to my mum."

"That also means that Uncle Joe is actually your uncle." Bea was still staring at the photo. "It might also explain how Ruby Turner, your auntie, knew your name."

"What do I do?" Reality was sinking in. "Should I call Charlie? Do you think he knows who I am?"

"Of course he knows who you are." Eddie reassured her. "I would say that Charlie has been orchestrating quite a lot of things in your life recently." Bea looked at him confused. "You said you saw him back in Birmingham and at the car show. How he turns up and disappears. How crazy Buddy goes around him."

"Now you mention it..." Bea remembered. "I saw the advert in the paper after I'd bumped into him in Birmingham."

"It all makes sense." Eddie pulled her towards him for a hug. "And I would say he is definitely not a ghost."

"But why wouldn't he have told Joe or Ruby?" Bea couldn't work out why if Charlie had been alive all this time he hadn't told his brother and sister. "And who's buried in his grave then if it's not Charlie?"

"Well that's where the mystery continues again." Eddie reached for the tea and toast. "I'm famished." He munched through two slices before speaking again. "It certainly isn't our place to tell them."

"I know." Bea picked at a piece of toast, her appetite gone. "And how on earth do I start the conversation with Charlie?"

"Just say it." Eddie grabbed a third piece of toast. "It's not going to be a shock to him is it? He clearly knows who you are. He's probably surprised it took you this long to work it out."

"How didn't I see it?" Bea put the uneaten toast down. "I should have at least guessed when Mum was dead set against me moving here and then in the hospital when I started talking about the *Sophie* and Bloomsdale. That's what brought on her heart attack." She couldn't hold back the tears.

"Hey." Eddie hugged her tightly. "You know it wasn't your fault."

"I know, it's just..." Bea sniffed. "Why didn't she ever tell me about my dad? All those wasted years."

"Are you eating that?" Eddie pointed to the picked-at slice of toast on her lap. She shook her head and he grabbed it. "There's one person who might be able to help you with it and all you have to do is pick up the phone and call him."

"Easier said than done." She watched as he devoured the last of the toast. "Easier said than done."

# CHAPTER 32

"**D**id you miss a party or did you miss a party?" Lisa greeted Bea on Monday morning as she walked into the office. "It all kicked off between Mr. and Mrs. Summers."

"It was the mother of all arguments." Giles had seen her arrive and hurried over, quickly followed by Steph.

"Everything had been going so well," Steph started to explain. "Your book was announced to everyone and then there was press all over Mr. Summers and Tanya."

"It was after everyone had gone home, just a few stragglers left and the servants cleaning up." Bea had been walking to her desk as they talked and now she sat down heavily in her chair as the other three perched on the edge of her desk. "Mrs. Summers had been absent most of the evening, as had Eddie now I think about it."

"You're right, Lisa." Giles agreed. "I saw him and that Charlotte at the beginning but I think they went upstairs."

"They were probably getting down with the Fireys." Lisa laughed. "Get it…the song from Labyrinth…and Eddie and Charlotte were probably getting down…" She stopped laughing when she realised no one else was joining her.

"We get it, Lisa." Steph chastised. "We just don't think it's appropriate in front of Bea."

"Actually its okay." Bea couldn't help smiling.

"What's happened?" Giles jumped off the desk and stood in front of her.

"Eddie and I are back together." There were screams of delight which caused everyone else in the office to look over at them. "It's early days so I would appreciate some discretion." She knew this wasn't going to happen but said it all the same.

"You can count on us." Giles pretended to zip his lips. "I'm so chuffed for you Bea, I really am." The door slamming open made them all turn and they hurried off to their desks in silence as Scott came scowling through followed by a very calm Mrs. Summers. Scott stomped straight up the stairs to his office whilst Mrs. Summers walked serenely past wishing everyone a good morning as she did.

"Good morning, Bea." Mrs. Summers said as she passed by her desk. "I'm so glad you're feeling better."

"Er...good morning Mrs. Summers," Bea stammered. "...Thank...you."

"Do call me Eleanor." Mrs. Summers smiled at her then continued on her journey upstairs.

"What the fuck!" Giles mouthed at her and she shrugged her shoulders in disbelief. What on earth had happened at the party and over the weekend to effect such a change in Scott and Eleanor? Bea couldn't wait to find out.

"Morning all." Eddie breezed into the office, a huge smile on his face and a confident stride to his walk. He walked straight up the stairs to the office.

"What's going on?" Steph looked at Bea as if she was in on everything.

"Why are you all looking at me?" She shrugged her shoulders. "I haven't a clue."

The entire office looked towards the stairs as if expecting some earth-shattering event to occur and when nothing happened everyone went about their jobs as normal, looking at the stairs every time there was a noise. Eddie came up and down, fetching various things from numerous cabinets. He had a strange smile on his face that Bea had never seen before and it made him seem older somehow, more self-assured.

It was almost lunch time before a panicked voice was heard.

"You can't." It was Scott. "I'll be ruined." No one answered him but Mrs. Summers and Eddie soon appeared at the foot of the stairs and stood together like a united front in the middle of the office.

"Can I have your attention please?" She didn't need to ask twice. "Now I understand it's been a bit different round here since I returned but things are going to get a bit different still." There were a few murmurs. "Nothing to worry about but while I was away I've had a chance to think on a few things and I don't like what this place has become." She took a breath. "I started out in this business a young girl with a passion but I allowed someone else to take control, all for the sake of profit." Bea knew she was talking about Scott. "Well, no more." She stamped her foot slightly as if to emphasise her point. "I want the contract and original manuscript of every book that has been released using a ghost writer." There was a gasp from the entire office, except for Bea who was a little confused.

"Every book?" Giles asked. "Even, you know, his ones?"

"Every book Giles, even those ones," Eleanor confirmed and even Eddie looked a little shocked at this. "I want us to be a publisher that works with the author to make their visions real not one that steals books and hoodwinks writers into giving up their stories so we can make a bigger profit."

Bea didn't have a clue what was going on and by the looks on people's faces around the office it was clear that only a handful of others actually did.

"Now I know it's going to take a while and I'm going to need help from all of you." Eleanor continued. "I've no idea how many there are so I don't know how long it's going to take but if we all work together we can do this."

"We need all the contact information for the ghost writers and the names of the people that were given the credit on the individual books." It was Eddie's turn to speak. "Everyone will be written to, explaining the situation. If their book was good enough before it was altered then they will be offered a new contract, if not then when the contract ends it will not be renewed."

"All current work will be put on hold for now and no matter what department you work in you'll be working on this for the foreseeable future." And with that Mrs. Summers headed back up the stairs and Bea was sure she heard Scott sobbing.

"What's going on?" Bea grabbed Eddie before he had chance to disappear. The whole office was in uproar.

"I can't tell you much at the minute but I'll fill you in later." He gave her a quick peck on the cheek. "Eleanor has been amazing. She's so different to the meek and mild woman that she used to be." Bea felt a little stab of jealousy at the look of admiration in his eyes. "Have you phoned Charlie yet?" She shook her head. "Do you want me to do it?" She shook her head again. "Putting it off won't make it any easier you know." He squeezed her hand and after another peck on the cheek headed back up the stairs.

"Why is everyone looking at me?" Giles had the eyes of the office on him. "I don't know anything."

"You've never been a good liar," Steph said walking over to him.

"Come on Giles." Lisa was followed by everyone else including Bea who had converged in front of Giles' desk. "You've been here years longer than anyone else and it's obvious you know the full story."

"Well I suppose it's going to come out sooner or later." He paused for effect, his eyes sparkling with enjoyment at being the centre of attention. "Let's just say that what happened with Bea's book isn't a first."

"We know that," Steph said.

"I didn't," Bea admitted and a few others agreed with her.

"What?" Giles was stunned. "You didn't know that now and again well mostly now, we use ghost writers?" There were a few people who shook their heads. "How could you not know? Especially you Bea, you do the accounts."

"But I don't know the names of all the authors so how would I connect the payments?" Bea was annoyed at herself for not realising but in all honesty how could she have known?

"You're still not telling us everything." The attention turned back to Giles again.

"Of course I am." But no one was convinced and he soon caved at the looks of disbelief. "Oh, for goodness' sake. Mr. Summers doesn't write his own books." Gasps echoed around the office.

"I don't believe it." Lisa said what everyone else was thinking. "Of course he writes his own books." Giles shook his head. "But…he's so famous."

"Then who writes them?" But Giles refused to be drawn any further and started tapping at his computer instantly dismissing them all.


Bea had been asked to work till the end of the day and by half past four there was already a huge pile of folders containing numerous contracts on the recently cleared desks of the editorial department. New USB sticks had been hastily purchased from the town and filled with original manuscripts for Mrs. Summers and Eddie to start reading through. Mandy and Beth had also been given the task of reading through these and deciding which were good enough to publish in their own right.

She was itching to speak to Eddie but he seemed to be keeping his distance, only popping in and out quickly or appearing with Mrs. Summers, their heads together in some secret conspiracy.

Bea had been given the task of matching the ghost writers with the credited authors and making sure all the contact information was correct. She had found this relatively easy until she'd started on Scott's. It felt wrong to be delving around in his files but what choice did she have?

She searched and searched but there was nothing. In fact if she hadn't have known any different she would have thought Scott had written the books. There was absolutely nothing to indicate that he hadn't. The contract was in the name of Mr. Summers and signed by Mrs. Summers.

"How very odd." She read and re-read everything but she couldn't find any answers so decided there was nothing for it but to go and ask the man himself. Surely he knew who had written the books he'd put his name to.

Plucking up as much courage as she could, Bea grabbed the folders and headed up the stairs. There was definitely a tense atmosphere. Scott was sitting by the window looking lost whilst Eddie and Mrs. Summers were busy looking through files.

"Could I have a word?" Her voice was almost a whisper but in the overwhelming silence she was heard instantly and three faces looked up at her. "It's just...well I mean...I can't." Her hands were sweating and her mouth was suddenly dry, she'd never felt this intimidated in her life.

"What's up Bea?" It was Eddie who spoke. Seeing her distress he came straight over to her then saw the name on the file in her hand. "I was wondering how long it would take." Mrs. Summers had now joined them and took the file from Bea.

"Scott?" she called over to him but he didn't answer. "Where is the name of your ghost writer?" Still he didn't answer and Bea felt the awkwardness in the room escalate. "Scott, answer me!"

she demanded and Bea felt herself backing away towards the stairs, her head bowed, hoping no one would notice.

"It's me." Bea stopped walking and her head shot up at Eddie's admission. "I write Scott's books."

"What?" Mrs. Summers' voice was high and shrill and as much as Bea wanted to find out more she didn't want to be in the middle of world war three so she escaped down the stairs. Unfortunately this didn't have the desired effect as seconds later Scott came storming down the stairs, Mrs. Summers hot on his heels. "How could you?"

"He'd never have made it on his own." Scott turned before he reached the door. The whole office thrown into shocked silence. "He's got no spine, just bows and cowers and I couldn't bear to see such good stories going to waste so I published them in my name instead." Mrs. Summers looked at him in absolute disgust. "He gets paid for them."

"How could you do it?" Mrs. Summers was visibly shaking as she spoke. "You stole his life, his career, for your own personal gain." She was standing in front of him now and Bea noticed Eddie had descended the stairs as well. "You disgust me." She spat. "How could you do that to your own son?"

# CHAPTER 33

**B**ea looked straight over to Eddie who looked like his whole world had come crashing down around him. She watched as if in slow motion, Mrs. Summers turn to look at Eddie. She didn't know who looked more devastated, him or her? Even Scott looked as if his whole world had just caved in.

Without a word Eddie brushed past the pair of them and out of the door, his heavy footsteps could be heard thundering down the stairs.

"I'll go after him." Bea looked at Scott and then at Mrs. Summers who seemed to be frozen to the spot as was everyone else in the office, their mouths wide open like a school of fish in mid breath.

She knew she was right behind, but when she got outside he was already out of sight. She knew exactly where he was going though. The same place she always went when she needed a quiet place to think. A place where every single inhabitant listened but never answered back.

The welcoming lamps from the church soon faded from view as she walked through the pitch-black graveyard. She was glad her phone was in her pocket and not in her handbag back on her desk as she switched on the torch app. The sudden brightness blinded her momentarily but it wasn't long before she was standing next to Eddie at his parents', *no, grandparents'*, she corrected herself, grave.

"Eddie." He turned to look at her and even in the darkness she could see he'd been crying. "I don't know what to say."

"It explains a lot though doesn't it." He sniffed. "Why he was always so jealous when Mum and Dad spent time with me, or stuck up for me."

"So does this mean that Mrs. Summers…" She stumbled on the unfamiliar first name. "I mean Eleanor is actually your…?"

"My mum?" She nodded. "I'm pretty sure it does."

There was a noise behind them and they both turned to find Eleanor stumbling towards them, her heels sinking in the grass. Eddie turned to leave.

"Eddie, please," she begged and he stopped but didn't face her. "You weren't meant to find out like that."

"Really?" The sarcasm in his voice was clear. "So tell me dear mother, how was I supposed to find out?" The use of the word mother was meant as an insult not an endearment.

"I've wanted to tell you for so long but Scott…" Eddie scoffed at his name. "Scott thought that it would hurt you too much and he didn't want to mar the memory of your grandparents."

"My grandparents!" Bea had never seen Eddie so angry. "Those people there are my mum and dad." He pointed at the grave stone. "You may have given birth to me and HE may have provided some DNA but you are not and never will be my mum and dad."

Eleanor collapsed in a heap at these words.

"Eddie." Bea placed a hand on his shoulder and this seemed to calm him a little. "Maybe we should find somewhere warm to talk this through." Eleanor looked up at her as if she was an angel.

"There's nothing else to say." Eddie was dismissive in his voice and his stance.

"It wouldn't hurt to hear what she has to say, would it?" Bea didn't want him to regret not listening to her. "We could go to the coffee shop?" She looked at her watch—it was after six. "Oh, it will be closed by the time we get there."

"That's okay." Eleanor stood up and tried to compose herself. "I've got the key." Bea looked at her confused. "Didn't you know we owned the coffee shop as well?" Bea shook her head. "Eddie?" There was such a vulnerability in her voice that it must have touched something inside Eddie and he nodded his head, taking Bea's hand as they followed Eleanor through the graveyard and back into the centre of the village.

The walk back was conducted in an awkward and tense silence. When they reached the coffee shop they could see it was all locked up and in darkness but there was still a light shining from the office above. Eleanor unlocked the door and turned on the light, beckoning them inside before locking the door behind them. Bea was about to head towards Eddie's favourite table in the corner but he stood stock still by the door.

"Go on then." His arms were folded and he looked as if he'd aged ten years as did Eleanor.

"We were fourteen," she began. "Just kids messing about one night then four months later I realised I was pregnant." Bea could see she was finding it a relief to finally tell him the story. "We wanted to bring you up ourselves and be a little family. We talked about nothing else for weeks. The little railway cottage that Scott's parents rented out had recently become vacant again. Such a sad story." She side-tracked. "Poor man's wife up and left him in the middle of the night taking their little girl with her." Bea's head shot up but now wasn't the time to ask about something that resembled a dream she'd had.

"My cottage?" Eddie asked. "On the abandoned station."

"The very same." Eleanor nodded.

"I find that hard to believe of Scott." Eddie seemed to relax just a little.

"He wasn't how he is now." She tried to convince him. "He was so sweet and kind, always giving me things, writing me silly poems, but losing you and then me…well it changed him."

"So what happened?" Bea asked. "Why didn't you move into the cottage and become a family?"

"Our parents went crazy, mine especially," she explained. "My father wanted something better for his little girl than a teenage pregnancy and a dead-end marriage, he said. Luckily by the time they found out it was too late for an abortion. Not that I would ever have had one." She stated at the look of horror on Bea and Eddie's faces. "But unless I gave you up for adoption, they said they'd disown me." Tears started rolling down her cheeks. "What else could I do?" She held out her hands to Eddie. "We were fourteen, still at school, no qualifications, how could we feed you? Clothe you? Give you a decent life? So we had no choice."

"So Scott's mum and dad adopted him?" Eleanor shook her head.

"They never adopted him," she corrected. "They were his grandparents and became his legal guardians." She wiped her eyes. "I thought it would be easier that way. I'd still be able to see you and hold you but they wouldn't let me. They said it would confuse you. So I had to watch you grow up from afar and it became so painful that eventually I started to leave whenever you came into the room. I couldn't bear to be near you knowing I couldn't kiss you or hug you."

Bea felt herself welling up at the pain she must have felt all these years.

"On the day you were born my father handed us the deeds to this place." She looked around. "'Make your dreams come true'," she whispered. "That's what he said to me. He knew I'd always wanted to own a publishing house. Books were and still are my life." She started walking round. "Upstairs was empty but this used to be a little café so we turned it into a coffee shop and then eventually started on the upstairs. Our parents gave us whatever money we asked for, I think they were just happy to see us getting on with our lives but we never forgot you, not a day went by when we didn't talk about you and how quickly you were growing up." She looked straight at Eddie.

"We should never have got married," she said. "We'd grown too far apart, each blaming the other for losing you. Scott grew increasingly jealous of you as well and we wanted different things for the press. Scott was just out to make as much money as he could but I wanted to help authors realise their dreams." She spoke with such passion that Bea believed every word. "We thought having a baby would fix things, give us something to bond over but when I lost it, it was like we were being punished for giving you away and I just couldn't cope with it anymore. We had a blazing row and I left. It's taken me all this time to get the strength that I needed to face up to everything and get my son back."

A noise from above made everyone pause and footsteps could be heard echoing down the stairs, the door locking and then the sight of Scott standing outside made Bea hold her breath.

"Can I let him in?" Eleanor asked Eddie who shrugged nonchalantly. Scott walked in, he seemed defeated somehow and kind of lost.

"I'm sorry, Eddie." Maybe it was the use of Eddie rather than Edmund or maybe it was the apology or the sincerity in his voice or maybe it was all three but Bea hadn't expected Eddie to react in quite the way he did. He flew at Scott, knocking him to the ground. Within seconds Eddie stood over him and grabbed him by the shirt, his fist hovering above Scott's face. Scott didn't put up any resistance, he just lay there looking Eddie in the eye, ready to take whatever Eddie threw at him.

Bea and Eleanor didn't try to stop him and after what felt like a lifetime he eventually relaxed his fist and let go of Scott's shirt. Scott stood up, brushing himself down as he did.

"You don't know the meaning of the word sorry." Eddie turned to look out of the window. "All my life you've been against me, jealous of me even. What brother does that? Let alone a father. I idolised you, respected you, looked up to you. My big brother who was so much cooler than me, I wanted to be you more than anything."

"That was the problem." Eddie turned and looked at him confused. "I couldn't stand it. I didn't want to be your brother, I wanted to be your father." Bea couldn't believe this turn of events, was Scott being honest? He certainly appeared to be telling the truth. "I needed you to hate me, I wanted you to hate me. It was the only way I could cope with it. I knew if you hated me you'd want very little to do with me and I could live with that. But then you showed me those amazing stories you were writing. I was so proud of you but you were so young so I thought it was best if I published them in my name. After all, who would believe a twelve year old had written them."

"You told me it was a fifty year old man living in Droitwich," Eleanor interrupted. "Why didn't you give him a pen name instead?"

"I thought about it," Scott explained. "But when you read them and said how amazing they were I knew they would be big and they needed a face to go with them and promote them so I decided I would do it."

"You were protecting me," Eddie said, not quite believing his own ears.

"That's all I've ever wanted to do." Scott sat down in one of the chairs. "I made sure you had somewhere decent to live when you didn't want to live in the manor. Always made sure you had money."

"It's a pittance to what you must be earning." Eddie had been about to sit down opposite him but the mention of money made him stand to attention again.

"A pittance?" Now it was Bea's turn to be confused. "You get paid thousands of pounds each month."

"I bloody well don't," Eddie laughed.

"You bloody well do, I've seen it with my own eyes." Bea watched as Scott pulled out some papers from his inside pocket and handed them to Eddie.

"What's this?" Bea peered over his shoulder to see what he was looking at and Eleanor looked entirely bemused by the whole thing.

"It's a trust fund," Scott said simply. "It's been in place from when the very first royalties came in and I've had all the royalties transferred into it ever since." Bea could see this was true, there were hundreds of thousands of pounds in there. "It matures on your 21st birthday."

"But…why?" Eddie had to sit down, the shock was too great for him.

"Because you're my son and I want you to have the best life you possible can." Scott placed a hand over his. "Imagine if I'd given you all that money when you were younger, you'd have squandered it but now you're older and you've had to work, you appreciate it more."

"So where does all your money come from?" Eddie asked the question that Bea was dying to ask.

"Personal appearances mostly and of course I do own half of a very successful publishing house." He tried to lighten the mood and it worked a little. "I know it's all raw and emotional right now but one day I hope you'll understand and we can at least be friends again." He smiled at Eddie who smiled ever so slightly back. "Come on, Eleanor, let's leave him to it for now." Scott stood up and took Eleanor's hand who reluctantly followed him, leaving the key for them to lock up on the table as she went past.

"Well," was all Bea could say as she sat down next to Eddie who was still staring at the statement in front of him.

"What just happened?" He looked at her, his face filled with sadness and confusion. "I don't understand any of it."

"Shall we go home?" She put her arm round him. "We can talk some more, or not if you don't want to. Whatever you want to do is fine with me."

"Can we go back to yours?" He looked at her, tears threatening to spill out of his eyes.

"Of course we can." She kissed him softly. "Shall we get some fish and chips?" He nodded and after turning off the lights they locked the door and walked back to the *Sophie*.

# CHAPTER 34

"I can't believe you still haven't told him that you know." Em said shaking her head. "If it was me I'd have told him that day." Bea was back in Birmingham along with Em and Al. They'd spent the weekend sorting through all the things Bea had put into storage and were now having dinner in TGI's before they all headed back to their respective homes. It was the only weekend they could all get together this side of Christmas and none of them wanted to leave the task until the New Year.

"And the poor man is working on your boat?" Bea nodded at Al.

"Has been for three weeks and he's hoping to have it finished by the time I get back." Bea couldn't believe she'd left it so long. "I've been at Eddie's most of the time helping him come to terms with his news so it's kind of been put on a back burner. I haven't even seen Charlie since he started. Eddie rang him and went through all the plans while I was at work. I think it's given him something else to think about."

"How is Eddie?" Em asked. "That must have been such a shock for him."

"He's getting there." If you could describe crying half of the night instead of all of the night as getting there, she thought to herself. "It's going to take a while but each day he seems a little brighter about it."

"Imagine finding out your brother is actually your dad!" Em looked at Al.

"Bloody hell Em, that's impossible." He laughed. "And we know I'm not Bea's because this Charlie is."

"Do you think they're still married?" Em queried. "I mean, Mum was still called Winters and you did say his headstone said Husband on it."

"I hadn't even thought of that." Bea could imagine anything of their mum though.

"I remember an Uncle Charles now I think about it." Em took a sip of her coke. "I think I was at university when Mum and you went to live with him."

"And you're just sharing this information now!" Bea looked at her sister.

"We had that many uncles over the years I didn't think it was relevant." Em started to rack her brain. "Oh God, I think it was in Yorkshire as well."

"Think Em, think." Bea pleaded. "Hang on, I've brought the wedding photo to show you." Bea pulled out the picture of their mum and Charles Winters outside Bloomsdale church.

"That's him, Uncle Charles." Em took the photo then showed it to Al. "He was lovely. I stayed with you one weekend and we baked chocolate chip shortbread. I always remember because the cottage was on a disused railway station."

"Emerald Gertrude Miniver!" Al scolded. "How could you forget something like that? All these years you knew who Bea's dad was." He shook his head at her in mock disgust.

"That just confirms it all then doesn't it?" Bea asked more to herself than to her brother and sister. "I think I've been putting it off just in case he's not but there's too much evidence now to be in any doubt." She smiled, a huge smile that spread from ear to ear. "So that dream I had wasn't a dream, it was a memory, and the reason Ruby Turner knows about me is because she's my auntie."

"She's still a little creepy if you ask me," Al commented. "I mean, surely she hasn't seen you since you were little so how would she know you now?"

"Perhaps she has the gift," Bea said in all seriousness.

"You know I don't believe in all that." All three of them were suddenly quiet as the waitress brought their dinners and it was a few minutes before the conversation resumed as sauces were swapped and dolloped on plates and the first mouthfuls taken.

"Why don't you believe in it, Al?" Em asked, wagging a chip at him. "There's so many unexplained things out there."

"Just because something is unexplained it doesn't mean it's paranormal." He tucked into his steak.

"I've always thought you had the gift, you know," Em said to Bea as she started piling a tortilla with chicken and sliced peppers. "You used to say some crazy shit as a kid and you are obsessed with graveyards."

"I am not obsessed with graveyards," Bea protested. "And what crazy shit did I use to say?"

"You once mentioned Uncle Geoffrey that lived in the sky." Al's face suddenly lit up.

"I remember that," he said, pausing for a moment. "And when she was a baby she used to look right past me and laugh at something behind."

"You're pulling my leg." Bea was sure they were winding her up.

"Scout's honour." Al made the Scout salute with his fingers.

"Bea?" A female voice interrupted them and Bea turned to see a familiar face.

"Jen!" She stood up and hugged her friend. "How's everything? How's your dad and everyone else at the accountants? How's Maureen?" She added the last name as an after-thought.

"You haven't heard, have you?" Jen's face was full of gossip. "She's been sacked."

"She's what!" Bea sat down.

"Turns out she's been on the fiddle for years." Jen nicked a chip from Bea's plate. "Her and Mrs. White, they've been defrauding the company. Dad was fuming."

"I bet he was." Bea couldn't believe it. "All that time parading around thinking she was better than everyone and all the time she was..." Bea looked at Jen. "What exactly was she doing?"

"They created bogus employees in some of the corporate businesses that we do the payroll for." Jen looked behind her. "I'll have to go in a minute, Steve's waiting." Bea looked over to see a handsome blond man staring over at them. "They took thousands and thousands between them and it was only found out because they got greedy and started on a new business. Luckily the owner checked his payroll figures otherwise we might never have known."

"So is this why the police were involved?" Jen nodded.

"It's taken this long to work everything out and get all the evidence together." Jen waved over at Steve who was tapping his watch. "There's talk of a trail and everything but I don't think Dad wants that. He doesn't want the company name being dragged through the mud." She stole another chip. "Well I'd best be off, so lovely to see you." And she was gone.

"You believe in Karma though don't you Al?" Bea asked. "Because that's what's just happened." She smiled again and tucked into her chicken smugly satisfied that Maureen had finally got what was coming to her.


The drive home was uneventful and it gave Bea the time she needed to lay some of the ghosts of her past to rest. The weekend with Al and Em sorting through their mum's things had helped

Bea come to terms with the anger and guilt she'd be feeling over her death. It wasn't her fault, she knew that now but she was still struggling with the fact that her mum had kept her dad a secret all these years. But like Al had told her, their mum always had a good reason for doing things, it wasn't always the right reason but to her it was always a good one.

She was a few miles from home when she heard her phone buzz in her bag. As per normal she ignored it. But it buzzed again and again and again. Reaching into her bag with one hand she kept her eyes firmly on the road. There were no street lamps on the country lanes and even though her head lights were on full beam it was doing little to cut through the fog that had come rolling in over the moors a few miles back.

She rifled around one handed, veering slightly off the road but correcting herself instantly. The phone showed texts and missed calls from Eddie and she wondered what on earth could be wrong. She decided to ring him on the hands free, far safer than texting. She clicked the appropriate buttons on the phone and as it started ringing threw it onto the passenger seat.

It wasn't a very good aim and the phone slid off onto the floor.

"Bugger," Bea said to herself, slowing right down and feeling for her phone on the floor.

"Are you nearly home Bea?" Eddie's voice sounded a little strange.

"Yeah just a few more...SHIT!" Bea hadn't noticed the flock of sheep appear as if from nowhere and she swerved to avoid them.


"Bea, are you okay?" Eddie was panicking. "Bea? BEA!" There was no answer and when he looked at his phone the call had been disconnected.

# CHAPTER 35

"Moonbeam, Moonbeam." Bea could hear the voice speaking to her but couldn't bring herself to connect with it. "Time to wake up my little Moonbeam." She felt a gentle shake on her arm and with enormous effort forced her eyelids to open, shutting them immediately at the blinding light.

"Why is it so bright?" she croaked, her mouth dry and sore.

"Come on my little Moonbeam, it's time to get up." Bea racked her brain for the name of the voice that was so familiar to her. "My little Moonbeam sent from the stars." She felt a hand brush her forehead.

"Mum, how many times have I told you not to call me Moonbeam?" She tried opening her eyes slowly, letting them adjust to the light in their own time. The room started to come into focus and she could see her mum smiling at her from the side of the bed. There was nothing else in the room except the bed she was lying in and her mum. No wonder everything was so bright, the walls and ceiling were white, the sheets were white and even her mum was dressed in white.

"But you love it when I call you Moonbeam." Her mum was smiling.

"When I was about four I did." Bea shocked herself at this memory, she thought she'd always hated her name. "Why did you call me Moonbeam?"

"There was a beautiful full moon the night you were born." Her mum was still stroking her forehead. "Your dad was holding you and he took you over to the window. The moon was so bright it was like you were standing in a moonbeam. I said this to him and he said that's what we should call you, Moonbeam Winters."

"You've never told me that before." Bea wiped a tear from her eye. "Why didn't I know my dad? Why did you hide him from me? I found the letters and cards in your things when you..." She paused as she tried to remember something that suddenly seemed incredibly important but she couldn't quite pull it from her memory.

"I didn't mean to hurt you." Her mum took her hand in hers. "I thought I would lose you."

"Lose me?" Bea was confused. "How could you lose me?"

"I wanted to settle down, I really did." Bea could see she was telling the truth. "I just couldn't do it. We had a lovely little house and you were just about to start school but I felt stifled, trapped almost. I loved your father but I couldn't live like that. I needed to be free."

"But why did that mean I couldn't see him?" Bea's voice quivered a little. "Al always saw his dad."

"Al's dad was different." Her mum sat on the side of the bed. "He was happy being a part time dad but your dad wasn't. He wanted full custody of you which is why we had to keep moving. Every time he found us I was frightened he would take you away from me and I couldn't lose my baby girl." Her mum was crying now, full thick tears that splashed down onto the crisp white sheets.

"Don't cry, Mum." Bea tried to hug her but her body felt like it was weighed down with lead. "I understand now. I understand it all and it's okay, I've seen him."

"You've seen him?" Her mum was surprised. "He's here?" She looked around.

"He's here." She didn't really know how to explain. "I think he's been looking for me, leading me here to Bloomsdale."

"But he died." Her mum's face seemed to take on a frightened look. "They told me he died, I went to his funeral. I saw them bury him." Her mum was starting to panic. "If he's not dead then that means he can take you away."

"It's okay Mum, calm down." Bea wished she could move. "You're not going to lose me, I'm not going anywhere. I can love you both you know."

"You have to come with me." Her mum shot off the bed and started helping Bea to sit up.

"Mum, what are you doing?" Everything hurt, her entire body ached from head to toe.

"Bea?" A strange male voice was calling her name. "Bea can you hear me?"

"Moonbeam please, you have to come with me." Her mum was still trying to move her. "I can't lose you."

"Bea?" The voice called her again and she felt drawn to it.

"Goodbye my little Moonbeam." Her mum's voice was distant now, her face fading from view.


"Bea?" The voice was more insistent now. "I need you to open your eyes, Bea. Can you do that for me please?" It took all her effort but Bea forced them open slowly, her eyes accosted by harsh strip lighting above. "Good to have you back Bea, you gave us quite a scare back there."

"I can't move my neck." Bea's voice was a whisper as she tried to look round but her head and neck wouldn't move.

"It's okay, Bea." Another voice, female this time said soothingly. "You're in hospital. You've had an accident and we have to keep you strapped up till we've checked for any spinal injuries." The unseen lady must have seen a look of panic cross her face. "It's just a precaution, don't you worry." Bea felt a reassuring squeeze of her hand. "There's someone here to see you.

You're very lucky you were born in this hospital and we had your blood group on record." She felt another squeeze of her hand. "And we've found your family as well, so don't go worrying about them either."

Bea's mind was in turmoil. She couldn't think straight. Accident? Family? Did they mean her mum? But hadn't she just seen her? Wait! She'd finally remembered.

"My mum's dead." It was a struggle to talk, her mouth and throat were so dry and she started to cry.

"Don't get upset now, Bea." A tissue was pressed against her eyes. "It's your Uncle Joe we've found. He's in total shock, poor man." Bea's mind raced again. Uncle Joe? Oh dear lord they'd rung Joe and told him his niece had been in an accident. He didn't even know she was his niece, no wonder he was in shock.

"Eddie?" she asked.

"He's here too, don't you worry," the female voice continued and in the background Bea could hear lots of chatter and beeps. She felt herself drifting back off to sleep despite her name being called over and over again.


"Bea?" A lovingly familiar voice was calling her. "Bea?" Her eyelids were heavy but she managed to open them and found a very worried-looking Eddie staring at her. "I thought I'd lost you." He kissed her gently on the lips. "I'm so sorry, it's all my fault. If I hadn't rung you…"

"What happened?" She interrupted him feeling more relaxed and free from pain than she had earlier and although it was stiff she was able to move her neck. She could now see that she was in a hospital room, hooked up to a SATs machine that beeped now and again.

"They found you next to your car, you must have managed to pull yourself out somehow." Eddie took her hand. "Your phone was smashed to pieces and you didn't have any ID in your bag so they had to trace you from the registration plate. That's how the police found Joe."

"I don't remember any of it." Bea tried to think back.

"The doctor says that's normal with this kind of trauma." He brushed her cheek. "You're lucky you've not broken anything. Just concussion and lots of cuts and bruises."

"I saw my mum." This memory was so vivid. "She was right in front of me like you are now."

"You know she's…" Eddie paused.

"Yes, I know." Bea didn't say the word. "It was so real though."

"You were unconscious for quite a while Bea, and you've hit your head pretty hard." Eddie looked at her. "It's no wonder your brain has got a bit mixed up."

"Can I come in?" Bea looked towards the door. Joe was standing in the doorway looking years older than she remembered.

"I'll leave you two to talk." Eddie squeezed her hand and moved away to be replaced by Joe just seconds later.

"I should have known it was you the first time I saw you." She stretched out a hand to him. "You look so much like Charles." He burst into tears. "He never stopped looking for you."

"I know, Uncle Joe, I know." Bea heaved herself up against the top of the bed with great effort and pain. "I found all the letters and cards he sent me." Did she tell him that his brother was still alive? No, he'd had enough of a shock.

"All these months you've been right here under my nose and I didn't see it." He was still crying. "Buddy only came back because of you." Bea smiled at the thought of the little black dog. "And to think I could have lost you without even knowing you."

"It's okay Uncle Joe, its okay." She reached up towards him. "We've found each other now."

"If only Charles were still here." The tears started to subside. "He'd be so proud of the woman you've grown into." Bea started to yawn.

"I'm so sorry, Uncle Joe." Bea could feel herself drifting off to sleep. "I'm so tired." Another yawn.

"You get some more rest, sweetheart." He patted her hand. "I'll come and see you tomorrow." But Bea didn't answer him, she was already fast asleep.

# CHAPTER 36

The clatter of a trolley woke Bea. She could hear the staff trying to go about their duties as quietly as possible and when she looked at the window it was still dark outside and she realised it must still be the middle of the night.

"Hello my darling." Bea looked to the chair opposite.

"Oh hi, Dad." She felt so tired still and her head felt like it was stuffed with cotton wool instead of her normal fully functioning brain. She closed her eyes and settled back into the pillows before flinging them open again and staring at the figure bathed in moonlight. "Dad?"

"It sounds so lovely to hear you say that after all these years." He smiled, a smile that reached his grey eyes and made them crinkle in the corners. "I'm so glad I finally found you. I've been searching such a very long time."

"I'm so sorry about Mum." Bea couldn't think of anything else to say. Her dad was here, sitting right in front of her and all she could think of to say was to apologise for her mum.

"Your mother always was a very complicated woman but she did what she thought was best." He was still smiling. "It was a strange relationship, sometimes I wouldn't see her for years sometimes it was just months but we loved each other."

"Wait." It was taking Bea a while to process what he was saying. "You used to see Mum?"

"Right up until I died." He smiled a wry smile. "She stopped visiting me then of course, but after it was easier for me to find you."

"All those years." Bea knew he was referring to his death metaphorically. "She kept you from me." Bea's anger was starting to rise again.

"It was my fault." He took her hand as if to calm her. "I would push her and push her, threaten her sometimes and I should have known that was the wrong thing to do with Kathleen."

"Why does everyone make excuses for her?" Bea couldn't believe it. "Al and Em are forever trying to cover for her and now you. Of all people I expected you to be different." She couldn't help her voice rising in anger.

"Don't get yourself worked up about it." Her dad patted her hand. "You've just had a traumatic experience and you need to stay calm."

"Everything okay in here?" A middle-aged nurse poked her head round the door. "I heard shouting." Bea looked to her dad who put his fingers to his lips in a shushing motion.

"Just a bad dream." Luckily the chair her dad was sitting in was high backed and faced away from the nurse so she couldn't see it was occupied.

"Well that's not unusual in the circumstances. I'll be back in a few minutes to check your SATs." She closed the door.

"I'd better be going." He stood up and pressed a feather light kiss on her forehead. "Don't think about the past anymore. I've found you now and no one will ever take you away from me again."


"Do you know you lost control of the car exactly where your dad and Ruby had their accident all those years ago? And on exactly the same date?" It was afternoon visiting and Eddie had arrived at the stroke of two o clock with a huge teddy bear and a box of her favourite Thornton's chocolates.

"He came to see me last night." Bea had already demolished most of the top layer, leaving only the fruit creams that Eddie had happily eaten.

"I didn't see him." Eddie was a little confused. "I was here the whole two hours of visiting last night and you were asleep most of it." He smiled. "No one else came and I didn't want to wake you up because you looked so beautiful and peaceful. I just sat staring at you."

"With two black eyes and stitches on my forehead?" Bea had seen herself in the mirror that morning and she thought she looked horrendous. Purple bruises were starting to form on most parts of her body and she had stitches in her head where broken glass had been removed.

"Even with four black eyes and stitches all over." Eddie replied then laughed when he realised what he said. "Well, maybe not four black eyes."

"I don't think it was visiting time." Bea thought back. "I'm pretty sure it was late, maybe the middle of the night even."

"You must be getting mixed up Bea." Eddie looked at her with concern. "You can't get on the wards at night. They're all locked up."

"I definitely saw him, Eddie," Bea insisted. "We chatted for a little bit before the nurse came in to do my SATs."

"And how was it?" He knew better than to push her on the issue of timing.

"It was fine." That was about all she could say. "I'd been asleep and I just called him dad without even thinking about it so there was no awkwardness or anything."

"I told you it would be okay." He smiled. "All those weeks of putting it off."

"I know." She shook her head in annoyance at herself. "We had a lovely chat, mostly about Mum." She paused. "He told me they still used to see each other. Can you believe it? All these years right up until he died."

"But he didn't die?" Eddie quizzed.

"To everyone else he did." Bea stated. "He said it was easier to find me after he'd died."

"So is he telling his brother and sister now then?" He started on the second layer of chocolates.

"I have no idea." Bea gave Eddie a death stare as he reached for one of her favourite pralines. "The nurse came in and he had to go."

"He's got to tell them." Eddie was oblivious to the looks he was getting as he reached for a second nutty one but the playful slap from Bea soon told him and he changed to a strawberry cream.

"Well of course he has." Bea moved the chocolates out of Eddie's reach before he could devour the rest of them. "But can you imagine how much of a shock it will be to Uncle Joe and Ruby? God, I can't believe she's my auntie."

"Now, now." Eddie scolded. "That's not like you to be nasty about someone."

"I know." Bea couldn't believe she'd said the words herself. "She just scares me a little that's all. She's so different to Charlie and Joe."

"Who's different to Charlie and Joe?" Bea and Eddie both turned to see Joe standing in the doorway.

"Erm…" Bea was lost for words but Eddie thought it was about time this man knew about his brother being alive.

"We were just on about Ruby and how different she is to you and your brother." He was rewarded with a scathing look from Bea.

"She always was." He sighed and pulled up a chair next to Eddie. "She was born a few weeks early and it was touch and go whether she would survive but she did. She didn't develop at the same rate as a normal child." He shook his head. "I hate to use the word normal but what else can I say." He took a breath. "She's very trusting and loving and when she met Mick she fell head over heels for him. Of course we all said she shouldn't marry him but she wouldn't have it."

"Blood pressure time, Bea." A nurse came in dragging a trolley behind her. "If it continues like this you should be able to go home soon."

There was a pause in the conversation as the nurse busied herself with the customary checks, writing them down in the folder at the bottom of the bed before promising to be back in a few minutes with some painkillers.

"And then after the accident she was never the same. Kept waffling on about seeing Charles and our parents. Started having strange visions." Bea looked at Eddie, was now the time to tell him about Charlie? "Mick took advantage of course and wheeled her out for fortune telling. She can no more talk to the dead than I can." He shrugged heavily. "Anyway young uns, enough about the past, what we going to do about the *Sophie*?"

"What about the *Sophie*?" Eddie groaned loudly and put his head in his hands.

"You didn't know?" Joe looked so apologetic. "Of course you didn't know and there goes me with my big foot."

"It's okay, Uncle Joe." Eddie patted his arm. "You weren't to know."

"What about the *Sophie*?" Bea was getting annoyed now that no one was telling her. It was obvious something was up.

"Charlie and I were just talking about it before I came to see you and I'm so sorry, I just forgot you didn't know." His face was full of remorse.

"Will someone please tell…wait!" All thought of the *Sophie* left Bea's brain as she realised what Joe had just said. "You've seen your brother?"

# CHAPTER 37

"M y brother?" Joe scratched his head. "Who said anything about my brother?"

"You said you'd seen Charlie?" Bea looked to Eddie who shrugged his shoulders in confusion.

"Well of course I've seen Charlie." Bea wondered how he could say it with such normality. The man had been dead for five years and he was talking like it was an everyday occurrence to see your dead brother alive and well. "He's been working hard on that boat, bless him and he's gutted at what happened."

"You've seen Charlie?" Bea repeated again, not knowing why Joe wasn't in complete shock.

"Why the sudden interest in Charlie?" Joe couldn't work out what was going on. "I see him nearly every week, don't know why you're so shocked about it."

"Because he's supposed to be dead." Bea didn't mean for the words to come out as they did.

"First I've heard of it." He looked at the baffled expressions on Bea and Eddie's faces then suddenly it came to him as if someone had switched a light on in his head. "Oh Bea, Sweetheart." He smiled sadly. "You didn't think Charlie was my brother did you?"

"Erm..." Bea was lost as to what to say.

"We did, Uncle Joe," Eddie answered for her. "Of course we did, same name, same age. What else were we to think?"

"Charlie is my cousin. My dad's brother's son." Joe explained. "He was born a week after our Charles, blooming spit of each other as well and it's tradition in our family that the first born son of a son is called Charles James Winters." He took Bea's hand and squeezed it tight. "I'm sorry sweetheart but your dad is long gone I'm afraid." Bea felt the loss hit her hard in the pit of her stomach. She thought she'd found him and to lose him again so suddenly was like a stab in the heart.

"It's okay, Uncle Joe." Bea smiled weakly. "Silly of me really. I just hoped with him having the same name that maybe, just maybe, he was my dad and he'd somehow survived the accident all those years ago."

"So your brother was known as Charles and your cousin Charlie?" Joe nodded at Eddie.

"My dad was Junior, Charlie's dad was James." He chuckled. "We've had Jimmy, Jim, Jamie, CJ, Chuck and even a Chip."

"So are you going to tell me what's happened to the *Sophie*?" Bea didn't want to talk about Charles and Charlie anymore, in fact she wanted them both to leave so she could burst into tears but instead she changed the subject.

"She caught fire." Eddie said it so softly that Bea wasn't quite sure she'd heard correctly. "We're not quite sure how, firemen seem to think it was an electrical fault, but there's only her hull left I'm afraid."

"Oh God!" Bea's hand flew to her mouth. "Was anyone hurt?"

"No one was hurt sweetheart." Joe reassured her. "Charlie managed to get himself out and call the fire brigade and luckily most of your things are at Eddie's." He wiped a tear from his eye. "End of an era."

"We can rebuild her, Uncle Joe," Eddie said.

"She wouldn't be the same." Joe sniffed. "Best to let her go."

"But…" Eddie tried to explain.

"No son, I should have let her go all those years ago when Charles died but I clung onto her, picking at her bones like a vulture. I should have cared for her and looked after her as Charles would have done for the *Mavis*." He broke down into sobs.

"Don't get upset, Uncle Joe." Bea wished she could get out of the bed and comfort him but her ribs were so sore she could hardly bend. She indicated silently to Eddie with a nod of her head and he went over and hugged him.

"It's not your fault, Uncle Joe." Eddie patted him on the back as the sobs subsided. "You did what you could."

The bell to signal the end of visiting time rang shrilly through the ward.

"Let's go and have a coffee shall we Uncle Joe?" Eddie asked and Joe nodded, each giving Bea a kiss on her cheek before leaving.

"Have your visitors gone?" The nurse from earlier was back with a small plastic cup containing various tablets. She poured Bea some fresh water and handed it to her before tipping the tablets into her hand. "Are you okay?" Bea was deep in her thoughts, going through the motions automatically. "Bea? Can you answer me?" The nurse looked worried.

"I'm fine." The nurse breathed a sigh of relief. "Just had some bad news that's all."

"I thought I was going to have to call Doctor Field." She busied herself with the folder at the end of the bed again. "You're very pale are you sure you're okay?"

"Just need some more sleep I think?" Bea started the agonising process of shuffling herself gently down the bed.

"You do that." She patted the bed. "If you're asleep when tea comes I'll pop it in the fridge for later." But Bea didn't really hear her, she was already closing her eyes and drifting off, at least in sleep she could forget everything.

"I don't want to lie in bed anymore, Eddie." It was a few days later and Bea had been released from hospital with strict orders to rest. Eddie had driven her back to his house and was now insisting that she get into bed.

"But the doctor said..." He was helping her out of the car.

"I know what the doctor said." She brushed his hand away, determined to get herself out of the car on her own. "He said I have to rest but that doesn't mean I have to lie in bed all day." She straightened herself up and walked slowly but assuredly towards the door of Eddie's cottage. As she opened the door a ball of black fluff threw itself at her. "Hello, Buddy Boy." She scooped him up as best she could and was rewarded with hundreds of licks all over her face. "Well I've missed you too."

Eddie took him out of her hands as she winced a little at his wriggling.

"Tea?" She nodded and walked to the sofa, relieved to be away from the hospital at last. The staff had been amazing but there was nothing like coming home. Then she remembered this wasn't actually her home. Of course she knew Eddie wouldn't throw her out but did he want her to move in? After all they'd only known each other a few months. Was she ready to move in with him? She didn't want to move in with him because she had to, because there was no alternative. That was never going to be the best start to a relationship.

"Penny for them?" Eddie had sat down next to her without her even hearing him, two mugs of steaming hot tea and a plate of chocolate chip shortbread on the table. "I got your favourites." She couldn't help it, she just burst into tears. "Hey, what's brought this on?" He pulled her into his arms.

"It's just everything." She cried for what felt like hours, Eddie just holding her tightly.

"Tell me what's going on," he asked when finally the sobs had turned to the occasional hiccup. "Is it your dad? Your mum? The boat?"

And Bea told him everything. How she felt like she'd lost her dad all over again, the anger she felt at her mum and the insecurity of the foundling relationship.

"I know it's daft to think like that about my dad." It was her dad that was at the forefront of her mind.

"I don't think it's daft in the slightest." He picked up the now lukewarm tea and drank it without complaint. "You're bound to feel like you've lost him. For the first time in your life you thought you had a dad and now that's been taken away from you." Bea knew he must be going through some dad issues himself but that was for another time.

"I just don't understand it though." She picked up the tea and wrinkled her nose up at the temperature.

"I'll make a fresh one." He stood up and went back into the kitchen.

"All this time I've been talking to my dad's cousin thinking he was my dad." She continued the conversation and Eddie stood leaning on the wall as the kettle boiled again so he could hear her. "But I saw him in the hospital. I had a conversation with him about being my dad." Bea couldn't work out what was going on. The man she'd seen out and about, had conversations with was the same man that had sat in the hospital with her telling her he was her dad. "Why would Charlie visit me in the hospital and tell me he was my dad? That's just cruel."

"I think you dreamt it." Eddie had to be honest with her, all this talk about seeing her mum and dad. "Just like you dreamt your mum." Bea was trying to rationalise it all in her head. "Look." He walked over and knelt down in front of her. "You know how crazy dreams get sometimes, how mixed up things get because your brain is just sorting out where to put things." She nodded. "So imagine your brain doing that after it's had a trauma. Nothing is going to make any sense at all."

"So you're saying because I believed Charlie to be my dad my brain used that in my dream?" She knew he was making sense but the conversations with her mum and dad had felt so real.

"Exactly." Eddie stood up again. "And obviously you were bound to dream about your mum because she's your mum and who doesn't want their mum when they're hurting." He swallowed suddenly and Bea saw a look of sadness cross his face but it was gone just as quickly as it had appeared.

A sudden growl from Buddy followed by barking made both of them look towards the door. There was the sound of a car door slamming and feet crunching on the gravel path. Buddy flew at the door growling and barking like some rabid dog.

"I've never seen him do that before." Bea was suddenly worried about who was coming up the path. "Pass him to me if you can." Eddie picked Buddy up who was now baring his teeth, never taking his eyes off the door. "Come here boy, what's the matter?" She held him by his collar as Eddie went to answer the door.

"Oh, hello Charlie." Bea heard Eddie open the door but didn't look up, she was still focusing on Buddy.

"I came to see how you were both getting on." Bea cocked her head, she didn't recognise the voice but hadn't Eddie said it was Charlie? And why was Buddy going so crazy? He'd always been so soft around Charlie before.

"But…" Bea lifted her head to look at the newcomer. "You're not Charlie!"

# CHAPTER 38

"What do you mean it's not Charlie?" Eddie looked at her as if she'd gone mad and Charlie was doing the same. "I assure you this is Charlie Winters."

"I have never met this man in my life." Bea had to admit he was very similar looking to the man she had been talking to, similar height, same short greying hair but the man she had met had grey eyes whereas this Charlie had bright blue eyes. Buddy was still going crazy although he had calmed down a little now he was sitting on Bea's lap.

"Well I know that." Charlie said and Bea relaxed a little when she realised she wasn't going mad then remembered that now she had no idea who the Charles Winters was that she had been speaking to.

"I don't understand." Eddie rubbed his head, heading back into the kitchen to finish off the tea.

"It's quite simple really." Bea started to explain. "Although this is Charlie Winters, it's not the Charles Winters that I've been chatting to these past months." Buddy growled again as Charlie moved to sit down in the living room.

"I'm not a dog person I'm afraid." He eyed Buddy warily. "I was bitten as a kid and I've been scared of 'em ever since, even the little ones." He accepted the cup of tea that Eddie handed him. "Me and Buddy have never seen eye to eye, have we mate?" Buddy barked his answer.

"So are we saying someone else round here is called Charles Winters?" Eddie sat down next to Bea.

"I don't think there is anymore, not in this family anyway." He took a great gulp of his tea. "I've got two girls who then had girls and Charles only had young Bea here so I'm afraid the Charles James tradition may have ended."

"I think we need to call the police." Eddie was already reaching for his phone.

"What on earth for?" Bea couldn't understand why the police needed to be involved.

"It's like you said all along." He clicked the phone on. "You've obviously got a stalker. This man keeps turning up, seems to know intimate things about you. I only thought it was okay because you said it was your dad."

"Sorry, I'm a bit lost." Charlie butted in. "Who did you think was Charles?" Bea and Eddie explained the story between them. "Well I have to say it sounds a bit suspicious if you ask me."

"My thoughts exactly." Eddie started searching through his phone for the local police station's number.

"Oi! Don't you dare." Bea snatched the phone from his hand and cancelled the call before it had connected. "I don't think he means me any harm."

"Bea please." Eddie held out his hand for the phone. "He's been in Birmingham, he turns up at the motor show, the graveyard and now he's been to visit you in the middle of the night in a locked hospital. What part of that doesn't sound like a stalker to you?"

"When you put it like that." Bea had to admit what Eddie was saying was true. "But how do you explain the things he knew about Mum? And that he is the spitting image of Charlie?"

"Lucky guess? Plastic surgery?" Eddie shrugged his shoulders. "I don't know."

"It was too true to be a guess." Bea shook her head. "No one would guess something like that, she wasn't your average mother or wife."

"Is that Kathleen you're on about?" Charlie had been content to let them talk, "She was a little minx that one. Many a night my wife and I spent with Charles and Kathleen. Such a wicked sense of humour she had. I was sorry to hear she'd passed away."

"You knew my mother?" Bea was intrigued by this piece of information.

"I did indeed have the great pleasure of knowing your mother." He smiled. "She was an amazing woman, her and Charles were so well suited but she just couldn't handle the pressure of family life." He smiled again only this time it was with sadness. "Such a shame. Charles was only ever happy when he was with her and those few months you all lived together here was the happiest I've ever seen him."

"Most people talk about my mother in a negative way," Bea stated. "Myself included. But I'm starting to see a different side to her now."

"Oh don't get me wrong," Charlie agreed. "She was feisty and unpredictable but deep down she had a heart of gold. Only ever wanted what was best for her kids. I don't think I ever met your brother and sister but she talked about them all the time. I don't think motherhood came naturally to her, she was a free spirit and found it hard to settle down and that's what she wanted for her children. She wanted them to be free and independent, able to make their own decisions and never have to rely on anyone for anything."

"I've never seen her from that point of view." Bea wiped a tear away from her eye that had appeared suddenly. "She certainly did that with all of us."

There was quiet for a few moments as Bea contemplated Charlie's words and thought about the new perspective she had on her mother. Eddie coughing interrupted the silence.

"We're still not getting anywhere with the identity of the other Charles Winters and what to do about it?" Bea could tell Eddie was worried.

"Why don't I ring him?" She remembered the business card he'd given her. "I should have the card he gave me somewhere in my bag." She rummaged around emerging triumphant.

"I'll do it." Eddie took it from her and Bea reluctantly gave him his phone back. "It's ringing." He said after dialling the number, instantly there was a bleeping noise from Charlie's pocket. "Well that answers that then." Eddie clicked off the phone. "He's obviously using Charlie's business card as well. Bea, I've really got to insist we call the police."

"Hang on a minute." Charlie's face was white as a sheet. "Ring the number again." Eddie did exactly as he was asked. Charlie pulled out a very old iPhone from his inside pocket, his hands trembling. "This is Charles' phone. The police found it close to the accident and Joe let me have it as it had all our business contacts on but now I just keep it with me for sentimental reasons. Always keep it charged as well."

"So the number on here..." Eddie handed him the card.

"Is Charles' number." Charlie took the card. "And that is one of his business cards."

"Now I'm totally confused." Eddie said what they were all thinking.

"Wait a minute." Charlie started flicking through the phone. "Have you seen any photos of your dad?"

"Well of course I have." Bea was a little put out by his comment.

"Recent ones?" She looked at him as if he was speaking a different language. "Obviously not recent as in just been taken but recent ones of just before he died."

"No." Bea shook her head. "We've only ever seen photos of him from a distance or when he was much younger. The one of him and my mother getting married is probably the most recent one I've seen and that was over 25 years ago."

"Here you go." Charlie handed her the phone. Bea didn't want to look at it to start with. She wasn't sure what she was more scared of, the photo not being the man she'd been talking to or definitive proof that once and for all she had in fact all this time been meeting with her dad who as everyone kept telling her was dead.

"Well?" Eddie was impatient. "Is it him?" Bea finally looked at the photo.

"Oh God!" Her hand flew up to her mouth. There smiling back at her with shining grey eyes was the face of her father. Buddy was on his lap and they were sitting on the bench by the church.

"Bea?" Eddie almost shouted but she couldn't really hear him.

"That's my dad." He looked so happy she thought to herself.

"For crying out loud Bea, we know it's your dad." Eddie's voice finally registered in her brain. "But is it the same man?" She scrutinised the photo, matching it in her brain to every little detail she could remember about the other Charles Winters. But she needn't have bothered. She knew the answer as soon as she had seen his face.

"Yes," she whispered. "It's the same man. It's my dad. He's alive."

# CHAPTER 39

"I don't know what's going on Hun, but your dad isn't alive." Charlie took the phone back. "I identified him myself with Joe."

"But that's not possible." Bea burst into tears. "I've seen him, talked to him." Eddie went to hug her but she pushed him away, not to be nasty, just that she needed her own space. "Even Buddy has seen him, you've seen him, Eddie. Remember, he went past on the boat. You waved to him and shouted hello."

"That was Charlie," Eddie stated. "This Charlie, the one that's standing here right now."

"But it can't have been." Bea looked at Buddy. "Buddy doesn't like Charlie, see how he reacted when he came. He didn't do that then."

"Perhaps you have the gift?" Charlie spoke with such sincerity but was met with a laugh from Eddie. "I'm being honest. Ruby has it, our Grandmother Rose had it and one of my granddaughters has it. Charles always believed in it but Joe won't have any of it and Ruby does say strange things sometimes. And my granddaughter Jess, well she's only five but she talks to people we can't see."

"So you're saying I see dead people?" Bea felt like she was quoting the film The Sixth Sense.

"This conversation just went to crazy town." Eddie walked off into the kitchen.

"Maybe not all dead people, maybe just ones close to you." Charlie explained. "Ruby's gift is very hit and miss."

"She knew who I was." Bea's mind flew back to the first encounter with her aunt. "She knew my full name, no one knows my full name."

"Perhaps you're like your Aunt Ruby then." Charlie concluded. "Mick puts her on show but most of the time she just spouts the same old same old but with you, well, you're family."

"Can you two hear yourselves?" Eddie came back in.

"What other explanation is there?" Bea asked. "If you have one, please tell us."

"I don't know." Eddie was lost for words. "He has a twin brother no one knows about?"

"I think that's more ridiculous than me being able to see ghosts." Bea laughed kindly, she felt more at ease now she knew what had been going on, even if it was kind of incredible. "A secret twin brother that not one member of the family know about?"

"Okay, okay." He put his hands up. "Being able to see ghosts is far more plausible than having a secret twin brother."

"Why don't you go and see Ruby?" Charlie suggested.

"She scares me," Bea admitted.

"She scares me as well," Charlie agreed. "But only because of what she can do, not because of who she is. She's such a kind person when you get to know her."

So a few days later and after a lot of scepticism from Eddie, Bea found herself outside the home of Mick and Ruby Turner. It was very different to how she remembered it. The cottage had had a fresh coat of paint, the garden was tidy with winter blooming pansies in hanging baskets and potted here and there to add vibrant colour to an otherwise dull day.

The last time Bea was here the place looked like two separate dwellings which at the time it was but now there were matching curtains at all the windows, which were clean and shiny. She couldn't believe the change in the place and wondered if it had been sold and no one had thought to tell her.

"Mick, she's here." The door opened before she even had chance to knock and standing before her was Ruby, impeccably clean with her hair tied back in a neat bun wearing a blue jumper and jeans. "Come in, come in, kettle's on." Bea found herself ushered inside the light and airy hallway. It was obvious the inside had had exactly the same attention as the outside.

"Fancy leaving it all this time before visiting your Aunt and Uncle eh?" She was pulled into a massive bear hug by Mick as soon as she stepped into the warm and welcoming lounge. Although still dressed in vest and trousers, these were at least spotlessly clean and in his size. "Wish we'd known it was you all those months ago."

"Sit, sit." At Ruby's insistence Bea sat down on what was clearly a brand-new sofa.

"Bet you don't recognise the place do you?" Mick sat down beside her. "Had a little win on the horses a while back so we've spruced the place up." Bea wondered how much a little win was. "Ruby can stop doing that fortune telling now."

"Oh no, Mick." Ruby had been heading into the kitchen but stopped in her tracks. "I like doing them, makes me so happy to see people's faces." Bea was a little taken aback by Ruby's words. Joe and Charlie would have you believe it was Mick that made her do them. "I just wish I was better at them that's all. Sometimes it comes, sometimes it doesn't." She carried on into the kitchen, coming back a few moments later with a fully laden tea tray.

"So what can we do for you?" Mick directed his question straight to Bea. "Charlie popped in and said you wanted a chat."

"Er…" She didn't have a clue how to begin this conversation. She felt suddenly embarrassed and silly. "It's just…I've been…well what I mean to say…"

"You've seen Charles, haven't you?" Ruby poured three cups of tea with a steady hand.

"I'll take mine upstairs." Mick grabbed his cup and walked off towards the stairs. "Need to study tomorrow's form anyway." Bea would never have expected this man to have tact. She had clearly misjudged the pair of them, formed her opinion on how they lived and not on the people they actually were.

"If I said I had would you think I was crazy?" Bea stared at her aunt, realising for the first time that she had the same grey eyes as her dad did. "I've eaten biscuits with him and touched him."

"Everyone thinks I'm crazy." She laughed, a kind, gentle laugh. "But I know what I see and what I hear. Charles and I quite often have a cup of tea when he comes to visit."

"But it's not real." Bea stated. "Only I can see him."

"Why does that mean it's not real?" She looked at Bea with a piercing gaze. "Give me your hand."

"Are you going to read my palm?" Bea hesitantly put her hand in Ruby's, not really knowing what to expect.

"He's here with you now." Ruby changed instantly, her voice almost a whisper. "And someone else, a woman." Ruby held tighter to Bea's hand, squeezing it hard. "They've found each other."

"Who has? What do you mean?" But as quickly as Ruby had spoken she stopped, dropping Bea's hand.

"Would you like a biscuit?" Ruby shoved a plate under Bea's nose.

"You just said he was with me, do you mean my dad?" Bea wanted to shake her. "And a woman? Who is the woman?"

"I'm sorry my dear." Ruby looked a little frightened at Bea's sudden change to a crazed madwoman.

"Don't worry about it, Aunt Ruby." Bea calmed herself down, remembering that Ruby's gift came and went and she clearly never remembered what she said. "We were talking about Charles."

They spent the next hour or so chatting about Ruby, Charles and Joe growing up. Their childhood on the boat. Bea found Ruby easy to talk to as long as you allowed for her to drift off now and again and completely forget what you had been talking about. When Bea left it was starting to get dark and beginning to rain and she was grateful that she had asked Eddie to pick her up in the car.

"Have a nice time?" He opened the door for her before running round the other side and leaping in just as the heavens burst open.

"I did actually." She kissed him. "I completely misjudged them both."

"So are you the next Mystic Meg then?" He started the engine. "Ow!" Bea slapped him hard on the leg. "No need for violence, I was only teasing."

"Just because you don't believe in it doesn't mean you have to make fun of it." Bea knew she would never get Eddie to understand, in fact she hardly understood it herself but she found comfort in knowing her dad was around, even if it meant he was dead and she would never actually have a proper relationship with him. But she'd seen him and spoken to him and who was to say that wouldn't continue. She smiled happily at the thought.

"Well you look like the cat that's got the cream." Eddie glanced at her while they waited at the traffic lights.

"I just feel…" Bea couldn't think of the words. "Like me."

"What do you mean by that?" Eddie drove off as the lights turned green.

"All my life it's been like something was missing." She tried to explain. "And now I feel like finally I'm home. Like this is where I should have been all the time. As if something or someone has been pushing me here all along."

"Bloody hell." They had pulled up on the drive of the cottage and through the pouring rain Bea could see Scott's Aston Martin. "What does he want?"

# CHAPTER 40

**B**ea had dashed inside as quickly as she could and was now standing at the window staring at Eddie and Scott who were arguing. The rain was beating down so heavily that she could hardly see them through the constant rivers that ran down the glass.

"Why on earth don't they just come in?" She said to Buddy who answered with a soft bark, then as if they'd heard her the two men ran into the cottage, dripping wet and shaking themselves off like a dog would shake his coat dry. "Tea?" Bea smiled her best smile but this did little to break the suddenly tense atmosphere.

Eddie disappeared upstairs, returning in dry clothes and with a towel for Scott.

"Thank you." Scott accepted the towel graciously.

"I'd give you some clothes but nothing I've got will even remotely fit you," Eddie said and Bea silently agreed. As fit and toned that Eddie was he was half of the size of his father. Bea reprimanded herself at the use of the word father knowing that Eddie would go mad if she ever let that slip out of her mouth.

"Doesn't matter." He started drying himself as best he could, taking off his shirt as he did. Bea tried desperately not to look, after all this was her boyfriend's father not his brother so totally inappropriate even if he was still gorgeously handsome and with abs to die for.

*Did I just say boyfriend?* Bea thought as she busied herself making the tea and keeping her back to the half-dressed Scott. *'Well you are living together.'* A little voice in her head reminded

271

her. She needed to sort that out, she couldn't live with Eddie permanently, could she?

The *Sophie* was gone now, gone to the shipyard in the sky Joe had said. She hadn't seen it since the fire, hadn't wanted to. It was too heart breaking to know that all those memories the boat held of her dad and now she knew her mum as well, even maybe herself as a child, were all lost. Luckily most of her things had been stored at Eddie's and now the manor on the kind insistence of Eleanor before Charlie had started work so nothing of any sentimental value had been lost.

Did she want to live with a man again? Could you even describe Eddie as a man? No, that was unfair, she scolded herself. He might be young but he showed more maturity than someone twice his age. *'Remember Trevor?'* The little voice was back and Bea groaned. *'And Rick?'* Apart from her brother and the various uncles, she'd only ever lived with two men, Trevor and Rick.

Rick was in her student days when she'd fallen head over heels for the biggest loser she could find. They'd quickly moved in together and it took Bea almost two years to realise that she was being taken for a fool. He hardly went to class, spent most of his time on his xbox, never cleaned, never cooked and after a full day at uni followed by a late shift at the local pub, he would expect Bea to cook them both dinner.

Trevor on the other hand was completely different. He was older than her, much older than her and took care of her like a princess. It had been lovely to start with. She came home from work to find a three course meal on the table, if they ate out he picked up the bill, even though he had a full time job himself the house was spotless and Bea never had to lift a finger even though she offered time and time again.

After a while though Bea had started to feel stifled. She couldn't do anything, couldn't go anywhere, couldn't see or talk to her friends. Then when she came home to find Trevor had brought her a whole new wardrobe of clothes and given all of hers to charity she flipped. She had grabbed what little was left of her possessions and ended up on Jen's couch.

"So will you listen to me now?" Scott's voice interrupted her day dreaming and she turned to find him still standing by the front door, a previously unnoticed briefcase at his feet.

"If I must." Eddie was standing in front of him and made no effort to move or invite him into the lounge.

"Your mother and I…" Scott reached for the briefcase and clicked it open, pulling out three different folders.

"My mother is dead, as is my father." Eddie's voice was calm but Bea could see he was holding his anger in check.

"Eleanor and I have decided to give you the publishing house and the manor." He handed two of the folders to him. "And I've arranged for all the Robin Sparrow books to be renamed and relaunched under Eddie Richards." He handed him the third folder. "I've arranged a TV interview for tomorrow."

"You don't get it do you?" Eddie flicked through the various papers. "I don't want this." He shoved everything back into Scott's hands who looked at him in shock. "I don't want the manor or Summers Day Press and I certainly don't want the books."

"I don't understand." Scott looked at Eddie and then to Bea who shrugged her shoulders, she had no idea where this was coming from.

"You and Eleanor built up Summers Day Press, it's yours not mine," Eddie began to explain.

"But it was only given to us because we gave you up." Bea could see the guilt and hurt in Scott's eyes.

"And we've all had to live with that every day since but you did it and I forgive you for it." Bea and Scott's mouths dropped open at the same time.

"You forgive us?" Scott's voice was a whisper.

"I do." Eddie nodded. "You were young and scared and I understand that now, I just wish you'd acted differently. I just wanted a big brother, someone to look up to. I wanted you to be proud of me."

"I am proud of you." Scott was starting to collapse. Tears were streaming down his cheeks and his whole stance had changed from strong and sturdy to looking like jelly. "I'm so sorry for what I've done to you and how I acted." He turned to Bea. "And I'm sorry about everything with you as well, Bea. I used you to make Eddie jealous and then to top it off I stole your book too."

"It's okay." Bea had long since come to terms with Scott's behaviour but she still had pangs of guilt over her own.

"At least let me give you the books back." Scott was starting to compose himself again.

"I don't want them." Eddie shook his head. "I'm happy as I am. I don't want to be famous, that's you. You're Scott Summers, it's what you do. I can't give speeches and make appearances. You may have done some shitty things but all that charity work you do and all that money you raise, I wouldn't be able to do that."

"But they're your books and you deserve it," Scott pleaded.

"I really don't want it." Eddie was adamant. "I want to write, I need to write but I'm happy for the books to continue under your name." He smiled. "I'm sure most of them only get read because of your face on the back anyway."

"Nonsense," Bea and Scott spoke together.

"They're amazing," Scott praised.

"I agree," Bea piped in.

"And how would you know?" Eddie laughed. "You've never read one."

"True," she said, glad that the atmosphere was starting to lighten. "But I will."

"Really Scott, you don't need to give me anything." Bea couldn't believe these words were coming out of Eddie's mouth but she was glad they were. "I've got my house, my writing and now I've got Bea." He pulled her in for a hug. "My life is perfect just the way it is." Bea's heart turned to molten chocolate at his words.

"You've grown up into such a remarkable young man Eddie, you really have." Scott held out his hand and after a brief hesitation Eddie shook it. "Eleanor and I won't be around for a bit, we're off to see if we can salvage what's left of our marriage by cruising round the Caribbean for two weeks, so if you could hold the fort for us that would be great." And with a quick wave he was out of the door and back in the rain.

"Now, that's Scott." Eddie smiled and turned to Bea. "Assuming I'll do whatever he asks like I always do." He laughed. "And you." He kissed her on the nose. "Should be resting."

"I don't need to rest anymore." She put her arms round him and hugged him tightly. "I've never felt better."

"Really?" He raised an eyebrow.

"Really." She agreed. "I feel like I could conquer the world right now."

"Well in that case." He picked her up. "Let's just conquer the stairs for now."

"You're just like Scott." For the first time she knew she could tease him about being like Scott without upsetting him.

"How so?" They were at the top of the stairs now.

"Just assuming I'll do whatever you ask me to do." Eddie laid her gently on the bed before crawling seductively up so their faces were level.

"And will you?" His brown eyes looked deep into hers.

"I will." She pulled him down for a kiss. "Sometimes."

# CHAPTER 41

"I don't think I've laughed so much in years," Bea said to Eddie as they almost fell into the front door of the cottage on Christmas Eve. "Giles and Richard sure know how to throw a party."

Buddy, who was fast asleep on his bed, took one look at them before deciding it wasn't worth getting off his warm, comfy bed and promptly went back to sleep.

"They always do." He hung his coat up and helped her off with hers. "This year seemed different though, lighter somehow. No one was on edge and even Scott made a few jokes which we laughed at because they were funny rather than because we felt we had to."

"You've really come to terms with it all haven't you?" Bea still couldn't believe the change in Eddie. He'd gone from being angry and resentful to happy and spending as much time as he could with Scott and Eleanor.

"Life's too short for grudges," he said heading into the lounge and switching on the Christmas tree lights. The room was immediately filled with twinkling lights that spread from the tree, along the fireplace and up the bannister on the stairs. "Your accident taught me that."

"What do you mean?" She kicked off her shoes and sat down on the sofa, tucking her knees underneath.

"When I was sitting there in the hospital with you unconscious I realised that all the hate and anger I had bottled up inside didn't mean anything. All it did was cause resentment and pain." He poured them both a glass of wine and sat down next to her. "Eleanor helped so much while you were in the hospital. She drove me around, looked after Buddy and made sure I ate. She even sat with you after insisting I went and got a drink and a breath of fresh air."

"I didn't know that." Bea was surprised.

"We spent hours and hours talking about everything and she made me realise that I wasn't the only one hurting, that she and Scott had been hurting for over twenty years." He looked at her. "I suppose I realised that it hadn't been their fault all those years ago, that it must have been so hard for them to stand up to their parents, and we've all been there."

"Haven't we just." It had taken three years at university to give Bea enough courage to stand up to her mum and even after that there were still plenty of times when she didn't. She smiled at the memory of her mum, something she did quite often now.

"They could have handled it differently, I know." He laughed. "Scott especially. But I even understand him now, to a lesser degree than Eleanor but I still get it."

"Well cheers to that Mr. Richards." Bea clinked her glass against his.

"Summers." He corrected.

"Beg pardon?" Had she heard him right?

"Summers." He repeated. "Eddie Summers."

"Really?" So she was right then.

"It's who I am." He shrugged his shoulders. "I used Richards a few times in my rebellious stage but I never intended to keep it, it was only because I knew how much it pissed Scott off that I carried on with it."

"You're as bad as him." She chuckled.

"I can't see me ever calling them Mum and Dad but it gets easier to build some kind of relationship with them." Bea's phone beeped.

"Oh wow." She read the message on her phone.

"Who is it?" Eddie took a glance at the screen as she showed him the message from Giles.

"You remember the girl I was talking to at the party?" Eddie shook his head. "Oh, you do. She had huge baubles in her ears and that amazing reindeer jumper she'd knitted herself."

"It doesn't ring a bell but continue." He looked at her, a blank expression on his face.

"Anyway, she was on about this house just out of town that a few people share and she was sure that someone was leaving in the New Year." Eddie wasn't sure where the conversation was going. "She's just texted Giles to say that she was right and if I want the room it's mine." Bea couldn't believe it.

"Why do you need a room?" Eddie was confused.

"I can't live here forever can I?" Bea started texting Giles back.

"I was going to give you this tomorrow but…" Bea paused as she watched Eddie start rummaging around under the tree. She had no idea what he was doing, she'd only looked through all the presents this morning and there hadn't been any to her from Eddie. "Where is it?" he said in exasperation.

"Where's what?" Bea asked knowing full well that he wouldn't answer.

"I only put it there this afternoon." He continued his searching. "A-ha! Here it is." He turned to Bea, one knee on the floor and a small box neatly wrapped in gold paper with a red bow in his hand. "Moonbeam Winters will you do me the very great honour of m…"

"Marriage?" Bea interrupted him. "Don't you think marriage is a little hasty?" She didn't want to hurt his feelings but she didn't want him to ask her and she have to say no. They weren't ready for marriage, not by any means.

"Open it," he said, simply handing her the box.

"But..." She continued protesting.

"Just open it." He put her hands gently on the ribbon and she pulled it undone. With absolute dread she unwrapped the paper and held her breath as she opened the box.

"Oh Eddie!" She couldn't contain her delight at the sight before her.

"Moonbeam Winters," he started again. "Will you do me the very great honour of moving in with me?" He took the key out of the box and she flung her arms around him. "I take it that's a yes then?"

"Yes!" She couldn't believe she'd made such an idiot of herself. "If you're sure?"

"I wouldn't be asking if I wasn't." He kissed her. "I love you Bea, always have. From that very first moment in the coffee shop. I'd been having the biggest case of writer's block for months but then when I walked in and saw you it was like everything fell into place. I had absolutely no idea who you were or even if I'd ever see you again but that night I wrote and wrote and I haven't stopped since."

"I thought you looked like a little boy lost." She laughed. "So cute and vulnerable."

"Cute?" he asked, moderately offended.

"Of course I don't think that now." She raised her eyebrows in what she hoped was a seductive manner.

"And what do you think now then?" Bea didn't have to tell him, she kissed him instead. A kiss so full of love that she started crying. "Hey, why the tears?"

"I'm just so happy." She sobbed. "At the start of this year I hated everything. I was stuck in a rut and couldn't see any way out of it and now…" She sobbed again.

"You deserve to be happy, Bea." Eddie reassured her. "We both do. It's been a tough year with some real ups and goodness knows some real downs but look where we are."

"I know, that's why I'm so happy." The sobbing continued and he pressed a gentle kiss to her forehead.

"Come here, you daft mare." He pulled her into his arms and they just sat there enjoying the closeness of each other until they both fell asleep.


"They're going to be here any minute!" Bea was panicking as she opened the oven to baste the turkey for what felt like the twentieth time in the same amount of minutes. "It's not cooking." She slammed the door shut.

"Calm down." Eddie soothed from the dining room where he was busy laying the table. "It's never going to cook if you keep opening the door."

"Stuffing!" she screamed. "I haven't made the stuffing!" There was lots of clattering and battering noises and Buddy who had been just about to head into the kitchen to see if he could scavenge some scraps decided against it and went over to see Eddie instead.

"I don't blame you, boy." Eddie ruffled the fur behind his ears before opening the crackers and placing them neatly on the table. He looked up as there was a knock at the door. "I'll get it," he called.

Scott and Eleanor were the first to arrive, swiftly followed by Ruby and Mick and just a few minutes later Joe had arrived to complete the party. The cottage felt suddenly small with all the extra people but it only added to the atmosphere.

"Merry Christmas!" There were exchanges of kisses and good wishes and introductions made. Eddie led them all to the table and promptly opened the bottle of champagne that Scott had brought.

"This is for you, Bea." Eleanor handed her an elegant silver box tied simply with a black bow. "Merry Christmas." Everyone was watching her as she took the present.

"You shouldn't have." The box felt heavy. "You've given me so many lovely things already." Bea thought back to the numerous presents of jewellery and writing books that she had opened this morning. "Oh my!" She gasped, dropping the box but holding the contents as if it was the most precious thing in the world. "My book!" She stroked the front page almost reverently. "The Tiller Girl, by Moonbeam Winters." The gaudy woman had gone and been replaced with a beautiful red head standing at the tiller of an exact replica of the original *Sophie*. "It's wonderful." She started crying again.

"Not the waterworks again." Eddie went over to her and hugged her tightly.

"I'm okay." She stopped crying almost as quickly as she had started. She looked around the room, full to bursting with family that just a few months ago she never even knew existed. "I just wish…" And everyone knew what she was wishing for without her having to say it. That she could have had just one Christmas with her dad and just one more with her mum.

Buddy went berserk all of a sudden and ran to the door, scratching and whining. Bea went to let him out while Eddie settled everyone at the table. He ran straight to the gate carrying on the whining but it was now interspersed with the odd bark.

"I knew they'd come." Bea turned to find Ruby standing behind her.

"Knew who would come?" But Ruby didn't answer, she just nodded in the direction of the canal. Bea followed her gaze and there in the distance was the *Sophie*, fully restored to her former glory chugging along. There were two figures at the tiller and Bea stared open mouthed as her mum and dad waved and blew kisses at her, their arms round each other, clearly madly in love.

"Merry Christmas!" they both called. "We'll see you soon." And Bea knew they spoke the truth. That even though the rest of the world thought they were just a figment of her imagination, to her they were real and that was all that mattered.

# EPILOGUE

Charles James Summers squirmed impatiently in his seat. He'd sat through most of the classes' stories about their grandparents and now there was just Maisey Robinson to go. Sometimes it was good having a surname beginning with a letter near the end of the alphabet but today on Grandparents' Day he was desperate to read out his story.

He was good at writing stories, just like his mum and his Grandad Summers. His mum said his dad was as well but he'd never seen any books written by Eddie Summers, only the numerous ones that adorned the shelves of his house all by Scott Summers and Bea Summers and his mum's first book before she was married under the name of Moonbeam Winters. He still giggled at his mum's full name.

"Charles?" His teacher, Miss Flowers called his name and he almost raced to the front of the classroom. Last year he had talked about his Grandad and Nannie Summers but this year was even more special, this year he had written about his visit to see his Grandpa and Grandma Winters.

The class listened quietly as he told them about their canal boat called the *Sophie* and how he had made chocolate chip shortbread with his grandpa and how he'd fed the ducks from the boat with his grandma.

"What a lovely story." Miss Flowers smiled. "Perhaps your Grandpa could come in one day and tell us about his boat?"

"He can't I'm afraid Miss, he lives in heaven most of the time." Charles sat back down in his seat.

"Oh…well I'm sorry to hear that Charles but you were meant to write a real life story not a made up one." Miss Flowers looked down the register for the next name.

"But it is real, Miss." Charles pushed his glasses up his nose as some of the children laughed.

"Don't be silly, Charles," she scolded gently. "Robbie, you're next." Charles leaned back in his chair and drifted away as Robbie started talking about his grandad who worked in the police. He didn't care that his teacher and the other children didn't believe him. He knew they were real, and as his mum and Great Aunt Ruby always told him that was all that really mattered.

# About the Author

I was born in Coventry but now live in Nuneaton. I married the love of my life over 20 years ago and we have two almost grown-up children. We share our lives with two mad dogs as well.

Writing is a great passion of mine. I love creating stories and characters, they help me escape from the world for a while and I hope readers feel the same.

I am a huge fan of All Creatures Great and Small, Call the Midwife and Bridgerton. I love history and romance.

I also write for children as Lily Mae Walters.

Printed in Great Britain
by Amazon

27722367R00165